NARCOPOLIS

NARCOPOLIS

JEET THAYIL

THE PENGUIN PRESS

New York

2012

THE PENGUIN PRESS
Published by the Penguin Group
Penguin Group (USA) Inc., 375 Hudson Street, New York, New York
10014, U.S.A. • Penguin Group (Canada), 90 Eglinton Avenue East, Suite 700, Toronto,
Ontario, Canada M4P 2Y3 (a division of Pearson Penguin Canada Inc.) • Penguin Books Ltd,
80 Strand, London WC2R 0RL, England • Penguin Ireland, 25 St. Stephen's Green, Dublin 2,
Ireland (a division of Penguin Books Ltd) • Penguin Books Australia Ltd, 250 Camberwell
Road, Camberwell, Victoria 3124, Australia (a division of Pearson Australia Group Pty
Ltd) • Penguin Books India Pvt Ltd, 11 Community Centre, Panchsheel Park,
New Delhi – 110 017, India • Penguin Group (NZ), 67 Apollo Drive, Rosedale, Auckland
0632, New Zealand (a division of Pearson New Zealand Ltd) • Penguin Books (South
Africa) (Pty) Ltd, 24 Sturdee Avenue, Rosebank, Johannesburg 2196, South Africa

Penguin Books Ltd, Registered Offices: 80 Strand, London WC2R 0RL, England

First American edition
Published in 2012 by The Penguin Press, a member of Penguin Group (USA) Inc.

Lyrics appearing on pages 164, 168, and 169 are from "Dum Maro Dum" from the film
Hare Rama Hare Krishna (1971, directed by Dev Anand). Lyrics by
Anand Bakshi, music by Rahul Dev Burman.

Publisher's Note
This is a work of fiction. Names, characters, places, and incidents either are the product of the
author's imagination or are used fictitiously, and any resemblance to actual persons, living
or dead, business establishments, events, or locales is entirely coincidental.

LIBRARY OF CONGRESS CATALOGING IN PUBLICATION DATA
Thayil, Jeet, 1959–
Narcopolis / Jeet Thayil.
p.   cm.
ISBN 978-1-59420-330-5
1. Bombay (India)—Fiction.   I. Title.
PR9499.3.T536N37 2012
823'.92—dc23
2011040210

Printed in the United States of America
1   3   5   7   9   10   8   6   4   2

DESIGNED BY NICOLE LAROCHE

DEDICATED TO

H.C.V.

CONTENTS

BOOK THREE
THE INTOXICATED

BOOK FOUR
SOME USES OF REINCARNATION

We made the whole earth a couch for you,
And the mountains its tent stakes.
We created you of two sexes,
And ordained your sleep for rest.

—SURA LXXVIII

Something for the Mouth

B ombay, which obliterated its own history by changing its name and surgically altering its face, is the hero or heroin of this story, and since I'm the one who's telling it and you don't know who I am, let me say that we'll get to the who of it but not right now, because now there's time enough not to hurry, to light the lamp and open the window to the moon and take a moment to dream of a great and broken city, because when the day starts its business I'll have to stop, these are nighttime tales that vanish in sunlight, like vampire dust—wait now, light me up so we do this right, yes, hold me steady to the lamp, hold it, hold, good, a slow pull to start with, to draw the smoke low into the lungs, yes, oh my, and another for the nostrils, and a little something sweet for the mouth, and now we can begin at the beginning with the first time at Rashid's when I stitched the blue smoke from pipe to blood to eye to I and out into the blue world—and now we're getting to the who of it and I can tell you that I, the I you're imagining at this moment, a thinking someone who's writing these words, who's arranging time in a logical chronological sequence, someone with an overall plan, an engineer-god in the machine, well, that isn't the I who's telling this story, that's the I who's being told, thinking of my first pipe at Rashid's, trawling my head for images, a face, a bit of music, or the sound of someone's voice, trying to remember what it was like, the past, recall it as I would the landscape and light of a foreign country, because that's what it is, not fiction or dead history but a place you lived in once and cannot return to, which is why I'm trying to remember how it was that I got into trouble in New York and they sent me back to Bombay to get straight, how I found Rashid's, and how, one afternoon, I took a taxi through roads mined with garbage, with human and animal debris, and the poor, everywhere the poor and deranged stumbled in their rags or stood and stared, and I saw nothing out of the ordinary in their bare feet and air of abandonment, I smoked a pipe and I was sick all day, hearing whispers in my stone sleep about the Pathar Maar, the stone killer, who worked the city at night, whispers that leaked upward from the poor, how he patrolled the working-class suburbs of Sion and Koliwada and killed them while they slept, approached those who slept alone, crept up to them in the night and killed them but no one noticed because his victims were more than poor, they were invisible entities without names or papers or families, and he killed them carefully, a half dozen murdered men and women, pavement people of the north-central suburbs, where the streets are bordered by effluents and sludge and oily green shimmer, and all that year he was an underworld whisper, unknown to the city's upper classes until he became a headline, and in my delusion I thought I understood his pity and terror, I thought I knew him as a Samaritan, a pure savior of the victims of a failed experiment, the Planned Socialist State of India, he was trying to end their misery, the Pathar Maar, he was on a mission to wipe out poverty, or so I thought, sunk in my own poverty in the back of the taxi, slumped against upholstery stained a Bombay shade of brown, telling the driver to slow down as we drove past the women, and I saw, I swear I did, the face of a maid who looked after me when I was a small child, a dark woman who smiled sweetly when I hit her, and I knew it was her, washed up in the dead-end district where the women were graded, were priced and displayed in every street and gully and house, women from the far north, from the south, from all over, bought new and used, sold or given away, bartered, almost free, I knew it was her but I didn't stop and the taxi slowed to a crawl behind a jeep with a printed sign, GOVERNAMENT OF INDIA, and when the driver found the address I'd given him for Rashid's he assumed I was going to the cages, the cheapest rooms on the street, where the women were five rupees and upwards, and he pointed to the houses with numbers printed on the window boxes and said, "Number houses better," nodding at the streetwalkers and the women in the cages, "these girls dirty," as I stepped out of the cab and into chaos because a buffalo cart had broken down and a crowd was quickly gathering to watch the animal kneel in the narrow road as the carter whipped it in sharp methodical bursts of fury, though otherwise he was calm, he didn't curse or sweat as his whip hand rose and fell, rose and fell, slabs of ice packed in sawdust melting in orderly rows on the back of the cart, and everywhere the poor and deranged waited and watched, as I did before climbing the stairs to the first-floor address I'd been given, to stand at the doorway and take it in, a smell of molasses and sleep and illness, a woman tending the pipe, using a long needle to cook the opium, her hand moving as if she was knitting, a couple of smokers lying on pallets, an old man hunched over a stove, inhaling as the opium bubbled, everything in the room happening on the floor, sleeping mats and pillows folded or spread, a calendar on the wall with a photograph of a mosque—listen, stop there and light me again, or let me do it, yes, ah yes, now that's it, lovely, such a sweet meditation, no, more than meditation, it's the bliss that allows calm to settle on the spirit and renders velocity manageable, yes, lovely—and now, in the same city, though it's a lifetime later and here we are, I and I, which isn't said in the Rastafari way to indicate we, but to separate the two I machines, the man and the pipe, the who and the who, telling this story about a long-ago time, when I smoked a pyali and I was sick all day, my first time on Shuklaji Street, new to the street and the city, separated by my lack of know-ingness, by the pace of human business on the sidewalks and shops, knowing I didn't have the skills, my gait too slow, paying too much attention to the wrong things, because in my head I wasn't all there and the partialness, the half-there distractedness, was apparent in my face, people looking at me and seeing jet lag, recognizing it as a spiritual deficiency, and I went into Rashid's room, placed my head on a wooden pillow and stretched out, trying to get comfortable, realizing with some surprise that the old man who was nodding over the cook pot was speaking English, speaking to me in the lan-guage of a death-mad, religion-obsessed country of living saints, asking if I was Syrian Christian, because he'd noticed the Coptic cross around my neck and he knew Roman Catholics wouldn't wear that kind of cross, and of course he was right, I was Syrian Chris-tian, a Jacobite, if you want the subsect of the subsect—so good, this good smoke, the last smoke from the last pipe on the last night of the world—the old man, whose name was Bengali, saying, "Ah, in that case, perhaps you can answer a question that has been trou-bling me, I mean the particular way Christianity caught on in Ker-ala and how Kerala's Hindus, instead of adjusting themselves to Christianity, adjusted Christianity to themselves, to the old caste divisions, and, this is my question, would Jesus have approved of caste-conscious Christianity when his entire project was the removal of it, a man who fraternized with the poor, with fishermen, lepers and prostitutes, the sick and dying, women, his pathology and compulsion to espouse the lowest of the low, his message being God's unconditional love, whatever one's social standing?" and what reply could I have made when he wasn't expecting one, was already nodding as I watched the woman, watched Dimple, and something calmed me in the unhurried way she made the pipe, the way she dipped the cooking needle into a tiny brass pyali with a flat raised edge, the pyali the size of a thimble, filled to the brim with treacle, a liquid with the color and consistency of oil, and she was rolling the tip of the needle in the opium, then lifting it to the lamp where it sputtered and hardened, repeating the procedure until she had a lump the size and color of a walnut, which she mixed against the bowl until it was done, then tapped the needle against the pipe's stem, indicating to me that my smoke was ready, it was, but the pipe was too long, I couldn't manage the heaviness of it, and though I sucked when she held the bowl to the flame, the mouthpiece was too large, the taste too harsh, and when the pipe clogged she took it briskly away to apply the needle once more, saying in English, "Smoke, pull hard," Rashid saying, "Watch Dimple, she'll show you," and she did, shaking the hair out of her eyes, expertly and elegantly fitting the pipe to her mouth, taking a long clean drag, the smoke seeming to disappear, so when she gave me the pipe I was very conscious that it had been in her mouth, and she said, "Pull deep and keep pulling, don't stop, because if you stop, the opium will burn and there's nothing you can do with burned opium but throw it away, so pull until you can't pull anymore," and I, in my ignorance, saying, "Do I take a single continuous drag?" "You can, but then you have to recycle it inside your lungs, better to take short pulls," "How long should I hold it in?" "So many questions, it depends how much nasha you want, hold it as long as you like, but don't put the whole pipe in your mouth, not polite," and I said, "Sorry," and quickly moved the pipe away and brought it back to my lips with care, fitting it carefully, taking my time, understanding that opium was all etiquette, a sense rhythm that centered on the mouth and the way you held the pipe in relation to your body, a lunar ebb and pull of smoke that filled first the lungs and then the veins, and when I looked up she was smiling and so was Bengali, and Rashid said, "Here people say you should introduce only your worst enemy to opium, maybe Dimple is your worst enemy," and I was thinking maybe she isn't, maybe I is, maybe the O is the I and I is unreliable, my memory like blotting paper, my full-of-holes, porous, shreddable nonmemory, remembering details from thirty years ago but this morning a blank, and if memory = pain = being human, I'm not human, I'm a pipe of O telling this story over the course of a single night, and all I'm doing, the other I, that is, I'm writing it down straight from the pipe's mouth, the same pipe Dimple made the first time, but that story's for later—okay, here we go, we're coming to the best part now, the dreams, which aren't dreams but conversations, visitations from absent friends, a raucous procession behind your closed eyelids, your awake and dreaming eyes, and sometimes a voice wakes you, your own voice talking to someone who isn't there, because you're alone, on your back, sailing the opiate sea, no, I'll pass this time, I'm fine, oh yes, beautiful even—the same I who, when they put me in jail, noticed the cell wasn't much smaller than the room I was living in at the time on the Upper East Side, when they caught me buying dope, stoned on downers, and the white cop pulled his gun and chased me down the alley and I saw the dead end and turned, reaching in my pocket to give him the baggies, and the cop didn't shoot, for some reason he didn't shoot, he put me in a van and took me to jail, where, as I say, the cell was the size of the room I was living in and I was happy enough to be there and alive, and later I was sent back to India and I found Bombay and opium, the drug and the city, the city of opium and the drug Bombay—okay, time now for a short one, the night's almost over, a short one to keep the O boat sailing on its treacle tide, and this time all I'm going to do, I'm turning my head and inhaling, you do the rest—and ever since I've tried to separate the one from the other, or not, because now I'm giving in, I'm not separating but connecting, I'm giving in to the lovely stories, I'm lighting the bowl, one for me and one for me, I'm tasting it one last time, savoring the color and the bouquet, the nose of it, yes, like that, so good, and then I'm stopping, because it's time now to subside into silence and let the other I speak.

BOOK ONE

THE CITY OF O

1

Dimple

Before Dimple came to be called Zeenat, she worked part-time for Rashid and disappeared every evening to the hijra's brothel. I smoked at her station even if other pipes were free, and we talked the way smokers talk, horizontally, with long pauses, our words so soft they sounded like the incomprehensible phrases spoken by small children. I asked the usual foolish questions. Is it better to be a man or a woman? Dimple said: for conversation, better to be a woman, for everything else, for sex, better to be a man. Then I asked if she was a man or a woman and she nodded as if it was the first time she'd been asked. She was about twenty-five then and she had a habit in those days of shaking the hair into her eyes and smiling for no reason at all, a sweet smile as I remember, with no hint there of the changes that would overtake her.

She said: woman and man are words other people use, not me. I'm not sure what I am. Some days I'm neither, or I'm nothing. On other days I feel I'm both. But men and women are so different, how can one person be both? Isn't that what you're thinking? Well,

I'm both and I've learned some things, to my cost, the kind of thing you're better off not knowing if you mean to live in the world. For example I know something about love and how lovers want to consume and be consumed and disappear into each other. I know how they yearn to make two equal one and I know it can never be. What else? Women are more evolved biologically and emotionally, that's well known and it's obvious. But they confuse sex and the spirit; they don't separate. Men, as you know, always separate. They separate their human and dog natures. And then she said, I'd like to tell you more about it, about the family resemblance between men and dogs, because I have plenty to say, as you may have guessed, but what would be the point? There's little chance you'd understand, after all you're a man.

SHE'D LEARNED ENGLISH by conversing with customers and she was teaching herself to read. She knew enough of the alphabet to recognize some of the words in the newspapers and film magazines that came her way, or the paperback novels forgotten by customers at the khana, or the print on detergent packets and toothpaste tubes. Bengali gave her books sometimes, usually history, but also philosophy, geography, and illustrated biographies with titles like *Great Thinkers of the Twentieth Century* and *One Hundred Great Men of the World*. He found the books in the raddi shops around Shuklaji Street, which was a center of the trade in used paper, rags, toys, junk of all kinds. He gave her books and she read in secret, because she didn't like to be seen reading. She read the way an illiterate person did. She liked to look at the covers and trace the title with a finger, and if she was able to make sense of a line or a word, it gave her a thrill.

I WAS STRETCHED OUT, the khana empty in the dead hour of the afternoon, when Dimple asked what kind of book I was reading. It's not a book, I said, it's a magazine and this is a story about an Indian painter who lives in London.

"*Time*. What a big name for a small book. Is your painter famous?"

"Here, no, in England, yes. He's a school dropout. No, I have it wrong, he was expelled for making pornographic murals in the boys' toilet. He put himself through art school and won a scholarship to Oxford. The genteel British expected him to be some kind of Hindu scholar mystic. Instead, it says here, he paints Christ with more authority than British painters."

"Read."

"'Newton Pinter Xavier's art is Catholic guilt exploded to devastating effect. He doesn't paint as much as eviscerate and disembowel. His altered Christs are more powerful than Bacon's because they come at us with no frame of reference, or none that we are able to recognize in a terrestrial context. They are adrift of history. As for geography, they remain firmly outside the purview of the British isles, and, I suspect, that of the Indian subcontinent. They drip sex, heresy, and indiscriminate readings from the psychopathology of everyday life; they—'"

"Enough, stop, it's too much. Let me see the pictures."

The editors had thought to include several reproductions of Xavier's paintings. There was a gory Christ figure wrapped in thorns the size of railroad ties, the figure appearing puny and abused against a backdrop of blood splatter. There was a self-portrait. And there were two pitiless nudes, soft white bodies spread-eagled on stainless steel, dead skin puckered in the harsh fluorescent light. Dimple was silent as she looked at the pictures. Then she handed the magazine back, squinting at me as if she couldn't see. She said, he's too angry to think. He's so angry he's homicidal. He wants to make everything ugly. He wants to kill the world. She said, how can you trust a man like that? How can you agree with him when he says that people are sick and deserve to die?

AFTER A WHILE, she asked if I would read something else and she reached under her pallet and produced a textbook wrapped with brown paper in the schoolboy way, *The New Combined Textbook for Non-Christians: History & Moral Science Examination Syllabus.* Under the title was the author's name: S. T. Pande, Professor of History, University of Baroda. She held the book out to me and turned to a page she'd marked and I read a few lines.

"'The founder of Christianity was the eponymous Christ, Jesus, whose personality, manic and magnetic in equal proportions, served a radical agenda that sought to overthrow the world's hierarchical social orders. His radicalism, which manifested itself most prominently in the guise of mystic uttering, can best be encapsulated by the following indirect quote: "Be not content with this state of things." He was possessed of a sharp tongue that aimed its barbs at priests, the rich, politicians, usurers, Jews, Gentiles, foes and friends. Some say his special gift was indiscriminate truth telling. Others say it was his curse. He was born of Mary, virgin wife and mother, who was blessed with a lovely pear-shaped face, whose devotees address her in the following manner: Hail Mary, Mother of

God, pray for us sinners, now and at the hour of our death. Amen!'

"'Jesus was, among other things, an unlicensed medical practitioner who could cure the sick with nothing more than a single touch of his right index finger. Whether this ability was of divine provenance or simply a matter of being adept in the use of herbs and plants is open to conjecture. What cannot be disputed is the miraculous effect he had on the sick and the dying. This is why diseased peoples became Christians, and the poor too; in other words, the lowest of the low converted to Christianity because they found in it a balm to counteract the caste-ridden ways of the world.'"

Was this Professor Pande's style, I wondered, to write as if he'd spent days and nights with Jesus and Mary, taking notes, accumulating the privileged information he was now sharing with us, his lucky readers? I told Dimple that the professor, if that is what he was, seemed to me an unreliable source, though he was entertaining enough. I said there was nothing wrong with being unreliable. Who wasn't? What, in any case, was the point in being reliable, like a dog or automobile or armchair? I said it was fine with me, as long as he didn't call himself a historian and moral scientist. Dimple wasn't interested. She was a story addict, the kind of reader—if she had been able to read—who hated to get to the end of a book. So I held Professor Pande's book open on my chest and I continued.

"'Jesus was crucified in a very cruel way, but he died smilingly. His happy face had a great effect on his disciples and so did the miracles he performed. In fact, he was a consummate performer: no matter what the circumstances, he managed several performances a week. He once fed five thousand people with five loaves of bread and two fish only.'"

Dimple said: "Five loaves of bread and two fish, which means with half a dozen fish he could have fed all the poor of Bombay—no, no, of course not, just the poor of Shuklaji Street. Even so, he should have been born in India."

SHE WENT TO the window and spat into the street. There were burns on her fingers and her toenails were painted black. She had a moon-shaped bruise on her collarbone and she pulled her shirt tight to cover it. She stood at the window for a moment, looking at the street, and for the rest of her life she remembered the way the dust from the handcarts boiled up into the sunshine and the way she lived then, the brothel with the red number on its door, 007, and the bathroom she shared with the other randis, the peanut-shaped hole in the floor they pissed in, all of them, customers included. She remembered the women she worked with, the new and not so new women from all kinds of cities and towns, from Secunderabad and Patna and Calcutta and Kathmandu, sent to Bombay to earn money for their families back home, money the families never saw because the brothel keepers neglected to send it. And Dimple would remember that it was around this time that she determined to make her own future, around the time she started to read, her head on a pallet, or cross-legged and hunched, laboriously deciphering letters until she fell into a nod. When she woke she knew that her stay at the brothel was coming to an end and soon she would be gone, that she had to sustain her determination and it would come true, the future, if only she persisted, and she knew that whatever happened, whatever she accomplished or did not, it would be in testimony to the brothel.

WAS IT THAT AFTERNOON or some other that she pulled out a copy of *Sex Detective*, the true-crime magazine that Bengali was addicted to? She flipped pages until she found a story in photographs, "Womanizer Hubby Gets Comeuppance." In the first panel, a man in a flowered shirt and bell-bottoms offered a sunflower to a bosomy woman. The text was enclosed in comic-book balloons. Dimple pointed to the parts she wanted me to read.

> "'You are very clever. You are offering me one flower and in exchange you want the flower of my youth.' Their hot breathing is merged. Eyes tell eyes how intense is the thirst. Prakash and Priya move together to drink the juice of love. 'Prakash, your titillating touch is exciting the flower, please touch the virginity of the petals with the drops of your manly vigor.' Prakash with his fingers touches the lip of Priya and awakens her body."

I read the passage with some involuntary inflection, a dismissive undertone or jokiness, and she asked me why I was laughing.

"Why are you so serious? It's a story, someone made it up."

"Stories are real. Can't you see that these people are heading for disaster? Give me back the book."

"It's not a book."

"No?"

"And this is not a pipe."

"Enough. You're dreaming with your eyes open."

———————

DIMPLE MAY HAVE picked up the idea from the tai, or from one of the randis at the brothel, but Dimple, being Dimple, developed it into a kind of classroom lesson, a mini lecture. She told me she had something to say, something I shouldn't take personally. She said she was telling me these things because of the questions I asked, and because her own thoughts were only now taking shape in her mind. She said that men, whatever their sexual preferences, had more in common with other men than with women. It was possible they had more in common with males of other species, with chimpanzees, goats, and dogs, particularly dogs, as she'd explained to me before, than with women. This was not a harsh thing to say, she continued, and especially not to a man. Correct me if I'm wrong, but isn't it true that men aren't interested in tenderness as much as orgasm? Isn't it true that the main goal of the sexual act, for a man, is the discharging of semen into a suitable receptacle, or even an unsuitable one if nothing else is available? I don't mean to be cynical, but the truth is that the gap between men and women is unbridgeable and it extends to everything, from the taking of pleasure to the meaning of marriage. Genuine union is impossible; all we can hope for is cohabitation. I said nothing in reply. What surprised me about the speech was not its content. She spoke in English, unbroken English, and I wondered how she'd gotten so good at it.

LATER, when the nod took me, I dreamed I was walking through the corridors of a house from which the electricity had long been disconnected. I followed the sound of water along unlit corridors to a dead end, and beyond that to a room. It took a moment to recognize the shape waiting on the bed. Old friend, I said, tell me the story of your death, and please, you have to make an effort, it's the only way we can speak to each other. Dimple smiled politely. She said, what? I can't understand you. I said: I said, make an effort, an effort. As you wish, she said, this is your house, but why don't you open the windows? You shouldn't use electric light on a full moon. Light a candle, instead, and open the windows. Outside on the street, only one streetlamp was working. A dog with a broken leg limped into the light. The street seemed to be moving and I realized it was underwater. I heard the water lap against the building and I smelled the chemicals that floated on its surface. Dimple said: be grateful, so many people don't have even this. Then she said: I died in December at three o'clock in the afternoon. People were walking on the promenade. A child asked, is this the sea or the ocean?, and her mother replied, just drink your coco water, shut up for one second. The memorial benches were empty except for the crows. A couple stood gazing out to sea and I noticed that the woman was pregnant and it seemed to me that they were dead, like everybody on the promenade, but of all the dead people who were out walking, I was deadest and I was covered in blood, my own or some other's, I couldn't tell. The sea lay among the dirty mangroves and I imagined I was the tide that pooled among the rocks near Bandstand, a dirty blood-ringed tide that ebbed and was gone. Do you want to know what happened next? I died and my spirit hung upside down in a cave of creatures yearning to be born, hung upside down for many years or hours. A sign had been painted on the wall long ago, PIT LOKA, it said, and though the letters were faded, a group of us hovered near it, as if the proximity of the words would ensure our return to the land of the living. But I can't return, except like this, partially.

"I'm glad you're back," I said.

"I've been here all this time. What have I been doing? I don't know. People tell me things, secret things. They're kind to me because they like me and they tell me what to expect."

"What do they tell you?"

"The same thing I will tell you, that we're here, close to you, invisible, of course, but we are here."

"Where?"

"I've never met anyone who asks so many questions," said Dimple, and she looked up at the window and smiled. "On the other side of the mirror, our hands are resting against the glass, trying to touch your face. Only a veil separates us from you, a transparent veil as flimsy as the one that separates you from your dreams. If you want to talk to us you only have to dip your hand beneath the surface of the water. We're waiting for a glance or a word, some acknowledgement that we are here. If you dip your hand you'll hear us. You should listen. Even if you can't bear it, you should listen."

2.

Rumi on Pimps

I overheard a conversation, or more than that, an altercation, between a pimp and a tall man with a caste mark on his forehead. The tall man was wearing cowboy boots that he refused to leave at the door. I didn't hear what the pimp said but the other man's voice was difficult to ignore. He told the pimp that the laws of supply and demand applied everywhere, including the cesspools of the fucking third world. You're being childish, he said. You shouldn't take it personally if your whores are unpopular. Ask yourself how you can remedy the situation. Could be all you need is a USP. Regular medical checkups, that's the answer, friend. Test result posted on the wall for all to see, but only if it's negative. The pimp was a pockmarked giant with teeth that were too big for his lips. His mouth was open, as if he was panting, but he kept his voice even. He said, did you call me childish? He used the same high Hindi word the other man had used, *bachpana*. He could have reached over and broken his opponent in two without raising a sweat. The thing that stopped him was the expression on the other man's face, which was serene, as if he had a gun under his shirt or at the very least a knife.

"Just stoned talk," the man said when the dog-faced pimp had left. He was wearing a pair of headphones around his neck and I could hear strange music pumping into the air. "I said something, he got upset, and then he calmed the fuck down. You want to know something?"

He dropped his voice slightly, which only served as a signal to the men around us. He said: the thing to remember is one small but supremely important fact: pimps are cowards. Pimps are worthless. Pimps make their money from the weak and the diseased, from men and women whose will has deserted them, who will never fight or put up any kind of resistance, who want to die. Once you know this, that a pimp is a cowardly little fuck, there's no problem; you can stand up to them like a man. You've got to face facts and the fact is life is a joke, a fucking bad joke, or, no, a bad fucking joke. There's no point taking it seriously because whatever happens, and I mean whatever the fuck, the punch line is the same: you go out horizontally. You see the point? No fucking point.

I thought: he's trying to impress me. I thought: chandulis are slaves to the pipe, which diminishes us in the world, and we make up the difference with boasts and lies.

Then the tall man sat up and yelled across the room at Bengali. He said, can I get a pyali, boss, today sometime? I've been here half an hour and I'm tired of waiting. Someone coughed and the room became still. Bengali, very reluctantly, it seemed to me, put a pyali on Dimple's tray.

"I don't think they like you very much here," I said.

"Ah, fuck that, I wouldn't come to a place like this without protection." He looked meaningfully at his briefcase. "So, where you from originally?"

"Kerala, South India."

"Undu gundu land, I know where it is. You get any trouble?"

"If I make the mistake of speaking Malayalam to the locals, yes."

"Locals? Like me, you mean? Well, not to worry, things are changing: you Southies will be okay. We're going after bigger game." He dropped his voice and said, "Mozzies."

"Is that the new strategy, guaranteed to win friends and generate income?"

He propped himself on an elbow to get a better look at me. "Chief? You should watch your mouth. Maybe you've got a bellyful of opium and you don't care. Or you want to go off and you're looking for an easy way. Or maybe your head is full of bugs, like me." He was smiling, a wide patronizing smile, and when he held out his hand, his grip was firm and moist. "Anyway, name's Rumi. And you?"

"Dom."

"With a name like that you're fucked. All you have in common with these people is smoke."

I said, "What's the music you're listening to?"

HE HANDED ME the headphones. The music was high-pitched, like the sound track of a movie in which random scenes had been strung together, or cut up and played backwards, or deliberately placed out of order. Bottles clinked and a door creaked open. A shot rang out. A child whispered, is he here? Where is he? A woman wept and said, nahi, nahi. There was the sound of water falling from a great height. A door creaked shut and a bottle smashed on a tiled floor. A woman's high voice fell deeply through the octaves and a shot rang out. A man panted like a dog. A child wept and water lapped against the side of a boat or a body. A bottle of champagne popped and a doorbell rang. James Bond guitars played against cowboy string orchestration. The child said, here he is. Where is here? The woman's voice, soaked in reverb and whisky, executed another perfect fall and I experienced a sudden drop in my head like a vertigo rush. I heard the sound of water and Dimple handed me the pipe. I put it against my lips and heard a man shout, Monica, my darling, and I felt so dizzy that I had to close my eyes. Then a woman said, is he here?, and a child whispered, nahi, and a shot rang out and everything went silent. I took the headphones off and gave them back to Rumi.

He said, "Bombay blues."

3.

A Painter Visits

I saw in the *Free Press Journal* that Newton Xavier was to make an appearance in the city. He would read poems and answer questions about his new Bombay show, the first in a dozen years, opening that week at the Jehangir Art Gallery in Kala Ghoda. I was excited at the chance to see him up close. I wanted to see what he looked like. I remembered the work I'd seen and the articles I'd read, which described him in lurid phrases that sounded like terms of endearment. Most writers agreed that he was an enfant terrible and brilliant; a postmodern subversive who rejected the label "postmodern"; a drunk whose epic binges were likened to those of illustrious alcoholic predecessors such as Dylan Thomas, Verlaine, and J. Swaminathan, though he had lately sworn off the booze after a violent blackout that landed him in hospital; a wild child now in early middle age who "outdid the Romantics' antics, at least in terms of tenderness and rage," this according to the *London Review of Books*. The *Daily Mail* put it in plainer terms: he was "permanently drunk on booze, broads and beauty"

and he was "art-obsessed, self-absorbed" and "mad, bad and slan-
derous to know." He was worldly, acerbic, photogenic, precocious,
and he wrote poetry. The *TLS* said his two collections, reissued
under the title *Songs for the Tin-Eared*, were more chaotic than his
paintings, though they explored the same themes, i.e., the world
as a manifestation of the estranged mind, and the three major
religions—Islam, Hinduism, Christianity—as evidence of estrange-
ment. I pored over the reproductions of the paintings that I found
in the magazines, especially the Hindu Christ series. These are the
paintings he will be remembered for, I thought, the pictures of
Christ with blue skin, with doe eyes, kaajal, and a caste mark. Christ
playing the flute or stealing the clothes of bathing village nymphets
or meditating in a cave: strange portraits in vivid Indian reds and
yellows.

Xavier was speaking at the PEN Centre in New Marine Lines.
I took a train from Grant Road to Churchgate, and then I walked
to the Theosophy Hall. There were about a dozen people waiting.
Ceiling fans on long stalks circulated hot air and dust around a
large room. The walls were filled with antique volumes locked away
in glass-fronted cupboards. You couldn't touch the books, which
looked as if they'd fall apart at the slightest breath. All three volumes
of *The Secret Doctrine* were there, arranged on long tables, small
leather-bound editions that had disintegrated in Bombay's humidity.
I opened one and flipped through it quickly and read the biographi-
cal note at the end. As befitted a famous author, Madame Blavatsky
divided her time between the world's great capitals: her ashes were
interred on three continents. Her portrait, which adorned the main
hall, was the most prominent one in the room. The old fraud had
posed with her great head cradled in one hand, trying with all her
might to hypnotize the camera. Not even the ghost of a smile played

on her lips. It was a strange setting for an appearance by the godless Catholic, Newton Xavier.

I TOOK A CHAIR at the front. It was May and people were fanning themselves with newspapers. I picked up a folded sheet that had fallen on the floor. There was a black-and-white reproduction of one of Xavier's early paintings, a blinded bleeding Christ, his shortened arms raised, his hands nailed so roughly to the cross that spurts of blood flew at the viewer. On either side of this brutalized figure were two pristine busts, a man in a robe and a nude woman in a summer hat. The reproduction was washed-out and all you could make out were the woman's large breasts and the signature, Xavier77. There was a poem as well:

SONNET

God & dog & dice & day
Live forever, like Man.
Nothing dies ; no way, I say.
The world turns according to plan,

Everything endlessly recycled
Into endless Life :
The way you laugh & say, "Like hell,"
This fly, the light, his gone young wife,

All are alive & will always live,
Here, or elsewhere.
So—open your arms to me, give

Me the scent of your skin & clean hair,
Hold me, your lost brother,
Love me so we live forever, everywhere.

The sonnet connected in a strange way with his paintings. There was the obsession with religion and sex, the grandiose self-regard, the eccentric punctuation. I wanted to read it again but a woman in the seat beside me was complaining in a voice that carried through the room. "Very bad, very bad. Already forty minutes late. Who does he think he is, Rajesh Khanna?"

And just then they appeared, a gray-haired man in a kurta supporting another gray-haired man in a kurta, both apparently drunk, and, bringing up the rear, a peon in a short-sleeved blue shirt with PEN stitched in red letters on the breast pocket. The peon at least seemed sober. The first drunk, Akash Iskai, was a poet and art critic whose name appeared frequently in the newspapers. He helped his friend to a chair on the stage and shuffled to the podium where he launched into a long, unexpectedly coherent speech about modern Indian art.

"Xavier and his old friends and colleagues in the Modern Autists Group invented modern art in India," he ended by saying. "I use the word advisedly, for these senior artists are."

"For god's sake," the other man interrupted, "don't call me senior, I'm not a fogey just yet. And don't call them my friends: we went our separate ways a long time ago. If anything we're old antagonists."

The poet appeared unfazed by the interjection. The Modern Autists were reckless originators, he said, going where no one else had dared to venture. They were truthful innovators even when they were false and dissolute, yes, because they were babes in the urban wood. He called them chinless wonders, though I may have heard it wrong, he may have said sinless. I was nodding off a little by then. These bold men, for they were all men, overturned the dictatorship of the Academies and the Schools of Here and There, Iskai said. They made it new, in Ezra's inimitable words, which, as poets know, is not a dictum as much as a piece of practical advice. At the mention of poetry, there was some unhappy murmuring in the audience. Sensing he had lost them, Iskai turned to Xavier, who sat motionless in his chair.

"Perhaps you can tell us what the falling-out was about?"

"Color, brother Iskai. What else? It brought us together and tore us apart. I should mention that things were more desperate then. We were at the J.J. School of Art, learning to paint by numbers, eating dead meat shipped out by the Royal School and the Bengal School, and then we discovered Picasso and Van Gogh and Gauguin. We were young, feeding off each other. Everything was wide open. Now of course things have changed. I don't agree with their ideas about color and I have no doubt they disagree with mine."

There was an uncomfortable silence while the painter, spent from his outburst, stared expressionlessly at his audience. The silence stretched until a small figure in the back of the room raised his hand and Xavier pointed at the man.

"Didn't art school teach you anything about color?"

Xavier said, "Certainly not, I learned about color by looking at flowers. Let's not talk about school."

Iskai said, "No more questions, question time is later. We will proceed in orderly fashion, please. First, the guest of honor will make a speech. Join me in welcoming India's own Newton Xavier."

But the guest of honor was unable to get up from his seat. The peon shoved his hands under Xavier's armpits and heaved. Nothing happened. Then Iskai suggested that Xavier read sitting down and the peon handed him a sheet of paper. The painter held the page in one shaking hand, the other pincering his spectacles in a two-fingered grip. He looked old and terminally ill. I wasn't the only one who expected him to topple from his chair, and it struck me that the people in the audience weren't interested in Xavier's poems or his views on color. They were there to see if the bad boy of Indian art would live up to his reputation. They hoped to see him combust in front of their eyes, or implode, or die of a heart attack, or leap from his seat and rape an audience member. The worse his behavior the happier they would be. It was voyeurism at its vilest and we were drinking in the details: the stains on his kurta—drink? blood? semen?—the disreputable rubber slippers, his binge stubble and rapid eyes, his death pallor, the wonderful fact that he was too drunk to stand.

"Now you know what legless means," said the matron beside me, in a stage whisper that carried through the room.

"Madam, I have warned you before about your bad habit. Please keep quiet or I will be forced to have you ejected permanently," said Iskai, suddenly furious.

Someone had placed a glass of water near Xavier, but in lifting it he shakily spilled some on the table and he put the glass down without wetting his lips. He was going to read a new poem, he said, speaking so softly that the audience had to lean forward to hear him. Then he started to read and his voice was mild, the words perfectly articulated, the accent round and rich and neutral, not British or American or Indian but godlike. Most striking of all was the tone of absolute authority. I heard the coldness under it and it gave me a shiver, even in that heat it gave me a shiver.

THE POEM, told in rhyming quatrains, was set in a future waste-land of war or famine or disease, where some unnamed catastrophe had culled much of the world's population. To protect themselves against the invisible, nations had broken up into smaller states, each with its own government, religion, language, and particular social customs. Travel between cities was insanely complicated and travel between states was banned by all governments. Citizens were required to carry passports with them at all times. Xavier's poem concerned a rural Moroccan boy who falls sick while getting ready for school. His parents take him to a hospital in Fez and are told by the authorities that their son will not come out of his coma and fur-ther contact with him will only ensure their own decline or impris-onment, because they are out of their municipal precinct and had broken the law by coming to Fez, and are in fact continuing to break the law by remaining there. The parents are forced to abandon their son and return to their village, where the mother soon develops agoraphobia and the father becomes a systematic abuser of the female inmates in the small mental institution in which he works. The boy wakes up in a city he doesn't know, alone in a room in the middle of the night, except it isn't night at all, because a red light is streaming into the window. He thinks: I am dead, like Jed-di, like Ammi and Abba. Everyone died and I am in hell because of the bad things I did. He doesn't know it but he has recovered. He continues to lie in bed, attached to a glucose drip and a monitor. Then he sees that the moonlight has become redder, so bright it seems the devil himself has come to pay him a visit. The boy walks to the window and sees the building is on fire. He runs down the endless corridors of the hospital, which, he soon understands, is deserted but for him.

Then follow two quatrains of landscape description, the desert at night and in the early dawn, the necessity of finding drinking water, the portability and efficacy of dried fruits and honey, and the miraculous restorative powers of some varieties of cactus plants. When the poem returns to the boy, he is in his late teens. He is the leader of a band of rebel nomads, youths who travel by night and hide by day, living off the generosity of villagers. In the winter of the boy's eighteenth year, he and his comrades come to a small town that the boy recognizes as his village, now grown into a place of some importance. From a hill the youths gaze at the sleeping town and the boy identifies the cemetery, the insane asylum where his father worked, the bakery and tea shop, and so on, but try as he might he cannot locate his house. "Let's go down and wander around," his closest comrade and second in command suggests. "We'll wander around until it's found, / Then we can rest." The boy does not reply. He realizes that the reason he could not identify his home is because the modest house in which he grew up is now a mansion with a pool and a garden and he can even see children's toys scattered on the lawn. The group begins to descend into the valley when the boy changes his mind. They will skirt the town and travel on, he says. The poem ended with these lines:

> *It wasn't that I wanted to go home,*
> *Who knew home? I only knew alone.*
> *What I wanted was to be elsewhere,*
> *Somewhere, anywhere but there.*

Xavier continued to talk, though he was no longer reading the poem. I woke up to bright sunshine this morning, he said, or it could have been yesterday morning, who's to know? In any case,

I woke to bright skies and I thought, for some of us it's a beautiful day. I—

"Why wouldn't it be a beautiful day for you? You come to India only to escape the winter. The papers say you are moving from the UK to the U.S., to become a citizen of a rich, or I should say, richer country. They say exile suits you."

It was the small man at the back of the room who'd asked the earlier question. Iskai said it was still not yet question time and he asked the man to wait. Xavier said he had never claimed to be a citizen of exile. The word was much too grand and fashionable to describe his condition, which was something less dramatic and had to do with restlessness and chance. It was never my intention to become a citizen of the United States, he said. I am and will continue to be a first-class citizen of my own country rather than a second-class citizen of elsewhere. What I am doing is applying for the status of alien of extraordinary ability. It's a visa category I recommend for green card aspirants.

My neighbor said, please wait. She took a notebook and pen from her purse. My son is interested in U.S. for higher studies. What are the details of your visa, please? She waited with pen poised but Xavier didn't reply. He was immobile, looking glassily in her direction. There was silence for four or five seconds. Then a single high-pitched snort burst from his mouth: he was sitting upright with his eyes open, but he was asleep. Several voices started up at once. Suddenly, it seemed, everybody had a question for Xavier. Iskaye made his closing remarks but an elderly man stood up in the front row and, by force of will, made himself audible above the crowd. His question was punctuated by Xavier's distinctive snore.

"Forster said patriotism was the last refuge of scoundrels. Johnson said he would rather betray his country than betray a friend.

Yeats said the worst are filled with passionate intensity. Your early paintings eschewed patrilineal posturing for flat evocation. In this light, I find your anticitizenship stance simply unconvincing. If U.S. citizenship doesn't matter, why not take it up? My question, therefore, is two-part. Aren't you pandering to the home crowd when you make such statements? And, connectedly, have you taken a position viz. recent developments in that most programmatic of all states, the Soviet Union?"

Iskai said, "Newton?"

Xavier got to his feet, said, "Yes, such as it is," and fell backwards into the arms of the peon, who lowered him gently to his chair. Then he said, "It is only now that I know what color means."

"What does it mean?" asked the short man at the back.

"What?"

"You said it's only now that you know what color means."

Xavier looked at the man for the first time.

"Color is a way of speaking, not seeing. Poets need color, and musicians too. But painters should forget it. Color, if you don't mind me saying so, is a crutch, like the necessity of god. For some nineteenth-century European painters, the absence of god was as intolerable as the absence of color. They used the entire spectrum for every negligible little thing, a rain-slicked street, a house on a cliff, boats on a lake. I'm sorry to say it makes little or no sense for a painter in Bombay or Delhi or Bhopal to use a similar approach. Where's the context? If you want to make something genuine in this climate you have to think about indolence and brutality. Also: unintentional comedy. But there's no use saying this to you. You'll only misunderstand and misquote me, and I will end up sounding pompous or foolish, which is really the same thing."

Iskai said the meeting was over. He said Xavier would not be signing books. He thanked the audience and pointed them to the exit. People talked among themselves and nobody got up to leave. Even the elderly critic in the front row seemed satisfied. Xavier hadn't let them down.

I SAT WHERE I was. I'd had a long and exhausting day. I'd just begun work at a pharmaceutical company where my job was to proofread the house newsletter. It was dull business. I spent long hours correcting articles on the umbrella benefits of broad-spectrum antibiotics, or the latest research in the treatment of fungal complaints. But the job put me in lovely proximity to high-grade narcotics. I had access to government-controlled morphine, to sleeping pills, painkillers, synthetic opiates, to all kinds of fierce prescription downers. That morning, unable to stop by Rashid's on my way to work, I'd taken two strips of Prodom from the shop stores. They were a miracle cure for whatever ailed you, two pills and you were staggering around as if you'd been drinking vodka all morning. It helped me forget that I was opium sick. Later I'd stopped at Rashid's for an hour and made it to PEN in time for the reading. With the downers and a pipe of O under my belt I was numb, if not rubbery. I wasn't as wasted as Xavier, but I was in the same neighborhood. When I opened my eyes, I saw I was the only audience member still in the hall. Xavier was asleep in a wheelchair and Iskai spoke to him in a low monotone. Nobody noticed except Madame Blavatsky, whose eyes followed me around the room.

"Come on now, Newton, do wake up. I promised to get you home in one piece. I know you can hear me, so wake up, old boy, it's a question of will." When he saw me getting to my feet, he said, "Look, could you help me out? The bloody peon has disappeared—it's probably past his official working hours. Would you mind taking Mr. Xavier down while I go find a taxi?"

I agreed, of course, and pushed the wheelchair with the still unconscious Xavier out of the building to the gate. But when the wheelchair stopped, he opened his eyes. He was perfectly composed.

"Okay, thanks. I'm assuming Akash left you here to look after me, but why aren't you looking for a taxi?"

"Mr. Iskai went to find one."

"That might take all night. Let's go."

I was still unsteady on my feet. And when I saw a taxi out of the corner of my eye and turned to hail it, my own momentum carried me twice around. I fell heavily to the road, hurting my elbow. The PEN night watchman picked me up and put me in the cab. Then he did the same with Xavier. He told the driver to take me to my hostel in Colaba and to drive Xavier to his hotel, which was in the same general direction. And so it was that Newton Xavier ended up dropping me home. He did it angrily and he made a bitter speech.

"Unbelievable. Where did Akash find you? You can barely walk and he puts you in charge of me. I end up minding the minder. What a lovely pile of shit."

"Let me understand this, you're berating me?"

"You're welcome, asshole."

HE STARED OUT the window as the taxi sped past Hutatma Chowk and the tiered breasts of Flora and her friends, toward the sodium lights of Colaba Causeway and the Victorian ruins piled one on top of the other, once grand facades behind which squalor lived, and more squalor, cobbled alleys lined with cots on which the better-off pavement sleepers settled for the night, as the speckled water, the septic seething water, the gray-green kala paani, the dirty living sunbaked water lapped against the sides of the broken city. This is how I would describe the taxi ride later, when I embellished the story of my evening with the famous drunk Xavier, who was taking small contented sips from a nip bottle of whisky.

"Wait a minute," I said. "Didn't I read somewhere that you were on the wagon?"

"On, off, off, on. I have a friend who says you never really quit, all you do is take breaks."

He nodded politely and took another sip. Then, as if he were asking about my job or the weather, he said, so, what are you on? I debated it. I did, for about half a minute, and then I thought how laughable it was that I was bashful about confessing my drug use to an alcoholic. I told him, and of course he wanted to see Rashid's. He'd tried opium in Thailand, had in fact spent a month in Chiang Mai smoking too much for his own good, but that had been many years earlier. He'd heard about Bombay's drug dens and he would be in my debt if I took him to the khana. If there was anything he could do for me in return, I should consider it done. And there was nothing to worry about; he would not talk about it. In fact, he had more to lose than I did if word got out that he'd been carousing in Bombay's red-light district. He could keep a secret. The question was, could I?

IT WAS LATE, but I knew Rashid's would be open and it was a simple thing to redirect the cab and keep the driver waiting with the promise of a tip. On the way, the painter continued to sip at his whisky without offering me a taste, and soon we were falling up the wooden steps to the khana, where Bengali sat bent over a newspaper and Dimple was making herself a pipe. For a moment I saw the room from a stranger's eyes; I saw a wavering image, unreal, something out of the sixteenth century. I stood there in my bell-bottoms and I felt like an interloper from the future come to gawk at the poor and unfortunate who lived in a time before antibiotics and television and airplanes.

I ORDERED TWO pyalis and let Xavier go first. Who's the old man? Dimple asked, having assumed from Xavier's subdued manner and tone of voice that he was from Elsewhere (a place where Hindi wasn't spoken or understood). But he replied in the same colloquial Bambayya she had used.

"My dear, I'm not that much older than you. My hair's white and my bones are rickety but that's because I drink. I look older than I am. Whereas you look your age."

I told Dimple she'd seen his work in a magazine some weeks earlier. She didn't remember, but Bengali did. He spoke from deep inside a nod. Christ, Bengali said, from the Sanskrit *ghrei*, to rub, which in Greek became *Christos*, the anointed, which may mean that Christ is an Indo-European concept, much as your paintings suggest. And that was when Xavier realized that though Bengali's eyes were closed he was looking directly at him. I reminded Dimple that she'd been disturbed by Xavier's pictures, which was a pure reaction, maybe the most gratifying response an artist could expect. I was addressing Dimple, but I was speaking for Xavier's benefit. I was showing him off to her, it's true, but I was also showing her off to him. Addicts are alike in that way, we're always eager to show civilians our subterranean relationships and outlaw skills. At the time, I still thought of Xavier as a civilian.

"And now here he is in person," I said. "Isn't it incredible?"

It was at this moment that Bengali whimpered in his dream and uttered a sentence nobody understood. We heard only the last word: *kaun?*

Dimple shook her head once. There was nothing incredible about it, she said. I thought it was so because I spoke English, because I read books, and because my parents paid for my education and my upkeep. For me everything was surprising, the world was full of wonder, the most random idiotic occurrence was incredible because my luck made it so. For people like her, for the poor, the only incredible thing in the whole world was money and the mysterious ways in which it worked.

SHE'S RIGHT, Xavier said. Only the rich can afford surprise and/or irony. The rich crave meaning. The first thing they ask when faced with eternity, and in fact the last thing, is: excuse me, what does this mean? The poor don't ask questions, or they don't ask irrelevant questions. They can't afford to. All they can afford is laughter and ghosts. Then there are the addicts, the hunger addicts and rage addicts and poverty addicts and power addicts, and the pure addicts who are addicted not to substances but to the oblivion and tenderness that substances engender. An addict, if you don't mind me saying so, is like a saint. What is a saint but someone who has cut himself off, voluntarily, voluntarily, from the world's traffic and currency? The saint talks to flowers, a daffodil, say, and he sees the yellow of it. He receives its scent through his eyes. Yes, he thinks, you are my muse, I take heart from your stubbornness, a drop of water, a dab of sunshine, and there you are with your gorgeous blooms. He enjoys flowers but he worships trees. He wants to be the banyan's slave. He wants to think of time the way a tree does, a decade as nothing more than some slight addition to his girth. He connives with birds, and gets his daily news from the sound the wind makes in the leaves. When he's hungry he stands in the forest waiting for the fall of a mango. His ambition is the opposite of ambition. Most of all, like all addicts, he wants to obliterate time. He wants to die, or, at the very least, to not live.

Dimple said, "I need a translator to understand you."

"I think I do too," said Xavier, "I think maybe I'm going off my head again."

I said, "Saints and addicts, I like that."

And that was when Dimple asked the question I couldn't answer for many years. She asked why it was that I, who could read and write and had a family that cared enough about me to finance my education, who could do anything I wanted, go anywhere and be anyone, why was I an addict? She didn't understand it.

At the time, I couldn't either. I didn't know my own compulsions well enough to reply. Instead, I broke out the pharmaceutical morphine I'd stolen from the office stores and made myself a small shot. Xavier had one too.

WHEN SHE TAPPED the stem he took the pipe and held it comfortably, the way a man holds a telescope, with two or three fingers. She said later that she felt his eyes travel the length of her body and settle on her cunt and all the while he pulled at the pipe, the sound loud in the room, and she felt that he was sucking at her amputated penis, sucking in a way that would end her life if she didn't resist him. Some time later, she heard the sound of water, running water, as if a tap were open somewhere, or not the sound of water exactly, but a voice imitating the sound of water, a voice that was low and uninterested and busy and she realized it was his voice and he was speaking to her. Eunuchs used to carry quills in their turbans, he said, like a portable penis that could be attached when they wished to urinate. I'm sure you could get something custom made, bone or hard plastic, a funnel of some sort, something you could carry with you. Imagine how much easier it would be. You wouldn't have to sit, you could stand and pee like a man. She noticed that his eyes protruded like the eyes of a snake or a lizard, pop eyes that didn't blink or waver. She understood that it was very important to close her own eyes and breathe calmly. But when she shut her eyes she felt him in her anal cavity, a dry grating pressure that threw words into her head she could not dislodge: Satan. Shaitan. Shat On. She opened her eyes in panic and just then he exhaled a great cloud of smoke, too great for a single pair of lungs, and she saw only his torso clad in white kurta and churidars: where the head should have been there was thick vapor, as if a burning sword had decapitated him, as if inside he was all smoke, a man-shaped river of smoke that was leaking into the room. Later she said it was at this moment that she began to pray and the prayer that rose to her lips was not Muslim or Hindu but Christian, and she said it to herself in English: hell mary midriff god pray fussiness now and at thee owruff ower death.

I GOT UP at midnight. There was a 12:30 curfew at my hostel and in any case it was time we were on our way. But Xavier wanted biryani and kebabs, which he hoped Bengali would be kind enough to bring from Delhi Darbar's late-night window. He wanted more whisky and maybe another pipe. When I got up, Dimple did too. Xavier asked why she was leaving. Was she afraid of being alone with an old man? She told me to go ahead. She would stay and shut up shop.

The cab was still waiting and I took it home to Colaba. In my room, which faced the street, there was a smell of camphor from the evening's antimosquito effort. I opened the window and the moonlight lit up the bed and desk and mirror (the only furnishings) as if I'd turned on an electric lamp. I arranged myself in the usual way, on my back with my hands folded across my chest. I slept and woke suddenly and found that the sheets were wet and there was a gash between my legs. I tried to stop the blood with my hands but it soaked into my trousers and filled my shoes. I fell asleep with my shoes on, I thought stupidly, touching the crusted blood on my thighs. I looked on the floor but there was nothing there except moonlight and dust. I was reaching blindly for the telephone when I woke up. It was noon and I was in the same position in which I'd fallen asleep. Though I'd slept for ten hours I was exhausted and sweaty. I had a shower and ate lunch in the mess. I did the laundry and went back to my room, where I arranged and rearranged the objects on my desk. By four in the afternoon I could think of nothing else and I was on my way out the door when the hostel manager said there was someone waiting to see me. In the lounge, a grand name for what was in reality nothing more than a corridor without light or air, was Akash Iskai reading a newspaper. He wore a blue T-shirt that had been washed many times and he looked slightly less like a Hindustani musician than he had at Xavier's event. The poet had gotten my address from the PEN watchman, who said Xavier and I had gone off together in a taxi. Iskai had assumed his friend would be fine, but he knew now his friend was not fine at all. Xavier had disappeared. He wasn't at his hotel and he hadn't turned up for a press conference at the gallery where the new show was about to open. Where was he? Did I know? Iskai said he felt responsible for the latest disaster that had overtaken the poor man. He would be blamed if something had happened because the PEN event had been his idea and he had organized the funds to bring Xavier to Bombay. I thought about what Xavier had said the night before, that he didn't want it to get around that he'd been smoking opium. And, I thought, Xavier is a man of the world. It would be wrong not to offer him the minimum respect one gave an adult, which was the option to let himself down, with a crash perhaps, if that was what he wished to do. I told Iskai that Xavier had dropped me off first and gone in the direction of his Colaba hotel, that he seemed fine at the time. And of course I hadn't noted the taxi's license plate number, why would I? Iskai went off, still upset, and I went to Rashid's.

THE KHANA WAS FULL, but Dimple wasn't there and neither was Xavier. I ordered a pyali and smoked it slowly, at Dimple's station, where Pagal Kutta was tending the pipe. He was the most incompetent pipeman in the khana. His pipes burned too fast and too strong. Worse, he was in a rush for you to finish so he could smoke the dregs. But it was the way he sucked at the pipe that had earned him his nickname, because he huffed and snorted like a mad dog. I endured the smoke he made me and I endured Rashid's stories while I waited for Dimple. Rashid was talking about the Pathar Maar's latest killing. He had struck late the night before and the newspapers hadn't gotten around to reporting it. He'd picked off a mother and baby who were sleeping under the Grant Road Bridge. He'd crushed the woman's head with a stone from the pavement and taken the baby by his ankles and smashed him against a wall. Others had been sleeping nearby but nobody heard a cry. It wasn't until someone woke to use the toilet that the murders were discovered.

"The Pathar Maar is a Congress stooge," said Rashid. "This is the culmination of the Garibi Hatao campaign. What do you say, Bengali?"

When he laughed, the others joined in, pipemen, customers, even Bengali laughed, though it was clear not everybody understood the joke: some among that group of career criminals and addicts didn't know if it was 1978 or 1975, much less the minutiae of government policy. Dimple came in an hour or so later and Rashid said something that made her duck her head and go straight to work. And when I asked Bengali about the man in the kurta who'd come to the khana the previous night, he looked at me blankly, as if he had no idea who I was, much less what I was talking about.

THE FOLLOWING DAY I resolved to stay home, but that evening I was back at the khana, and on the floor, smoking a pipe with Pagal Kutta, was the painter Xavier. His white kurta had turned the color of sawdust but his beard was trimmed and he'd had a haircut. In fact, he was looking fresher than he had any right to. Dimple was nowhere to be seen. I told him that Iskai had been to see me, that people were worried about him. Where had he been?

"Sampling the wares of Shuklaji Street. No reason for Akash to upset himself. My show opens tomorrow. I'll be there in a suit, charming the press. Tell him to stay calm."

I asked again where he'd disappeared to. He said, may I buy you a pyali of Mr. Rashid's excellent product? If Baudelaire had extended his survey of paradise to opium, and this opium in particular, I think it would have won hands down. And I am making no idle speculation. As you may have gathered, I am a wino, and it is as a wino that I aver, this opium is superior, uniformly consistently superior. Xavier was drunk, but not so drunk he needed a wheelchair. He thanked me for my help, paid for my pyalis, and left the khana in a respectable fashion.

A day or so later I asked Dimple if she knew where Xavier had been. She said he'd been with her at the hijra's brothel. But she didn't want to talk about him. In our language the word for evil and chaos is the same, she said, to speak of evil is to invite it into your life. She never mentioned Xavier again, not even to me.

DIMPLE KEPT her word when she said she would not speak of what had happened. But she did not forget the man with the pop eyes whose bloody gums and whisky sweat gave her the superstitious feeling that a devil had entered the room. After I left and Bengali went out to buy food, they were alone in the khana for about half an hour. She busied herself setting out a pyali, but he prepared the opium himself. He did it expertly, tapping the pipe when it was ready, offering her the first smoke. She felt as if she were the customer and he the pipewallah. She would have enjoyed it too, if she hadn't felt so controlled by him. While she was still smoking, he took the pipe from her and put the mouthpiece, still wet from her lips, to his, his eyes locked on her belly. Then, looking her in the eyes, he sucked slowly at the pipe and she felt as if he was penetrating her through her clothes, or as if she had fallen asleep in an unfamiliar town and had been slapped awake by a stranger, a man whose face she could not see, who fucked her without mercy and paid no heed to her pleas for lubrication. She had never felt so naked, not even in the brothel.

As soon as Bengali returned, she went home. She walked quickly to the corner and turned into Hijde ki Gully, where she walked past 007 and stopped as if to buy paan and checked to see if she was being followed. Only then did she go into the building. She ate dinner and washed herself. She exchanged her salvaar for a sari and was touching up her lipstick and face powder when Xavier entered. He chose the most uncomfortable chair in the house, a pink plastic armchair built for a child. Lakshmi brought him a beer and before he'd taken a sip he ordered another. He asked the tai how much it would cost to spend the night in one of the cubicles. With or without a girl? the tai asked. Without, he said, and the tai gave him the first figure that came into her head, three hundred for the night. How much with a girl? he asked. The tai said, six hundred. So a room costs the same as a girl? The tai laughed at him. He pointed at Dimple and said, I'll take that one. But ask her to put on a burka for me. You should make them all wear burkas, you'll make more money. The tai laughed again. Xavier told her, put half the girls in burkas and half in saris and see what the customers prefer. Not once in his exchange with the tai did he look at Dimple.

The tai told her to get a cubicle ready. Dimple chose the least private one, the one nearest the entrance, next to the tai's own room. She put a fresh sheet on the cot and cleared the bucket of used condoms and cigarette butts. Then she changed while Xavier and the tai continued to talk business in the hall, a strange conversation that filled her with dismay because of the way he said the English word eunuch, as if to disparage her and women like her; he never used the word hijra. Take a eunuch with a penis and no testicles, he said, which operation, as the tai knew, was accomplished at little cost, could in fact be accomplished with a minimum of expenditure; take him, and this was the important point, augment the basic armature of penis, no testicles, with a pair of good-quality breasts, the larger the better. He said the tai should invest in a new surgical procedure called silly cone, with which she could fashion a new breed of randi with big breasts and a show penis. For such a randi she could double the regular price, or even triple it. She would recoup her investment in the space of two months if not less and from then on it would be pure profit. The tai was no longer laughing, or she was laughing too softly to be heard. More likely, she was listening very carefully and would probably repeat the whole story to the seth, owner of the brothel and the randis. Dimple lay on the cot, taking as little space as possible and trying not to fall asleep, but it was late and she was tired.

SHE WAS IN a corridor that stretched and curved like a road in the country. The only light came from the thin strips of blue light glowing under the doors she passed. On her left was a wall and on the right were the doors, an endless succession of them, each with a strip of blue below it. Sometimes she heard voices, but mostly she heard the sound of splashing, or the hum of a large body of water, and she knew without being told that she had to keep walking, that it would be her error to stop and see what lay behind the doors, which were set at irregular intervals though they were all of the same size and shape. It doesn't matter, she heard herself say, nothing worse can happen to me. All those who loved me have died and I too am dead. She felt such unbearable loneliness at the thought that she stopped and opened a door at random. The room was enormous, taken up in its entirety by a pool filled with blue water. She knew the water was very cold, because no condensation had formed on the tiles and the air was frigid. Around the pool was a ledge, but it was too narrow to walk on. The room had walls that went so high that the ceiling was invisible to her. On the far side of the room she made out a figure sitting with his legs in the water. She couldn't see his face but she saw the lighted end of the cigarette he was smoking and she thought she smelled clove tobacco. She closed the door and walked on and her own footsteps sounded strange to her. She thought: I am losing myself one step at a time. And she opened the door to an identical room with a pool in which someone had recently been swimming. There was a thin mist on the surface of the water and bits of algae. It was cold and someone laughed. But when she looked into the darkness at the other end of the room there was no one. Then she noticed the shapes in the water and she went to take a closer look. Fat round shapes with long tails slept on the floor of the pool, and, as she watched, one detached itself from the mass of its brothers and torpedoed up towards her. She stepped back as an old man's head broke the surface.

Mr. Lee? she said.

AND SHE WOKE beside Xavier, who was still asleep. She bathed, changed, ate breakfast, and was at Rashid's by noon. When Xavier came in around two, her station was busy and he went to Pagal Kutta's. He acted like he didn't know her. He smoked a pyali and ate lunch in the khana and then he went out for a haircut and a beard trim. The barber pointed out a hammam, a couple of cubicles set up by the side of the road where they gave him a sliver of soap, a bucket of lukewarm water, and a thin cotton towel. The bath cost him forty paisa and he emerged feeling clean despite the dirty clothes he was wearing. He felt good enough to take a little stroll. He thought of picking up a T-shirt and a pair of slacks in one of the shops on Grant Road and he turned right at the end of Shuklaji Street. Then, walking past Delhi Darbar, he smelled food and forgot about buying clothes: he wanted a drink. In a shop window he saw the reflection of a raggedy man in a dirty kurta and he stumbled lightly. He saw biryani cook pots and flies and piles of horse dung. A man approached with a double cross on which plastic sunglasses and hair clips were arranged in the vague shape of a crucifix. He saw a man driving fast with his windows up and in the back of the car a little girl leaned her forehead against the glass. He saw men walking towards him with their hands around each other's shoulders, and a man had collapsed on the street, his pockets turned inside out, and a group of boys panted in unison with a radio song in which the singer imitated a dog. A woman in a yellow blouse and petticoat made up her face in a splinter of glass. She held the jagged splinter like a knife. When he walked past her cage their eyes met in the mirror. She nodded to him and he went to the cage. She reached through the bars and grabbed his dick. Her hand was small, the grip very firm, and the bottle green bangles on her wrist chimed like small bells when she massaged him. He asked her where he might find a wine shop and she let go of him. No wine. This is a Muslim locality, babuji, what do you expect? When he walked away she made a fist and grabbed herself by the elbow, gesturing to his dick with her lips. A man standing near her cage laughed. Xavier passed a movie theater, its front wall streaked with piss. He bought a ticket and went in just as a song sequence began. A man in a matador's costume gyrated in a giant birdcage. It was the tune he'd heard minutes earlier, in which a man panted like a dog. The matador took off his jacket and shouted, Monica. Xavier thought of saints and felt a powerful emotion, elation or fear, he wasn't sure. A woman slid down a ramp to a dance floor. There was an artful shot of her figure framed between two bottles. She held the bottles up to her face and Xavier got up and went out into the sunlight and took a cab to Chowpatty. He found a permit room where a waitress served him whisky and poured him a beer. There were many tables and all the drinkers were men. On a tiny stage a woman in a chiffon sari danced to muddy music. He couldn't tell if it was jazz or Hindustani classical. The woman moved her hips but not her feet. She held up her hands and gazed at the floor as if she was being robbed. Her expression said she was trying to remember something very important, something that could save her life. The drinkers gave her money but it wasn't enough because she was still unable to remember the important thing. When the song ended she dropped her hands and walked offstage. Somebody clapped.

Late in the evening Xavier went back to 007, getting there before Dimple. He told the tai to send him the same girl dressed the same way and then he took a beer with him into the cubicle in which he'd spent the previous night. When Dimple came in, changed and washed, he fucked her standing up with her arms propped on the cot and her clothes pushed up around her waist. Later, he fucked her again and yelled something in a language no one could identify, French maybe, or Italian, some European language other than English, shouting the same two words again and again, *Sa Crenaam*. The cubicles next to theirs were occupied, the tai on one side and Lakshmi on the other. Lakshmi clapped her hands in the chakka salute when Xavier came, because it took him so long. She shouted her congratulations, to Dimple for her stamina and to Xavier for his technique.

SHE WOKE INSTANTLY, with the sensation that she'd forgotten something. She knew it was late because the night-light had been turned on in the main room. She was alone on the cot. Then she became aware of a figure sitting motionless on the floor. She put the lamp on and saw Xavier, fully dressed, with his back against the door. The night-light made red slashes in his face when he spoke. She thought: he looks like a lunatic. Find yourself a patron saint, he told her in a dog's hoarse voice. Everybody needs at least one and some of us need two or more. I'm not saying the saint will protect you, he might, but there's the question of companionship, not to mention peace of mind, which you need. I need protection too, Dimple said. Then listen carefully. I suggest that you think seriously about the patron saints of amputees, Anthony of Padua and Anthony the Abbott, who are also the patron saints of animals. The Anthonys of animals and amputees, now there's a pairing that goes beyond the merely alphabetical and alliterative, wouldn't you say? I suggest too the services of Agnes of Rome and Thomas Aquinas, who, among lesser or greater achievements, depending on your point of view, are the patron saints of chastity. Which isn't of much concern to you though perhaps it should be, if you see what I mean. Between the two your best bet is Agnes, who is also the patron saint of orphans and virgins. It might interest you to know that the patron saints against sexual temptation are all women, the Marys of Edessa and Egypt, Mary Magdalene and Mary Magdalene of Pazzi, Angela of Foligno, Margaret of Cortona, Catherine of Siena, and Pelagia of Antioch, who martyred herself at fifteen with the help of a ladder, a house, and a small battalion of Roman soldiers. Then there's Maximilian Kolbe, the patron saint of drug addicts and journalists, which, if you ask me, is an inevitable pairing. Most important of them all, in your case, is Dismas, who will be of particular service to you and those around you: he is the patron saint of criminals and whores. And of course the twins Damian and Cosmas, Arab physicians who practiced together and were martyred together and became the patron saints of medicine and pharmacy, a useful bit of information for drug fiends. My own preference is Martin of Tours and Monica, two of the patron saints against alcoholism, and between the two I choose Monica every time. Of course Martin is also the patron saint of recovering alcoholics, which facet of his personality I am willing to overlook on some days. Teresa of Ávila is praised for her poetry, though it's slightly too florid for my taste. But she is also the patron saint of aches, head and body, and someone you would do well to petition. I recommend too my namesake, Francis Xavier, the patron saint of Goa and Japan and of navigators and aimless travelers. There are twenty-five patron saints of unhappy marriages, including Hedwig of Andechs, Margaret the Barefooted, and Thomas More, but only one patron saint of happy marriages, Valentine. Memorize the patron saints of the poor, for they are plentiful yet in short supply, Philomena, Giles, Martin de Porres, Nicholas of Myra, Lawrence, Anthony of Padua, Ferdinand of Castile, and Zoticus of Constantinople. And eventually you will need the services of Ezekiel Moreno, the patron saint of the ailment smokers are susceptible to, and of course Ulric, the patron saint of a happy death, which is the least I wish for you.

4.

Mr. Lee's
Lessons in Living

She was getting aches in her shoulders and her back and she woke up sometimes with the pain, woke too early, and the tai gave her an oil massage, told her to eat moong, told her she was smoking too much. Mr. Lee said, exercise, take a walk on Chowpatty Beach, good to get out, take a look at the sea, because that's all you can do, you'd be crazy to swim, it's so dirty. He went with her sometimes. He dressed up, put on a hat, socks, tan English loafers—for a walk on the beach. And he carried a walking stick, the most elegant thing she'd seen, dark polished wood with a jade handle in the shape of a leaping dog. They walked for some of the way and he received steady attention on the street. They both did. He was a foreigner, a refugee from mainland China, but they could have been father and daughter, they looked so similar.

He wanted to stop at Rajasthan Lassi for a chikku milk shake. They sat on the steps of Brilliant Typing & Shorthand Institute and looked at the life on the streets. She was content to watch and listen and Mr. Lee, understanding this, said little. The milk shakes came in tall glasses with a pink napkin stuck to the side and she drank half in one go, then realized she was expected to take the napkin off, hold it in one hand, and sip at a straw like the other women. She copied them, she took small sips and dabbed her mouth. She watched the people walking home from work or to evening classes at Wilson College, the parents and grandparents and children, the extended joint families who came to the beach from who knew where and never got out of their cars. They ordered meals from the windows of new Ambassadors and Fiats and ate quickly and ordered more. She watched them as if she too were in class, a student of the college carrying out field studies for a course on the Mores and Practices of India's Middle Class. Or a course in Parental Love, she thought, as the milk shake curdled in her mouth and the image of a woman flashed in her head and was gone. She had very few memories of her mother, but they were vivid and she would carry them with her for the rest of her life. She remembered a tall woman praying in a temple, her sari the exact shade of red as the kumkum in her black hair. But the woman also prayed in a secret church she had made at home. The woman prayed in Hindi and English. The Hindi prayers were said aloud, recited in public, but the English was hidden from the world, whispered to her kitchen cupboard, where her church was. The woman was very poor but she wore starched salvaars and saris, and, every morning, strings of fresh jasmine appeared in her hair. Dimple remembered that the woman's hair was thick and very long. She loved the woman's smell, like woodsmoke and milk and old wool, and she remembered that her skin was the color of milk. But then she remembered the sound of bells, death bells, and the woman's wails. Afterwards, the woman stopped wearing red; she wore only white and she covered her face with her sari. She stopped speaking, even to Dimple, and then she gave her away. This was the clearest memory of all, her mother's crushed, fearful face as she handed Dimple to the priest.

They walked towards the beach and passed a beer bar and heard a tinny insistent beat. Men exited the bar at all hours of day and night and stopped at the adjacent paanwallah, whose Bedbreaker Special with its secret hit of uncut cocaine would keep a man going all night, or so some of Dimple's clients said. Do palang tod, she told the paanwallah, who handed over two Bedbreakers wrapped in newspaper. Then they walked past the wrought-iron railing of Wilson College to the beach, where crowds of men strolled on the sand or lingered in the darkness under the trees. They stood by the water and ate the paan and spat the juice on the sand and laughed or chewed their teeth. The paan was astringent and sweet and it numbed her mouth and put a happy jitter in her eyes. The men looked at her the way they did, their eyes lingering on the freshness of her, her white skin and black eyes and the red leaves of henna that trailed from index finger to wrist. Her hair would come loose and she'd stop to gather it into a bun and her admirers would stop too, watching every move. They saw health and good nature in her roundness, and something more, a calculation, a professional distance in the eyes, a kind of premeditated shine on her teeth and skin. And some heightened awareness, a ripple of interest skimmed above the heads of the strollers on the beach and returned to her from the men.

HER BREASTS WERE fuller and the space between her legs had healed long ago into a scar, but the ache in her back and elbows was something new. She was always aware of it, a dormant ache even when there was no pain. The tai gave her massages, an hour with the curtains drawn first thing in the morning before the giraks arrived. If anything, the aches got worse. She'd get up stiff, so numb she felt nothing in the tips of her toes. A ghost ache would stay in her bones all through the day. She'd be irritable and preoccupied and the customers would go to someone else. Some of her regulars continued to see her but they did it as if they were duty bound and paying a conjugal visit.

This is how she met Mr. Lee. Her income had dropped and the tai took her to see him. First thing in the morning, the tai said, meaning sometime around noon. They had to get there early or he wouldn't answer the door. He's a Chini, she said, as if that explained everything, every oddity in Mr. Lee's personality. Dimple washed her hair and put on lipstick. She'd taken to wearing trousers because it allowed her to walk with a little strut in her step, or lounge on the couch with her legs spread, or slouch like a pimp, or climb a tree if she felt like it. It allowed her to act like a man when she wanted to. But that day she wore a starched salvaar with the pallu wide on her chest. She put on slippers with small heels and placed a pair of silver hoops in her ears. It was a conservative look: Nargis, offscreen, circa Raj Kapoor: a good Indian girl going to meet her elders. Dressed this way she almost believed it. She thought: clothes are costumes, or disguises. The image has nothing to do with the truth. And what is the truth? Whatever you want it to be. Men are women and women are men. Everybody is everything. She thought: who do I look like? Do I look like my mother? Do I look like my mother or someone else? She had no idea and for that she was grateful. Forgetfulness was a gift, a talent to be nurtured.

THE TREE WAS a peepal, very old, with shreds of fabric caught on its branches, shiny bits of silk and crepe. It was a common Indian tree, but the ribboned fabric made it look like some rare import. There was a shrine under it, incense bunched around a porcelain plate of oranges, and a box in which squares of colored paper had been burned. They were in a side lane off Shuklaji Street, a place for refugee families from China and Burma, two or three generations living in small rooms facing a courtyard. They went directly to a room on the far side, the only room with a locked front door. The tai made her stand in front of the peephole so he'd see her easily and then she knocked. Dimple heard a shout on the street, a man's voice saying an English word. Paper. Or: papa. The tai knocked again and Dimple's first thought when he opened the door was not a thought exactly but a word, *old*. He ignored the tai and spoke only to her. Nee ho ah? And then a longer sentence she couldn't follow.

She said, "Can you please speak English, please?"

"You not Chinese?"

"No, my family is from northeast of India."

"Okay, northeast, I understand. Very close to China, VERY close."

"I don't know from exactly where. I grew up in Bombay, here, on Shuklaji Street."

The tai said, "Leeji, we have come for your help. She is having pain. Can you give her afeem?"

INSIDE, they sat on a low bed covered with bamboo matting. He gave them tea without milk or sugar, a rust-colored liquid with a taste she couldn't identify, a dusty earth tang like dried flowers or herbs. The room was dim and tidy, all the windows closed except for a skylight set low on the tile roof. When her eyes adjusted she saw two men, asleep, one to a bunk on adjoining beds, or not asleep exactly; they didn't move or speak but their eyes were open, seeing nothing. They were all eyes, as if their faces had caved in around their mouths. Mr. Lee sat on the floor on a woven bamboo seat and sipped his tea. She'd never seen such a room. Everything in it was floor-level and old and beautiful. She loved the desk's polished wood, set on a stand made of darker wood. It had a hinged top and no legs. The closet was horizontal with a usable surface. It was a toy room filled with toy furniture. Mr. Lee screwed a cigarette into a holder and tapped the ash into a saucer that said CINZANO, his eyelids heavy; for a moment he seemed to forget that she and the tai were in the room.

He said: heat is very much. Drink tea is best thing, better than cold drink if you thirsty. He held the cigarette holder like a paintbrush and waved it around when he asked questions. Had she taken opium before? Did she know the taste was very bitter, strong enough to make her sick? Was it her own idea or did the tai want her to take it? What was her name? Yes, she replied, when she was cut at the age of nine; she knew it tasted bad but the pain was worse; she wanted it, the tai had nothing to do with how much she wanted it; Dimple, like the actress of the hit movie *Bobby*, who was younger and prettier than she.

MR. LEE WAS on the floor with his legs stretched in front of him. A single lamp burned in the room and its yellow light shone on his bald head and clean undershirt. His actions were slow, economical, planned ahead so there was no wasted movement. He boiled more water on a pump stove and poured it into their cups, reusing the leaves he'd measured out from a tin. In another pan he heated milk. From a tin trunk he drew tiny scales and a bowl. He put a sticky black ball on the scale, weighed it, broke off a bit, weighed it again, and put the ball into her palm. He gave her the warmed milk in a steel glass and told her to place the pellet on the back of her tongue and swallow quickly. She did exactly as he said. The pellet was unbearably bitter and it stuck to her tongue. She panicked and swallowed too much milk, but the pain disappeared in fifteen minutes, to be replaced by its opposite, something enveloping that told her she was loved, no, beloved: she was beloved and not alone.

THAT NIGHT SHE was sick, throwing up quickly and repeatedly, so quickly it was almost pleasure. She had many dreams, separate dreams that seemed to pass through her simultaneously, or was it a single dream that stretched in all directions for most of the night? She dreamed of a house she had never lived in and of a family she did not know. The neighborhood was unfamiliar, but she knew it was somewhere in Bombay, Malabar Hill maybe, or Breach Candy, or Marine Drive, or Cuffe Parade, some neighborhood where the rich lived, because everybody in her dream was rich. She had friends with names like Queenie, Devika, and Perizaad. She was popular with her teachers because she did well in class and for the same reason she was not popular with her classmates. She was often happy. Even in her dream she knew she was happy because she was a student and reading was her proper occupation. Her favorite book was a slim collection of prophecies by a nun who wrote in Konkani, who wrote every day, who filled up exercise books with her tiny handwriting and threw away most of what she wrote. Only three of the slim books survived her severe self-editing. The nun's name was Sister Remedios and after her death her writings were published in Konkani by the convent where she had lived and died. Dimple's edition was an English translation that appeared two decades later. The book was terrifying, not because it contained endless descriptions of civil butchery and mass suicide, but because of the serene accompanying sketches of trees, streams, and sunbirds. The drawings were scattered throughout, small drawings the nun had made that were sometimes related, though only cryptically, to the catastrophic visions she described; more often they had no connection to anything at all. In eighty or so pages Sister Remedios described a ruined world shaped by landslides and floods, a world in which "fissured cities rose and fell in a cement tide, and trees upended their roots into the air, and birds fell to the ground like stones, and the moon fell into a crack that had appeared on the earth, the old earth that was breaking itself into pieces." She wrote in the past tense, as if the terrible scenes she described had already happened and had been witnessed by thousands, by hundreds of thousands of doomed souls and only she, Sister Remedios, had returned alive to tell the world of its death. The nun did not record the cause of the cataclysm, she did not say whether it was war or some unnatural planetary upheaval that had caused it, but the scenes of suicide were faithfully rendered. The book ended with two pages about a great pit filled with black blood, its surface pocked with toxic gas bubbles, and the army of ghosts that fought to drink at the pit: whenever one succeeded in clawing his way through, a hooded swordsman decapitated the weeping creature with a single broad stroke. In this way the ghosts were left headless though not extinguished. Only one among them managed to reach the pit and drink its fill. When the ghost lifted its oily black mouth to the moon and howled with joy, Dimple recognized her own blind face and then she saw the face of the hooded swordsman and recognized him too. And though she knew she was dreaming, that Sister Remedios's book was her own invention and the world was as intact as it had ever been, she whimpered in her sleep at the ferocity of her own visions.

Toward dawn she fell into a deeper sleep and woke up late, unrested, with a taste in her mouth, a sweet-and-sour residue like pani puri water. She bathed and the tai gave her money for new clothes but a customer arrived as she was leaving, a regular, with two boxes of mithai. He was the seth of a sari shop on the main road and it was what everyone called him, Seth. Lakshmi said even his own family called him Seth. She said he'd answered to it for so long he must have forgotten his real name. The seth wanted to drink a few bottles of beer and toss handfuls of salted cashews in his mouth and brag about how much money he would spend on his daughter's wedding. It had just been arranged, he said, and he wanted to celebrate. He wanted French, no handshake, and then he wanted to lie back and sip his beer while she danced for him, lip-synching to the radio. When she sponged him, he cleaned his hands and groin carefully so no trace of her remained. It was the ritual shared by all her married customers. After he left, she slept some more, very deeply, and woke up late in the evening and the next day the pain was back and it was as if she'd never been free of it and would never again be free. She was on out call. An Arab customer had telephoned the tai. Send Dimple, he said. He wanted her to stay the night at his hotel in Colaba, a new building in one of the alleys behind the Taj. The Arab came to Bombay every year during the monsoon to see the rains that didn't come to his country. He expected very little by way of service: he wanted her to lie facedown on the bed while he rubbed himself against her, both of them fully dressed. He was a big tipper and she couldn't afford to be unwell. She went back to Mr. Lee's. She began to visit him a few times a week. She kept an emergency hoard of eating opium for the times she couldn't make it to the khana and it was as easy as that to acquire the habit of opium, for that's what it was, a habit, like bathing twice a day or eating vegetables.

SHE WAS LEARNING to live with the pain. It was always there, in her shoulders and her back. The opium reduced it to something manageable, but she woke with pain. And then, taking the pipe one morning from Mr. Lee, she realized that her arms were getting longer. She was sure of it, her arms were out of proportion to the rest of her. She went to a real doctor in Colaba. She took a train to Churchgate and a taxi from the station to his office. He was an English-speaking man with a degree from London and a second office in Worli. His room was full of books on glass-fronted shelves. He picked up a heavy black volume with indentations on the pages and after a few minutes of reading he told her that the lengthening of her arms was a biological change brought about by her gelding. He said, you were castrated so young there have been hormonal spikes in your physiology. In a way the growth of your arms is a compensation for the profound change you've undergone, perhaps the most profound change a human system can experience short of dying. She thought: I don't care. As long as my knuckles don't drag on the floor I don't care. What does it mean if my arms are longer? It will be easier to make pipes. She thought: this is nothing, just one more of the body changes I have to live with, like the way my Adam's apple disappeared and my mustache and the veins on my arms. Where did they go? When she asked the doctor, he made no reply. He nodded politely and wrote out a bill. The doctor wore glasses with gold frames and he didn't actually examine her. He didn't touch her at all, not even to shake hands, as if he knew her, knew where she lived and what she did for a living and the exact amount of opium she took on a daily basis, and even if he made no moral judgment about her life, he had made a medical or personal judgment, which he had every right to. He didn't touch her but he washed his hands with soap at a sink near his desk. He was like a bhai on Shuklaji Street: he did not handle money or maal. He didn't get his hands dirty until he had to. He gave her a note and asked her to take it to the front desk. She paid the elderly woman in the outer room, paid in cash, paid more for fifteen minutes of the man's time than she earned in an entire night. She thought: all he did was look in a book. I wonder how much he would charge to touch me.

MR. LEE'S KHANA existed outside the street's usual lines of supply and demand. It was Mistah Lee's, or Mister Ree's, a place of fable, the Chinese den with the antique pipes, where customers were unwelcome. Wooden cots were stacked like bunk beds, each cot with a pipe, each pipe on a tray. Smokers tended to their own pyalis. The door was always closed and because there were few customers the police didn't bother asking for chai-paani bribe money. Two or three middle-aged Chinese men arrived around noon, smoked their quotas, and left without saying much. Mr. Lee wasn't interested in more custom. There was enough money to keep himself in opium and food—plenty of one and just enough of the other—and that was as much business as he wanted. When they were alone, he liked to open up his battered tin trunks and show her relics from his old life. There was an English identity card in an envelope of documents.

The image was creased and faded but the lettering was still legible. She read his name slowly; she was teaching herself to read English.

"Lee ka see."

"No," he said. "Lee Ka Tsay."

She read aloud his birth year, 1929, and province, Canton. He'd been an officer in the army.

"Wrong army," he told her. "I on wrong side in war. You know why? Because we lose. If you lose, you wrong."

SHE WANTED TO know what it was like to lose a war and a homeland at one stroke and to travel for a long time and arrive in a place where no one knew you. He told her it was like dying or being paralyzed, a catastrophic occurrence that no one was equipped to deal with, however strong or well trained they were. She said she liked the city because it was big and there were many strangers who became friends. She said he was lucky to start again somewhere new. He made a gesture with his shoulders, a tiny gesture that told her the precise extent of his unluckiness. And she understood that while his memories of home had softened with time, everything he told her of India was sharp with dislike. He said, here everything too fast, too loud, too crazy. Indians don't care for past, only care for now. They too busy thinking of food to think of tomorrow. So? You do what you want do. Dare to dream. Dare to dream. You have to turning round like snowball otherwise you don't become big. He had to explain to her what a snowball was.

There was a uniform in the trunk and she asked him to put it on. It had high collars and narrow epaulettes and insignia on the breast; it suited him, and the peaked cap transformed him. He filled out, as if he'd grown younger and taller. She saw the markings on the uniform and she understood that he'd been an important man. Go out in that and the girls will pay you, she said. His smile was shy, a small shy flicker, like the ghost of a smile that had occurred a long time ago.

IT TOOK HIM a while to work up to it, to ask the questions she'd been asked many times. How did they do it? And: how much did it hurt? Her reply was casually made, as if she were talking about a haircut or a school outing. It affected Lee more than if she'd wept or cursed. When you're cut young you become a woman quicker, she told him, and since she had not yet been ten, they did both at one go. With older boys, they removed only the testicles. Gelding. They used the English word. In her case: gelding and docking.

"I was nine or I might have been eight," Dimple said. "It was about a year after I came to Bombay, to the hijra's brothel. A woman was called, a famous daima, Shantibai. There was singing and dancing and whisky. The daima told me to chant the goddess's name and she gave me a red sari. She made me drink whisky. I hated the taste but I drank it. They gave me opium. Then four of them held me down. They used a piece of split bamboo on my penis and testicles and held me down. The bamboo was so tight I felt nothing, until afterwards, when they poured hot oil on my wound. That was when I felt the pain, and more, something strange, I was sure the pain would set me free. It burned when they poured the oil, but it was a good thing, it meant the bleeding would stop."

"They not take you to doctor?"

"I could have asked for a doctor, but nobody respects the doctor nirvan. You get anesthesia and medicine. You're not risking your life."

Lee asked more questions.

"My mother gave me to a priest, who brought me here to 007 and sold me to the tai. I was seven or eight. I don't remember much about my mother or my life before I came. I don't want to remember."

"Best. Forget is best."

"Why remember and make yourself sad?"

"Why remember when anyway you memory wrong, ALL WRONG."

"Yes, yes, best to forget."

"What I said."

HE TOOK HER to Chowpatty for milk shakes at Rajasthan Lassi or a pista kulfi at Cream Center and a sandwich on the beach. It was December, the time of year he liked best. He said, this Bombay? Only nice two month of year, December and January, rest of time it no place for human being. To clinch the argument he nodded at the scene around them. It was a weekday but the beach was crowded: men ambled aimlessly and stray dogs lay curled under the trees. Here and there lamps burned where vendors sold peanuts, sugared tamarind, and coconut oil head massages. A small boy lay buried in the sand. Only his hands and head were visible. Beside him was a handkerchief with a pitiful collection of coins. The boy's eyes were closed and he was muttering. Mr. Lee planted his walking stick in the sand and watched the lights on the near horizon, a wavy line smudged silver and blue, strung with spray. There was a yellow moon in the sky, like the half-shut eye of a giant bird of prey, and there were no stars to be seen, not a single one, not anywhere. Where have the stars gone? he thought. How will the ships navigate without stars? And then he remembered that the stars were dead, long dead, and the light they shed was not to be trusted, was false, if not an outright lie, and in any case was inadequate, unequal to its task, which was to illuminate the evil that men did. He thought he saw a junk that was at least a hundred yards long, with nine masts and immense sails and attended by a flotilla of smaller boats—supply ships, water tankers, transports for cavalry horses, and fast-moving patrol boats. He knew the junk and its master. In the dusk the big ship's lights on the water were violet on violet and he thought if he waited long enough one of the small boats would come to fetch him. The ship was a long way from home but seemed in good shape, sitting solidly in the water, so close he could see the rigging. It is the eunuch admiral Zheng He, he told Dimple, the great Chinese Muslim navigator, and he's come to take me home. Then he heard drums, jungle drums, and he thought of witch doctors and the image of the great junk faded to violet mist. He heard the sound of surf and he heard someone speaking or cursing in Hindi. Your mother's cunt, the voice said. Or the voice was saying someone's name, Marky Chu. Lee told Dimple he was sick. He had a grating in his throat and he didn't want to go to a hospital because there was no point, he knew what it was. He said he needed opium for its painkilling properties, just as she did. He had a list of aches and pains. It was a bond between them, the itemizing of pain. In pain, he said, as if it were a country. As if he were saying, I am in Spain.

HE SAID HE'D TEACH her the important things, starting with the most important thing of all, the correct way to make tea and rice, so the tea wasn't overbrewed and the rice wasn't overcooked. He said: "You want make food forget Indian way. Indian's system is like American system, everything overdone. They have no subtle." He sent her to buy octopus. She brought the tentacles home in a bag of ice and cut them into thin slices, at a sharp angle. She put the sliced octopus in a saucepan with ginger and green onions and added a black bean paste. He told her to touch the octopus to the flame and serve. But she let the dish cook for a good five minutes until the flesh was tough and rubbery. "You overdid," he told her. "Old Chinese saying, you don't need take off your pant to fart." This is how he talks, she thought, he makes pronouncements, as if each thing he says is the final word on the subject. He talks in proverbs. There's nothing I can say in reply.

Lee taught her how to make pipes because he was finding it difficult to do even this. Soon he would become a feeble old man and he'd need help to eat and shit. He would end up in a hospital, he said, at the mercy of Indians. He wanted to pass on his expertise, such as it was, while he was still able. He told her the most important thing was to take your time; that the making of the pipe should take longer than the smoking of it; that hurry went against the meaning of opium. "Patience," he said. "Be patient. You not patient you no good." He taught her posture, how to recline so her head was at the same height as her right shoulder. He told her to close her eyes for a few minutes before she picked up the pipe and to bow to the lamp when she lit it first thing in the morning. She thought: only, this is a chandu khana and we are smoking opium. We're not praying, we're getting high. But she followed his instructions and began the day with a few minutes of silence, the pipe resting across her lap.

He taught her some Chinese. *Ho leng ah* and *ha tho*, so she could haggle with the vendors at the Chinese shop where he sent her to buy vegetables and fish. She told him that the Hindi for how much, *kitna*, sounded a little like the Cantonese, *kay dow cheen ah*, especially if you said it fast. It made him angry. There was no similarity between the two languages, he said, none at all. She was being stupid.

He taught her how to curse, comprehensive terms of abuse that wished disaster on descendants and forefathers alike, phrases as thorough and devastating as Chinese martial arts. "Repeat after me," he said, enunciating the words very slowly and much too loud. "Dew lay low mow chow hai siu fun hum ka chaan." He taught her the intonation, the staccato monosyllables, the plosives that detonated in the mouth. He taught her the proper pronunciation of *dew*, the Cantonese for fuck, telling her to stretch the vowel. He encouraged her to employ variations.

"Enjoy sound of word. Is only way to say correctly."

And he repeated the phrase, chanted it, because he was having such a good time with this.

"One question," Dimple said.

Mr. Lee took a cigarette out of a pack and considered it. He was rationing himself, taking his time instead of lighting up right away. They heard muffled explosions, four in a row, and he froze, then half a dozen louder bangs went off.

He lit up and said, "Nothing, only firecracker for their festival. Indian are crazy."

They were in the courtyard, sitting in the sunshine, Dimple wearing Mr. Lee's straw gardening hat. She was protecting her complexion, a phrase she'd learned from *Stardust* magazine. Mr. Lee put his cigarette out to cough. He spoke around his hack: "Wha-a-at question?"

"Why am I learning to swear in Cantonese? Who will I swear at in Bombay? Nobody will understand."

"Best. If they don't understand, you can curse as much you want, like I use to."

He's taking his leave, she thought, he's absenting himself.

BOOK TWO

THE STORY OF
THE PIPE

I.

In Spain with Mr. Lee

He's absenting himself in stages. He's making it easier for me, she thought, he's teaching me how to be alone. His cough had become constant. The smoke made it better, but only for a time. He spent entire days in his bunk, dreaming and coughing. She heard the scrape in his throat, a private, deeply intimate sound, and it embarrassed her. She heard the bray of it and it reminded her of the people she knew, all of whom carried the sound deep in their chests, from where it would someday emerge. She shook her head to dislodge it but the cough or its echo stayed with her all day.

His fifty-fifth birthday came at the end of December when the city moved into its brief winter. She took a taxi to a Parsi bakery at Kemps Corner and bought a cake in the shape of a heart. On the way back she rolled the window down and felt the breeze against her face. It smelled of camphor. There was a traffic jam on Grant Road Bridge. For ten or fifteen minutes the cab stood in one spot, trapped in a tight squeeze of vehicles. Then a procession passed, a small group of mourners in single file, behind them four men carrying a stretcher. The body, covered in a single sheet, bounced with every jolting step the bearers took, bounced so much she wondered if it would fall to the bridge. The sight filled her with such unease that the pleasure she'd felt a moment earlier vanished and she remembered something a customer had read out from an English newspaper. It was a quote from the Mahabharata that the newspaper had placed on its editorial page as a thought for the day: only eunuchs worship Fate. The girak had made a joke of it, asking her if it was true, but the words had stayed with her. For she did believe in Fate and ghosts and bad luck, and if this made her doubly a eunuch there was nothing she could do to change it. It was Fate.

The door of the khana was open when she walked in, late, the cake held in front of her. Mr. Lee was on the floor with his eyes open, his knee bent under him. She took him to the hospital where they operated on his leg. The doctor told her he'd had a stroke, a minor one, but he would need to be looked after. He came home with his leg in a cast and fear in his eyes. His mind skipped years, slipping backward or forward without regard for chronology. He lost faith in linear time. He told her his autobiography by describing the rooms he had lived in: the house he'd taken as an officer, the mud-floored house he grew up in, hotels he'd lived in for weeks on end, rooms in Rangoon, Chittagong, Delhi, and cities he'd forgotten the names of. His first place in Bombay was a shared room in a hostel near Grant Road and he ate in an ashram kitchen, the food vegetarian, heavy, hard to digest. Disgust, he said, meaning: it was disgusting. He said, I enjoy return to my room at night because I speak Cantonese to myself in mirror. I like to hear sound of my language. He carried on long interrupted conversations with the mirror about the city's terrible food, the dirtiness and bad manners and the sharp body odor that all Indians shared, because spicy food smells were exiting through the pores. As he spoke, he became the person in the stories he told her, a young officer in the army, a student, a refugee driving from town to town, a child. He spoke of bicycles and books, a fur cap he received when he turned eight and a village of people named Lee. He spoke of a woman with rope burns around her neck and a man who froze to death in the summer. His voice rarely rose above a whisper and it regained its authority only when he uttered the word *China*.

2.

White Lotus,
White Clouds

His mother wore glasses with heavy black frames. When the frames broke she fixed them with tape. The glasses were not correctly aligned and they made her look cockeyed but she continued to wear them. He went with her to exchange their ration coupons for rice and he walked ahead and pretended not to know the woman with the bandaged spectacles. On the street a group of boys imitated her walk and crooked eyes. When they laughed at her the woman with the bandaged spectacles laughed too. She laughed shyly, covering her mouth with her hands like a child. The state of her spectacles did not stop the woman from reading the *Red Flag* every day. She refused to read anything else. She denounced the *People's Daily* and other publications as reactionary organs, or revisionist, or feudal, decadent and counterrevolutionary. The woman worked in a factory and she complained to the bosses that her fellow workers were indulging in pornography. The seriousness of the charge brought the deputy secretary to the floor to investigate. When he discovered that the workers had been discussing a foreign news magazine, in particular the skimpy dresses worn by the models in the advertisements, the deputy secretary chided the woman, but it went no further than that, because after all she was an example of revolutionary fervor. She believed in herbal medicine and acupuncture. She carried a bottle of eucalyptus oil, which she used to treat everything from headaches, period pains, upset stomachs, and inflammations to more serious events such as burns and cuts. She wore black or blue tunics all year round and black canvas shoes. On her head was a green peaked cap, a man's cap. Despite the lecture she received from the deputy secretary, she continued to denounce her fellow factory workers as decadent or reactionary, and she refused to have anything to do with them because they discussed frivolous matters such as clothes and monetary troubles. She had a hatred for money. She handed her wages back to the supervisor and said, I don't want to be contaminated by filth. Then she told him: be careful, be very careful or it will corrupt you without your knowledge. When the workers were given a bonus she refused to accept it, because, she said, a bonus was revisionism in its ugliest form. At the same time, his father looked after the expenses of the household, including food, clothes, and medicines for the three of them, and for this service he received only contempt from the woman.

His father smoked from the moment he woke to the minute he fell asleep. He smoked a Chinese brand of Virginia tobacco that he bought by the carton. When there was no money for cigarettes he bought loose black tobacco that he smoked in a pipe. His father wasn't much of a communist. At the height of the fervor, the villagers dug a tunnel through a nearby mountain, dug it with their bare hands and the most rudimentary of tools. Some army officers and a revolutionary leader visited the site and named it "Tunnel of the People's Triumph." His father took no part in the construction. He was heard to say that the villagers, his relatives, all of whom carried the surname Lee, would have spent their time more profitably by building a road around the mountain or by using a truck. He voiced this opinion loudly but there was no reprisal from the Party. The village of Lees was known not only for the ideological correctness of its inhabitants but also for his father, who wrote a series of novels about a tramp named Ah Chu. The tramp had a knack for disaster and his inner life was reflected on his face, which was covered in boils. Ah Chu's life unfolded in real time, for there was a book every year or every other year, and readers waited to discover what foolishness he'd been up to since the last installment and how much further his life had unraveled. The reason for the popularity of the series, particularly with the communists, was because Ah Chu was seen as a symbol of Republican China and because there were plenty of jokes. The first of the series, *The Childhood of Ah Chu*, opened with a joke about Ah Chu's father, a corrupt government official who carries his cynicism everywhere, on display, like a great open wound. He believes in nothing and trusts no one and has no interests except wine. One afternoon a friend visits and finds Ah Chu's father calmly cutting off his pigtail. What are you doing? asks the friend. Have you gone mad? I'm cutting my hair because my son has left home. The man notices something that surprises him even more than his friend's mutilated pigtail. Tell me, he says, why are you sober today? I've decided to give up drink until my son returns to the bosom of his family, says Ah Chu's father. Where has your son gone? asks the friend. To buy more wine, says Ah Chu's father. It was not the best joke going around at the time, but readers loved it, for they loved jokes, even bad ones, and the book went into reprints.

———

LEE WAS STILL in school when his mother decided she wanted a degree, though she didn't know what kind of degree or which subject she would study. She didn't believe in culture. She didn't believe in books. She didn't believe in knowledge that did not benefit society as a whole. She believed that indiscriminate individual reading was detrimental to progress because it filled the populace with yearnings that were impossible to identify, much less satisfy. Societies with the highest literacy rates also had the highest suicide rates, she said. Some kinds of knowledge were not meant to be freely available, she said, because all men and women were not equipped to receive such knowledge in an equal and equally useful way. She did not believe in art for art's sake; she did not believe in freedom of expression; she did not believe in her husband, whose stature as a novelist she regarded with suspicion mixed with shame. Despite her lifelong aversion to culture she would go to university because she wanted to be a teacher. Teaching was the noblest profession in the world, she said. It was selfless, revolutionary, and critical to the nation's well-being. It concerned itself not with money, which was irredeemably dirty, but with the future of the mind. As she made these stunning proclamations, Lee's mother watched herself in the mirror. She held her head up and straightened her back. What was she doing? Was she imagining herself as the heroine of a revolutionary movie? Or was she imagining her role at the forefront of the new China? When she turned to face the boy her expression was cold and inhuman, as if she were staring at a pitiless desert landscape, a featureless yellow vista where all crimes were condoned and anything was possible except hope.

"You are my son," she said.

"Yes."

"You are my only son. Do you know why?"

"No, mother."

"Because I do not want some fat boys and girls running around the house. I do not wish to perpetuate your father's family name by helping to produce a dynasty. I took a vow to have only one child and I made your father take the vow too. Do you know why?"

"No, mother."

"To distance ourselves from the reactionary bourgeoisie. To make sure our only child developed intellectually, physically, and, most important, morally. To help you become a good laborer with socialist awareness and discipline."

Her lips curved upwards as if she was smiling but she started to weep. She turned to the mirror and looked at herself. She stretched her big lips and lifted them on one side to show the broken teeth that jutted out of her mouth. The boy realized that she was trying to make herself ugly and that he had never before seen her tears. He became frightened.

"Don't worry," he said. "I'll be a good laborer."

"Look at me," said his mother, her cheeks blotched. "I should have concentrated my vigor on speeding up our country's modernization. Instead, I'm a class dissident. I want to go to university."

SHE WOKE AT an odd hour, having slept in snatches. She was no longer able to sleep uninterruptedly through the night. Anxiety would pull her awake and keep her up, her eyes wide and a pulse thudding in her ears. She woke and lay still, listening to the noises of the night and her husband's steady breathing in his bed near the window. She heard her son in the next room, talking in his sleep. What was he saying? The words were too muffled to make out. She pinched her fingers and thought about the White Lotus Society, the group of rebels and mystics whose descendants became the heroic patriots of the Society of the Righteous and Harmonious Fists. The Fists won fame for taking up arms against the foreign conspirators who tried to partition China, but for her their significance was much greater. She revered them for the simple fact that they continued the great work of the White Lotus, a secret society led by the peasant who overthrew the Mughal armies, named himself emperor, and founded a dynasty. The dynasty, like all dynasties, eventually became decadent and corrupt, but not so the White Lotus, which, according to her, was the single pivot on which Chinese history turned; it was the fount from which all greatness ensued. She repeated to herself the alternative names the White Lotus had used to disguise itself in the years in which it was forced to go underground. She said the names very softly, because to say them aloud was to invite catastrophe. White Clouds, she said, and waited. She said, White Fans, and waited. Then, because this was the most dreaded one of all, she mouthed silently the name White Eyebrows. She sat up and put her feet on the floor and listened. She listened and walked through the house in the dark. It was a bright night and snow was falling. Moonlight dropped straight onto the kitchen floor with a curious sound, a sound it took her a moment to recognize, and then she felt the hair rise on her arms. It was the sound of money. She placed her fingernails against her neck and pressed until she felt the skin break. She closed her eyes and focused her thoughts on the pain, but it wasn't sharp enough. She found her nail file with the flat steel hook. She put the hook into her mouth, wedged it between her gums and teeth, and twisted until she tasted copper. Then she went into the front room where her son slept. He lay on his side with his hands propped under his face. He'd placed his sleeping mat against the front door as if to guard the house against intruders. She tiptoed up to him until she was close enough to hear what he said. It was a prophecy meant only for her ears. He said: "Nothing."

LEE AND HIS FATHER didn't give much thought to his mother's new regard for education. She'd wanted to take driving lessons though there was little chance the family would ever own a car. She'd attended a class in martial arts but didn't return after the first lesson because she was unused to physical exercise. She'd wanted to be a structural engineer because, she said, bridges were the key to the future. But nothing had come of these desires. This time it was different. She actually enrolled in the night college, though she hadn't passed the requisite exams and could not officially register for classes. She read aloud from textbooks of modern history, her voice shrill, as if she was arguing with someone, an old argument that had only gotten worse with the passage of time. As the day for the exams approached she became increasingly nervous. She slept very little and she forgot to eat. One night his father brought home a carp that someone had presented him and he made a stew with scallions, peeled ginger, some cloves of crushed garlic, and half a spoon of sesame oil. His mother stayed in her room, not emerging even though delicious smells were wafting through the house. His father put some of the fish stew in a bowl and served it to her with a side dish of rice and barbecue pork. Her wail was loud enough to wake the neighbors. You're trying to destroy me, she said. You want to corrupt me with food. You want me to die, die. How many times have I said it's wrong to eat so much pork when two hundred and fifty grams is the quota per person per month? She went into the other room and shut the door. Lee heard the sound of furniture being moved and something falling to the floor. They went outside and looked in through the window. Lee's mother was levitating. She wanted to rise to heaven but her progress was impeded by something caught in her throat. Her face had turned dark and her glasses were missing. Where were her glasses? He looked around and saw them on the floor, broken in three pieces, though the bandage was still intact. His father smashed the window and held her by the legs while Lee untied her. The rope left a gouge, a deep red furrow that she carried for the rest of her life.

3.

"Opium-Smoking Bandit"

Around this time, some writers were summoned to the communists' headquarters to attend a series of talks by Mao Tse-tung. On the fourth day, in the session titled "Talks on Art and Literature," Mao laid down a number of guidelines for writers. They must seek neither fame nor literary merit, he said, for these were avenues of self-gratification. Fame served no purpose other than to puff up the writer's ego, which was already inflated by the self-absorbed nature of his or her work. He did not make this observation lightly, said Mao, for he too was a writer, and a reader, and this fact gave him a vantage point from which to view the literary world's numerous pretensions. Very few writers were willing to face the truth, that their work was no more important than a peasant's. In fact, without the peasant the nation would plunge into a crisis. Without writers, the nation would most likely prosper. Yet writers were prone to endless egotism, which was the worst of the bourgeois mannerisms that continued to infect China. Bourgeois ideas manifested themselves in several ways, said Mao, some insidious, some obvious, but all marked by the self-indulgence known as individualism. Only a process of continuous purification would cleanse society of the menace. As for literary merit, it was as dangerous a preoccupation as seeking out fame since such merit served only to perpetuate the writer's posthumous reputation. What was the use of such a reputation? How did it serve society? The proper use for literature, said Mao, was in the service of the political cause. Writers who did not understand this had no place in the new China.

Among those summoned to the talks was Lee's father, who experienced a contraction in his stomach when he heard Mao's words. He kept his feelings to himself. His friend, the prolific novelist, essayist, and translator Ling Ling didn't accept the chairman's view of literature and its purpose, and was heard to say as much. She said a work of art had its own rules and was subject to no limits other than those imposed by its creator's imagination or lack thereof. The characters in a work of fiction could not be depicted in mere black and white as in some overtly political work. Heroes, she said, were not always pure in motive and character, sometimes they told lies or were deceived; and villains were not wholly villainous, more often they were conflicted and unhappy and caught up in the tortuous relationship between socialist ideals and the age-old engine of self-interest. For her views, Ling Ling was denounced as a rightist and sent directly to a labor camp where she was expected to qualify to work as a peasant. It took a little less than a week before her work was judged unsatisfactory and she was sent to prison. Ling Ling had trained as a medical doctor and she was able to withstand some of the hardships of prison, but three months after her internment she made a spectacular address to the National People's Congress. "Everything I have ever written should be destroyed—everything, everything, destroyed and burned to ashes and the ashes flung into the wind," she said. "I have not sufficiently studied the works of

Chairman Mao Tse-tung and therefore my own work is worthless. However, I am only sixty-seven years old and I can still be of use. If I am asked to fight the enemy using only my bare hands I shall do so. I will fight until my hands are stumps." Though Lee's father was spared prison, he and two others seen as close to Ling Ling were given reeducation classes in the fields that surrounded the encampment. He was allowed to smoke and sing but he was not to speak to his fellow workers or look at books or use a pen.

WHEN HE CAME HOME three weeks later he was silent about what had occurred during his visit to the headquarters of the communists. If neighbors asked he replied that it had been an instructional stay and he would say nothing more. He took to smoking opium with new vigor. For as long as Lee could remember his father had smoked a pipe on rare occasions. He smoked in the disciplined way of a connoisseur, rarely taking more than one at a time. He bought good-quality opium and stretched a pipe over the course of an evening. This was different. With his wife confined to her room and his mind full of questions about his work, he dedicated himself to the pipe, smoking six to eight in the course of a single day, and in between he smoked cigarettes. He lit a cigarette, left it in the ashtray, and lit another. When he took a break, he went to his writing desk and worked for an hour or two, no more, and in this way he finished the last of the Ah Chu stories, *The Eruption of Ah Chu*, which centered on an outbreak of psoriasis suffered by the unfortunate old man. There are long descriptions of the virulent nature of the disease, of the different kinds of scratching that Ah Chu resorts to in the vain hope of finding relief. Throughout the book's two hundred or so pages, winter darkness prevails. There is rain and sleet and never a chance of sunshine, because Ah Chu, plunged into insomnia and irregularity by his complaint, leaves his bed only at night. At the end, reduced to a puddle of bile and pus on a pungent sickbed, Ah Chu hangs himself from the chandelier in his dining room. Minutes later, the sun rises, which is the only moment in the dense and claustrophobic narrative that light appears in the gloom. *The Eruption of Ah Chu* didn't sell many copies and it brought some unwelcome official attention. The *People's Daily* said Lee's father had flirted too much with metaphor and as a result his book was full of confusion. However, since it was the work of a writer who had established his reputation as a critic of decadence, a single lapse was excusable. This appeared to be the official line because other publications echoed it, as did those cadres who were considered knowledgeable about party affairs. Lee's father paid no attention to the criticism. He was busy working on a real book. With Ah Chu dead at long last, dead with no possibility of resurrection, he was free to concentrate on a new kind of writing, a long-pending project he had put off for many years. He worked in his usual offhand manner, writing in half-hour bursts, as if his only aim was to take a break from the opium pipe. And in this way he produced a slim volume titled *Prophecy*, which disappeared from the bookshelves almost as soon as it was published. It was 1957, the year of the first purge, and when booksellers realized the nature of the book's contents, they either destroyed their copies or hid them or deliberately lost them. The official reaction was swift. Lee's father was a revisionist, it was said, and he should be sent to the countryside for manual labor. He was an opium-smoking bandit. He would be made to wear a placard that said: I AM A MONSTER. One self-described ultraleftist, a writer of short stories, said the book was the product of a diseased mind "fit only to be a maggot on the corpse of its putrefied revisionist masters." He recommended that the author be sent to prison. The most sustained criticism came from a novelist who was known to be a party favorite. All his books shared a similar plot and similar characters, though names were changed from story to story. The hero was always a handsome young peasant who was persecuted at work by a superior. The peasant was a student of the works of Chairman Mao. His superior was a former landlord or government official, a smooth talker and seducer, in short, a lecher and villain who has sabotaged a cherished village project, the building of a dam, say, or a bridge, or a telegraph office. After much struggle, the hero succeeds in unmasking his superior as the cause of the sickness that has plagued the children of the village and the reason the region has not prospered despite its hardworking inhabitants. The older man is ousted from his job and the young worker takes his place. At the end, the young protagonist quotes an aphorism of Chairman Mao's concerning the permanent nature of class struggle: "What was taken from the peasants must be returned to them. That is the law, today and forever." Or: "Revolution must follow revolution without interruption." Or even: "People say they're tense because vegetables and soap are in short supply. I'm tense before midnight but I take sleeping pills and feel better. Try pills." The formulaic nature of the novelist's work had not reduced his sales; in fact, they'd risen steadily over the years. The novelist was the first to publish a long critique of *Prophecy*, saying, among other things, that Lee's father deserved execution because his book celebrated decadence as a virtue. He was "a stinky dog who likes to defecate in the dark" and he deserved to be punished for his failings. The novelist also took advantage of the turmoil in the capital to put up a big-character wall poster that denounced Lee's father as a "counterrevolutionary parasite of the Khrushchev type." It was one of more than a hundred thousand posters plastered on the walls of

Peking at that time, but even so it was noticed and some lines were quoted in the *People's Daily*: "A fly cannot topple a giant tree. What can a decadent daydreamer and bourgeoisie do? We will not let you pollute the socialist future of China!" This appeared to be the verdict of the Party, for it was clear that the novelist was only echoing what his masters had told him. Lee's father's career was at an end but before he could be taken to prison he fell ill.

4.

His Father, the Insect

One afternoon, Lee came home to find his parents sharing a bed for the first time in years. It was not because they had made up their differences but because the bed was the only item of furniture left in the house, other than the shrine and his father's pipes. Money was short and his father had been selling things, small and not small, family heirlooms and clothes and furniture. In the newly spacious room his parents seemed to be strangers to each other and to him, damaged strangers with no claim to make and nothing to say. His father had placed a pipe on the bed. There was a tray with a lamp that tilted precariously on the lumpy mattress. When he took a drag his cheeks appeared to cave in. He had become very thin and it seemed to Lee that his father no longer resembled a human being. He was a pipe attached to a head with stick arms and legs. Or he was an inanimate object, a piece of knobbed wood, a walking stick or polished figurine. He was an insect, possibly a dangerous insect, a succubus with vertical eyes and internal antennae. Even the sounds he made were insect sounds, clicks and sucking noises. It was very interesting that the transformation which had overtaken his father had occurred so gradually that his family hadn't noticed. When exactly had his father stopped being human? Was it a permanent transformation or would he return one day to his natural state? While his father smoked, his mother lay on her back with her eyes open, pinching the fingers of her left hand with her right. Though she said nothing she managed to convey a sense of immense dissatisfaction with her surroundings and with the man who lay beside her. Lee climbed into the bed and turned his back on his parents and went to sleep. He dreamed he was an orphan who lived on a mountain inhabited by dragons. There was no food or water and for his survival he depended on one of the dragons to bring him bits of meat and fruit. The years passed and he grew tall, but the bigger he grew the more his dragon protector seemed to diminish, until one day he realized that his friend, the dragon, had become a living skeleton, an intricate network of interlocked bones without flesh or blood or breath. He woke one morning and found a pile of broken bones beside him, and then he felt a rumble under his feet and he realized that the mountain was heating up from below, that there was smoke emanating from its crevices and the trees had dissolved into ash and the sun had disappeared. He resolved to walk off the mountain and keep walking until he found food or he died, but no sooner had he started to walk than a rain of cinders began to fall around him. He ran faster and faster, until, exhausted, he lay down to mourn and die. He woke to the sound of drums. There was a fog so thick it was difficult to breathe. When his eyes adjusted he was in his parents' house. He might as well have been outdoors because the weather had come inside. He heard someone knocking and he stumbled across the room, unable to see through the fog. His eyes were streaming and when he took a breath he coughed. He walked slowly in the direction of the knock and then he saw a shape coming towards him, a shape that pushed him back on the bed. His terror vanished when he recognized his mother and he wrestled her to the ground and opened the door. The fog thinned and many people rushed in. His uncle and another man poured pails of water on the smoking mattress. They took his father outside, where, sick with fever, he shivered uncontrollably in the warm sunshine. His uncle was overcome by a rush of emotion and he took off the silk jacket he was wearing and cut off the sleeves with a pair of scissors. He slipped the sleeves over Lee's father's legs. They took his father to a hospital, where he died the next day, not of asphyxiation but from malnutrition. Rich Uncle Lee came to the funeral with a two-story house made of paper. As the house burned, Uncle said, brother, I give you a big house. Lee laughed at his uncle. He said, Rich Uncle, you should have given my father a house when he was alive.

Lee and his mother went home after the funeral. Under the charred mattress on the bed he found a copy of his father's last book and he read aloud the first sentence that caught his eye, "No remnants remained of the old ship except a splintered mast that the villagers planted in the sand, and so it happened that the rocky shores of the South China Sea became a deterrent to all but the most desperate of seafaring men." He turned back to the beginning and started to read the book through. What kind of story was it? It was presented like a biography but there were things in it that no biographer could know, for instance the things that men and women were thinking at important moments in their lives; and there was secret information as to how many years in the future one or the other important personage would die, and of which ailment; and there were wide pronouncements regarding the final outcome of Chinese history when unchecked enterprise would turn its cities into repositories of waste and poison; and there was a timeline for the world that charted how many years it would take for different parts of the planet to crack up and boil over into waste gas; and at the center of it all was a character who was neither man nor woman, a charismatic autodidact who changed identity at will. Was it a kind of imagined autobiography? Or was it a historical novel, true fiction, because so much of the detail was accurate, no, more than accurate, it was indisputable? Lee read a page or two and then, overcome by sudden melancholy, he closed the book and put it under the mattress. Over the next few days he would pick it up and read as many pages as he could before sadness got the better of him and he put it away. It took him a long time to finish and when he got to the end he understood that the book had been his father's true life's work.

PROPHECY BEGAN a hundred years in the future, in 2056, when a young archaeologist, a Cherokee, fleeing an unnamed cataclysm in an unnamed city, arrives in a landscape that's somehow familiar to him. He recognizes it from the remembered stories of his tribe, though the stories are no longer heard because the elders who knew them have died. He is in the land of his ancestors, the ancient place described in song and prayer. It is now an abandoned urban mesa. He wanders around for days. He is the only living thing. There are no coyotes or birds or insects. There is no running water. When he feels hunger or thirst he injects himself with vegetable extract, animal protein, and sugar, and when tired he takes a four- or eight-hour sleep tablet that allows him to stay alert for as long as he needs to.

One morning his belt pack emits a warning buzz followed by a mild siren. He starts to dig, reciting the names of the colors in his dye pack. Alice Blue, he says. He says, Mayan Sun. Then, very quickly, Electric Pink, Flesh Pink, True Pink. He says, No Color Blue. He says, Medium Bastard Amber. When he runs out of colors he starts again, Alice Blue, Mayan Sun, and so on. Late in the afternoon he finds what he's been digging for, the object that set off his siren, a cache of blue-and-white porcelain crockery in a rusted chest and a small brass medal with an inscription, AUTHORIZED AND AWARDED BY THE GREAT MING. He dates the medal to the late fourteenth century and then he makes another discovery. The porcelain had been brought to the United States by the explorer Zheng He on the last of his seven voyages around the world. The first section ends abruptly at this point with the young Cherokee lifting the tiny brass medal to his eye in the fading light of the sun.

The second section is told from the point of view of an assistant to a Chinese shipbuilder. The assistant is one of thousands of men working in shifts to complete a flagship junk to the emperor's specifications. There are pages of minutiae about shipbuilding, contentious passages as to the best wood, the ideal conditions for varnish and tung trees, the correct method of instruction for carpenters, how to make the lightest possible armor plating, and how to make certain that the compartments belowdecks are watertight. There are knowledgeable references to the giant junk's unique design and the exact dimensions of its enormous poop deck and cunningly placed storage cabins. The most revolutionary features are the masts, of which there are nine, a number considered wasteful by traditional shipbuilders. There is talk that the old builders are jealous but the emperor demands more junks, he wants a thousand in all and there's no time for jealousy. Every shipbuilder in the land is called in to help build the new fleet. At the worst possible moment, after completing the design and some of the construction of the flagship, the master ship-builder dies. The young assistant, who is never named, takes over. He works all day and sleeps in snatches and as the junk nears comple-tion he begins to talk in a voice that is not his own. He talks with the authority of a seafaring man, or a man who knows the secret of ships at sea, who knows how to recognize the traits that make each vessel unique. The men look to him for instruction though his ideas are radical and not entirely feasible. The rumor spreads that the young assistant has been possessed by the spirit of the dead shipbuilder. How else would he know the things he does? The assistant does not address these whispers: he has no time. When the junk is completed it is four hundred and seventy five feet long and a hundred and ninety feet wide. It is at this point in the story, that is, at the very end of the second section, that the author's voice is heard, Lee's father's authen-tic voice, which tells the reader that the junk "was larger by far than the *Santa María*, which was a mere ninety feet by thirty, a dwarf in comparison," and that "Zheng He commanded sixty such ships and many smaller ones, with more than twenty-seven thousand soldiers, shipwrights, poets, and physicians, whereas Columbus commanded less than a hundred men." Then the author makes a controversial suggestion: "I do not make the comparison with Columbus lightly, I make it deliberately and with forethought, for it is my contention that the voyager Zheng He discovered America seventy years before Columbus."

The third and last section is the shortest and most problematic in political terms. It concerns the life of a young Muslim named Ma, who is born in a province on the southwestern border. The boy is captured by the Ming, castrated, renamed, and made a servant to the prince. He is taken to the imperial court, where he is instructed in the ways of the Sons of Heaven. When the prince becomes emperor he decides to announce his ascension by beginning the sea voyages that have been planned for years but never attempted. He makes the Muslim eunuch (now called Zheng He) the admiral of his fleet and tells him to sail to the end of the horizon, beyond the known earth, to spread the glory of the Ming. The story is told in the third person but for long passages it dips into the head of the admiral, who is not above making political forecasts: "The Emperor believes China is the center of the world and he is the center of China therefore he is the center of the world. Try as he might to disguise it, he suffers from the ailment peculiar to Chinese leaders—the delusion that they are the most important form of life in the universe and their struggles and idiosyncrasies are worthy not only of emulation but of reverence." But the admiral also composes poems of praise that are craven and banal:

> Waves are high, the storm fierce, the sea's valleys deep;
> Preparing to die, brave men rush in every direction
> Praying to the goddess. Who will keep them safe?
> Who else but a valiant emperor, the great Ming?

The narrator of the last part of the book is a young grandnephew of Zheng He's, a boy named Soporo Onar, who sets off to find his illustrious relative's final resting place. The quest is ultimately unsuccessful and most of the last section is taken up not by Zheng He's triumphant early voyages, but by his desperate final one. It ends with his death in India and his burial at sea and Soporo's decision to build a monument to him in the pages of a book. Where in India did Zheng He die? Somewhere on the west coast, possibly some spot that wasn't too far from present-day Bombay, said Lee to Dimple, which may have influenced my own decision to live here. Then he said: I wish there was a translation of my father's book, because if there's anyone who would benefit from reading about the life of the eunuch admiral, it's you.

5.

"Light Me a Cigarette"

He told Dimple he was thirty-eight when his life changed in a way he could never have foreseen. That year, at a banquet in Peking, he found himself seated beside a slender woman whose hair was curled in the new style. She wore a plum-colored suit with white lapels and she accompanied a navy commissar who chain-smoked unfiltered foreign cigarettes. Early in the evening the commissar switched to brandy and soon he became silent and unexpectedly agile for such a heavy man. He told the waiters to replenish the teapot and the wine and water glasses. He spoke only when giving orders; he didn't converse with his dinner companions. Then his elbow slipped off the table and he spilled the slender woman's wine. A deep stain spread across the tablecloth and the commissar watched in fascination, as if it were the stain of communism itself, the unstoppable stain that had spread across the world and dyed it the color of blood. The woman—or girl, since she couldn't have been more than twenty or twenty-one—picked up the glass and placed it beside her untouched plate. She refilled it with a little wine and took a sip. Then she asked Lee to help her with the commissar.

They took the man to a room above the banquet hall where the girl put him to bed and took off his shoes. He was already asleep. The girl smoothed her skirt over her hips as she regarded the man on the bed. She sighed in an exaggerated way and put her hands on her waist and didn't look at Lee. She said: the first Ming, Tai Zong, drew up a list of capital offenses for government officials that included such things as the formation of cliques and flattery. Public drunkenness too was a capital offense. Do you know what the punishment was? The official was flayed and his skin was stuffed with straw and he was installed in a government building to serve as a warning to other officials. She sighed once more in a slow theatrical way and it must have felt good, because she did it again. She said: light me a cigarette if you're going to stare like that. Lee did as he was told. She stood in the middle of the room and blew smoke at the ceiling. He thought: even her silence is expressive, even the inhaling and blowing out of smoke. See how animated she is. Is she an actress? Is it too bold a question to ask? Before he could say anything, she led the way back to the restaurant, and, sometime later, she left the table and didn't return. Some days afterwards, he saw her wheeling her bicycle into the commissariat compound. She had her hair up in a bun and she was wearing work pajamas. She looked very different from the girl with the cigarette whose image had taken up residence in his head. He went to her and blurted the truth, that he had brought something for her. She seemed so disoriented that he wondered if she knew who he was. He gave her a carton of cigarettes, half a cooked chicken, and some stalks of sugarcane. She looked towards the compound and hesitated for a moment before putting the gifts into a carrier bag on her bicycle. She said: I am twenty-three years of age. I'm not interested in being a kept woman. Thank you for the gifts, she added, speaking so solemnly that he wondered if he had displeased her in some way. He watched as she pushed her bicycle towards the commissariat. Was she telling him to leave her alone? Did she think he wanted to pay her for sex? The idea put a ball of fear in his stomach. Then it occurred to him that she was saying something very different. She didn't want to be a kept woman: she wanted to be his wife. This idea also filled him with fear. She was a kind of classical Chinese heroine, a prototypical leader, and she wanted to be his wife. It was hard to believe. He had to talk to someone, someone senior whose advice he could trust. The next morning, unrested, he went to the administrative governor of the region, his boss, Wei Kuo-ching. Wei wasn't alone and Lee asked permission to marry in the presence of his boss's colleagues. What is the woman's name? asked his boss. Lee didn't know. He described her and how they had met. Oh, said the administrative governor, you mean Pang Mei, Commissar Hu's assistant. The older man clapped Lee on the shoulder and told him to go ahead if that was what he wanted. Then he said: I hope you know there's no need for such a drastic step.

LEE'S QUARTERS WERE out of the question. There were too many people around at all times and if she was seen coming out of his rooms there would be trouble, an official investigation perhaps, followed by humiliation, punishment, even prison. The only way they could be alone was to meet in his office, late, when there was no one around. He waited nervously until she came and took her to the supplies room where he had arranged blankets and a pillow behind a desk in the back. He locked the door and turned off the lights and they held each other in the dark, the girl's slender form like a child's in his arms. There was some inadequate illumination from the streetlights outside, just enough light to see her face. She seemed very serious, which only made him more nervous. When she reached for his dick he jumped and when she put it in her mouth he whimpered, he actually whimpered, and then he was ashamed. She took a tube from her purse and smeared a small amount of cream on herself with a single deft gesture. In the ass, she told him, fuck me in the ass. Then she got astride him and guided him into her and played with her clitoris while she rode him. He came instantly and again he was ashamed. Later, as they lay beside each other, she said: I am taking a precaution. In case we're caught a medical examination will prove I'm still a virgin. Then Pang Mei turned on her side, curled herself into a small ball, and went to sleep. Lee thought he'd let her sleep for half an hour, then wake her and tidy up and get out of the building. If he fell asleep too it would be catastrophic. He propped himself on an elbow to look at her. He thought about the Yellow River's summer floods and the steamed buns he bought sometimes from the railway terminus. He thought about the horses of Mongolia, about the Tartars' subjugation of Russia, and about the wise and solitary dragons that live in the heated air above the mountains of Szechwan. The girl's lips were moving silently in her sleep and he could see her eyes moving under the lids. He thought about the melancholy dragons of Szechwan and just then a tremor struck the room. The air seemed to shift and the temperature dropped and there wasn't enough oxygen. A sound of waves or mosquitoes washed against his ears. The floor shook as if a large animal was trapped under the building. Every object in the room, the standing lamp, the desks, the chairs and file cabinets, everything was shaking. He took a deep breath but couldn't fill his lungs. He stood up and fell to his knees. When the earthquake stopped he was kneeling on the blankets with his hands clasped around the girl's ankles, and he knew her as his savior.

6.

To Wuhan

In the morning a cadre came to his quarters with a summons to the commissariat. He thought: how did they find out? What did I do? What did I do? He dressed quickly and followed the man to a room where Commissar Hu stood in front of a blackboard with a dozen or so others. There was a table with sweet cakes and tea and cigarette packs arranged in the shape of a pyramid. There were men who were so important that no one knew their names. They smoked and interrupted Commissar Hu's speech with rude jokes. Commissar, we heard you last night. The earth shook so much we thought the building would surely fall. Later, Wei Kuo-ching also made a speech and Lee tried to pay attention but he heard only some of the words, blockade and industrial production and railway shipments and sabotage and military supplies. He heard the words but he was unable to fit them together into a coherent pattern. He thought about Pang Mei, how she'd slept through the earthquake, how delicate her feet were, and how lucky he was. At noon Lee was told he would be going to the province capital of Wuhan, where he was to meet the regional military commander, General Lo Tsai-ta, and negotiate an end to the factional fighting that had paralyzed the city. Commissar Hu told him he had an hour to pack. As he left the commissariat he looked for Pang Mei but she was nowhere to be seen.

The trip to Wuhan took a little less than four hours. He was traveling with a group of Red Guards who changed seats throughout the flight. They pointed out the window and laughed. What were they laughing at? Nothing could be seen except a gray wall of clouds and rain or condensation. He heard a high whine from the small plane's twin engines and he felt the vibration from the metal under his feet. When people walked up and down the aisle the plane wobbled. At times, it shook so violently that he thought it would surely fall from the sky and he found he was gripping the armrests. There was an announcement. Passengers carrying guns, ammunition, or radioactive material were asked to hand them over to the attendants, who would return said items when the flight landed. At this, some of the Red Guards handed over an assortment of weapons, including rifles, pistols, and army-issue knives. Traditional music followed. Lee listened until the music faded into a hiss. He slept for a little while and was woken by another announcement: the plane was approaching Wuhan, which was a great industrial city of central China. Passengers were forbidden to take pictures from the aircraft window or on the ground. There was a pause. Then the voice said that those who wished to alight could do so. The plane circled several times before landing. The attendants returned the Red Guards' weapons. More music was heard on the intercom, not Chinese selections but a song from the Western movie *Mary Poppins*.

When Lee stepped off the aircraft he saw that the runway was in disarray: planes and trucks were parked pell-mell and groups of young men and women walked around issuing orders that only added to the chaos. They strolled across the tarmac as if it was a village lane or they squatted and smoked and wrote slogans on the dirt. The sun was out and as Lee walked toward the airport building he heard his name called by the young guards who were on the flight with him. They were gathered around a jeep that had driven right up to the plane. They waved to him and Lee walked back. The guards had convinced the driver of the jeep to take them to the city, they said, and Lee was welcome to ride with them. They all crowded into the vehicle. As it left the airport and took the road into the city, the guards decided they wanted to eat at a restaurant. Hey, hey, hey, driver, said one, if you see a pig run it over, we're hungry. The driver smiled and said nothing. The guards seemed to Lee like teenagers, they were obnoxious and without shame. They were never silent. At the restaurant they ordered char siu fan and beer and when it was time to pay they told the proprietor they had no money. Lee had cash but the younger men wouldn't let him take out his purse. No, no, you are our guest. Do you want us to lose face? They turned to the proprietor. We invite you to Peking, they told him. Come to Peking so we may exchange revolutionary ideas. You will be our guest. The man knew better than to argue.

FROM HIS HOTEL that night, Lee made a phone call but the operator said she was not in her room. He tried the number at hourly intervals and gave up around dawn. The next morning he was late for his meeting with the man Commissar Hu had described as a warlord. General Lo Tsai-ta got up when Lee was shown in. But instead of making him feel welcome, the general picked up his cigarettes, excused himself, and left the room. Some time later an assistant appeared to tell Lee that the general would not be available until later in the day, there was a crisis at the railway terminus that required his presence. Lee left the compound and walked to the end of the street and turned right as if he knew where he was going. There were no buses or taxis but the street was full of people. Uncleared garbage and old newspapers lay on the corner. He kept walking and came to a bridge, the famous bridge known throughout the country as a marvel of modern engineering. At its base, a man was cooking rice for his family. There were people swimming in the river and clothes spread out to dry on the parapets. Lee walked past a lecture group of some sort, a group of five or six who sat in a circle and listened to a woman reciting something. Was it poetry or the words of a song? He caught a few lines:

> *The world is on fire; time is a bomb.*
> *Ten thousand years are not enough*
> *When so much remains to be done.*

Now he could see the entire span of the bridge. He noticed that there were small groups of people sitting throughout the length of it and some kind of obstruction at the other end. He stopped when he saw what it was, stopped, turned around, and went back the way he'd come. A bus had been parked crossways and on the far side of the bus was a snaking line of cars and trucks and military transport vehicles, a line that stretched farther than he could see. The drivers had disappeared and the vehicles looked like they hadn't moved in a long time. Below him the muddy Yangtze too was immobile, as if it had turned to cement.

IT WAS NIGHT when he returned to the general's office. Lo Tsai-ta was on the couch, a Panama hat worn low over his closed eyes and a cigarette burning in his hand. He wore a white shirt and linen trousers to go with the hat, but the overall effect of the ensemble wasn't elegance as much as exhaustion. He seemed too tired to speak. There were two other men in the room who greeted Lee as if they knew him well. One, an officer known only as Tung, took him to a table where a bottle and glasses had been arranged. Lee poured himself a brandy and soda. He took a quick swallow of the drink and carried his glass and stood at the window. Sit here, said Tung, and Lee took a seat on the couch opposite the general. He noticed that General Lo's eyes had followed his progress from the window to the couch but otherwise the general was inert, like a convalescent. Lee placed his drink on the floor and waited with his elbows on his knees. After a time the general lifted his arm and took a slow sip of his cigarette. Tung and his colleague were having a whispered conversation. Lee couldn't hear Tung but the other man's one-word responses were clear enough. Kaolu, he said, whenever Tung stopped for breath.

Eventually, Tung turned to Lee. "Wuhan is a test case," he said. "Everything happens here: the plague, riots, surplus productivity, famine, tremendous industrial output, the end of everything. We believe Peking is using us as a kind of social experiment. They want to see how much punishment a city can take before it shuts down. They've posed an interesting question or set of questions, I will say that much. For example, how much chaos can the human system absorb? What are the uses of insanity? Is there intelligence in negativity? How far can destruction extend before it stops being creative? How useful is chance? Can the individual imagination apprehend the last beach, the last birdsong, the last sunset in the last sky? The inhabitants of Wuhan have thought about all these questions, we've thought about and discussed them in great detail. We've answered them too, if only to our own satisfaction. There's only one question we are incapable of answering. Do you know what it is?"

Lee thought: why do you continue to stay here? But he shook his head. "No," he said.

Tung said, "What are you doing here?"

At this all three men looked at Lee as if he had just then appeared out of thin air.

"I've been sent by the Party to look carefully at what is happening in Wuhan," said Lee. "I am expected to make a report and that's as far as my responsibility goes."

Tung was shaking his head even before Lee finished. "No," he said. "No, no, no."

It was then that Lee chose to make a comment about the Mao Tse-tung Thought Million Fighting Wuhan Revolutionary Heroic Workers Troops, a coalition the general was known to support, though not openly. The Workers Troops was larger than its older rival, the Wuhan Area Proletarian Mao Tse-tung Thought Fighting Workers Center, which had the support of Peking. Lee said he thought the Workers Troops was the cause of much of the rioting and disorder on the streets.

Tung made a spitting sound. "You are ignorant," he said. "It is the Workers Center that has caused unrest in Wuhan."

Lee nodded slowly. Then he said, "There's talk in Peking that the Workers Troops should be disbanded."

At this the general got to his feet and gestured that Lee should do the same. "This meeting is at an end," he said. It was the first time he'd spoken in Lee's presence and it served as a kind of signal to Tung, who threw his cigarette to the floor and shouted a slogan against the Workers Center. Lee wasn't sure what he was shouting because Tung was too angry to properly articulate his words. He marched around the room and stopped in front of Lee.

"I am prepared to sacrifice my life," Tung said. "We are soldiers. This is what we have trained for, self-sacrifice. You tell them that." Then he walked out and let the door bang behind him.

7.

Twice Abducted

When Lee returned to his hotel and placed a call to Pang Mei it was well past midnight. He heard the phone ring at the engineering college hostel and then he heard a siren and people shouting in the courtyard below. Wei? said the operator in Peking. The noise in the courtyard became louder and there were announcements on a public address system. Lee hung up and went to the window. A fire truck and a covered transport vehicle were entering the hotel's gates, and a loudspeaker van and men carrying rifles and choppers and homemade spears. He went to the door and locked it and placed another call. He was talking to the receptionist at the commissariat when they broke open the door and punched him to the floor. He got up and a man who looked somehow familiar slapped him on the side of the head, so hard that his glasses flew off his face and landed on the carpet halfway across the room. There was a ringing in his ears and someone hit him low in the stomach and someone else kicked his feet out from under him. Lee landed on his back. There were flecks of blood on his shirt and his ribs felt bruised. They pulled him to his feet and bound his hands behind his back. Then they marched him out of the building and towards one of the vans. The lobby was in pandemonium. The hotel's official cars had been overturned and gutted and a tree in the courtyard was ablaze. The staff stood under the portico. As Lee was brought down the steps he saw a man run towards the gate. A small mob set upon him with bare hands and rifle butts and brought him down. The man shouted: help me, comrades, help me. Who was he talking to? How odd, thought Lee, that fear should make you ask for help from the exact source of your torment. A man with a chopper stepped up and cut off the fallen man's arms with precise and economical strokes. The man twitched and shivered as he gazed at his severed arms and the ropes of blood that joined them. His lips moved and the words he spoke, if at all he was speaking, were inaudible. Blood pooled around his hips. He sat up and vomited and the crowd stepped back in disgust. Then the man with the chopper cut off his head, though this took some effort because the chopper was no longer sharp and wouldn't cut through the neck bones.

Lee was the only prisoner but there were so many men escorting him that the van was cramped and humid. His clothes were soaked through with blood and perspiration and without his glasses he felt crippled, though he was able to see the faces of his abductors clearly enough. He wondered what time it was and then he thought about Pang Mei's complicated virginity and for some reason the song-like words he had heard earlier that day, or had it been yesterday?, repeated in his head like a prayer. Time is a bomb; the world is on fire. He couldn't remember the rest of the words, though he heard very clearly the voice of the woman who had recited them. The men in the vehicle spoke as if he was not there, or as if he was already dead. They talked about barbecue pork and homemade rice wine, about how long one could swim comfortably in the summer before the silt of the river weighed you down (no more than an hour), about the comparative advantages of cards over mah-jongg (less wastage of time, more chances of quick money), about the efficacy of deer penis as an aphrodisiac (excellent), and about Lee's fate, whether he would be executed publicly or disposed of with minimum fanfare (the consensus: publicly, with a shot to the back of the neck). Kaolu, said one of the men, and it was then that Lee recognized the man who had been in General Lo's office. His abductors were soldiers. They wore armbands that identified them as members of the Workers Troops but in fact they were soldiers, no, they were mutineers. It was they who were already dead, thought Lee.

THEY TOOK HIM to a building that looked like the garrison headquarters; they took him to a cell and left him alone. Some hours later, two men came in and stripped off his clothes and beat him, very methodically, until he passed out. He was woken by pain. He knew he'd been unconscious for some time, minutes maybe, or hours: it was hard to tell because time had expanded. Every part of his body throbbed or burned. The pain slowed time and a single moment became something impossibly complex that took all his resources to endure. His pulse throbbed in his ears and hours passed between each beat. He slept and woke and slept again and he felt like a visitor to an unknown solar system where time speeded up and slowed down at random intervals. They gave him congee and he slept. And then the men returned and beat him again. This was how he knew a day had passed, two days, three and four days. He was settling into a kind of routine, he was beginning to focus his mind around the pain and he was preparing himself for worse when, suddenly, a new set of abductors took over from the old. They opened the door of his cell and someone he hadn't seen before said, is this him? Yes, said Tung, whose hands were tied. The new abductors put Lee in a jeep and took him on a long drive. It was nighttime and the stars were low in the sky. There were more stars than he had ever thought possible, so many stars that it was easy to lose himself among them, all he had to do was let his head loll back on the seat and look up at the infinite. There was a smell of eucalyptus and manure. He heard birds and wondered why they were awake in the middle of the night. Were they as confused as he by the hitherto unseen elasticity of time? The new abductors drove out of Wuhan and stopped on a dirt road that curved upwards into the hills. They didn't beat him. They fed him and gave him a change of clothes and put a bandage around his ribs. They drove some more and stopped at an airfield, where they put him on a plane to Peking.

HE MADE PHONE CALLS from the hospital and discovered that Pang Mei was no longer working in the commissariat or registered at the engineering hostel as a resident. He made more calls. He learned that a teacher he knew, one of his father's old friends, had committed suicide. Others had simply vanished and were thought to be dead. He was still being treated for his injuries when Wei Kuo-ching came to see him.

"The killers are barely out of their teens, rabid youths, so-called radicals who hunt in gleeful packs," said the usually dapper Wei, looking bedraggled, and was he smelling of wine? "Anything can happen to anyone at anytime. Did you hear what happened to Commissar Hu?"

A big-character wall poster appeared one day, said Wei, denouncing Hu as a "son of a landlord," a "degenerate dog," and a "seller of scars." Those kinds of names are thrown around a lot these days, so maybe he should have ignored it. But the poster also said Hu was guilty of sexual perversion with degenerate like-minded women. You know Hu or you don't, but he's not the kind of man who will take abuse without fighting back. He called a meeting. He said his accusers were reactionaries and rightists. They were a danger to the Party. He said they were cowards, hiding behind the anonymity of wall posters. He challenged them to come out into the open. The same night fresh wall posters went up accusing Hu of counterrevolution. The accusations and counteraccusations were noticed and the Party sent a work team to investigate. The work team banned the students from putting up any more posters, but it also reproved Hu, saying he should confess to some of his mistakes. Instead of restoring the peace, the team's actions had the opposite effect. The students defied the ban and plastered posters all over the city. They mobilized student groups in other cities and they sent spokesmen to the highest levels of the party bureaucracy. The response must have been favorable because they stepped up their attacks. The next lot of wall posters gave details of Hu's alleged perversions. Prostitutes. Group sex. Sodomy. Homosexuality. And it was at this stage that Hu made his terrible mistake. He denied all charges and then he said, so what if it is true? Even the chairman isn't a eunuch when it comes to sex. They came for him the next day. They put black paint on his face and paraded him through the streets. They put him in a cage and hung a sign on the bars, ANIMAL EXHIBITION. They didn't let him sleep or wash or talk. It took two weeks for him to confess that he had impugned the chairman and that he was guilty of sexual and other crimes. Pang Mei testified that he had taken advantage of her and introduced her to foreign perversions. His own daughters were forced to denounce him. He's being purged, said Wei. But the only question Lee could think of asking was: what happened to Pang Mei?

SHE WAS DISGRACED, said Wei. The students took turns to work on her in groups. They humiliated her, taunted her, called her names on the street, talked to her family and colleagues, raided her quarters at all hours of day and night. After a few weeks, when they knew she was nearing her breaking point, they put up a poster that said she would not be allowed to commit suicide. I heard she was sent away for reeducation through labor. Isn't it a good thing you decided not to marry her? What a mistake you would have committed. Then Wei said, I'm here to warn you. There have been posters attacking our department, and me personally. If I am under attack you are next. There are few things you can be certain of at this time: bloodlust; group attacks against those who are alone or isolated; packs of dogs running wild through the streets; the end. This is our reality. Anything can happen to anyone at anytime.

8.

To Bombay

He put an official requisition through for a jeep. The requisition was a lie from beginning to end. He expected to be found out and arrested and punished, but nothing happened and the jeep came through. He found a map of old Asia. Names change but geography stays the same, he told himself, and he put his trunks into the jeep and drove south and never once looked back. He drove long stretches, drove as long as he could before the necessity of food or sleep made him stop. He traveled at night and slept in his uniform. When necessary, he said he was on special assignment for his division. He stopped in Sian and Chengdu and Kunming. He found that his map was so out-of-date it was inaccurate. He burned it and bought a new one. Once he left China travel became easier. He didn't have to worry about being caught: Burma was primitive and India was chaos, nobody asked for papers or explanations. He lived in Dacca, Calcutta, Cuttack, Amritsar. He lived in Delhi. In many places he found people who looked like him, Indians from the country's northeast provinces. He lived in cities and towns that he never learned the names of. He lived in hostels and guesthouses and ramshackle lodgings. He learned to drive like an Indian. He abandoned his jeep and bought an Ambassador and he thought he would keep driving until he got tired of it, but he never tired of it. Then why had he chosen to stop in Bombay instead of Delhi or Calcutta? The truth was, he had not chosen. He came to the city with no intention of staying: it was the last of a series of random events set off by his flight from his own country. He got into the habit of taking long walks in his first months, a time of aftermath and distrust, his perils behind him but vivid in his head. It was only when he left his small room and walked by the waterfront that he felt at ease. He discovered the sea by accident, in his first week, on an exploratory walk that began around the neighborhood of Grant Road and ended at Nariman Point. He walked for three hours and during most of that time the water was either in his sight or just beyond. He began to see it as a gift, the sea, because it was always nearby, wherever you were. It was the only thing about Bombay that did not disgust him.

"MY FATHER WAS an important man and I."

"I know, you told me before. You were in the army, you were important too."

"I was, in the old days."

She said, "You should rest, don't agitate yourself about these things."

He shook his head. He wanted her to understand. He pointed at the trunk that held his uniform, his identification documents and photos, paid and unpaid electricity and water bills. He said, you. He pointed to the pipes, pointed twice, his hand traveling slowly from cot to cot. He said, now I not important. I just old man with sickness, not much to give you except pipe. I want you take them. They only valuable thing I own: they your dowry. He nodded at her.

Ah Lee, I want you to live for a long time, she said.

AND MR. LEE made a small sound. She would remember it whenever she thought about him in the years after his death, the involuntary vowel that ascended from deep inside his lungs. It communicated more clearly than words the thing he was trying to say, that it was a humiliation to die and a double humiliation to die in a foreign country. And she remembered the lie she'd told him. Fourteen years later, in 1998, when she was diagnosed with the same ailment, she remembered her lie. A man who does not return to his native place is like a man who dresses in finery and sits in the dark, he told her. He had always planned to return to China in his old age, to die there and be buried beside his ancestors. He said, you promise to rebury me in China. However long it take, you rebury me. She wanted to calm him. She said, Ah Lee, don't worry, I promise. Later, long after he was gone, she would recall all this with terrible clarity; most of all she remembered his last days and the instructions he left. She was to place his ashes in a vase she would find in his trunk. Cremation was quicker than burial, he said, and ashes were easy to transport and easy to store. Beyond these points of business, he hardly spoke or ate; all he wanted was opium. He was willing himself to die.

ON A DRY morning in April, she took his ashes by taxi to the Chinese graveyard in Sewri. The front seat of the Ambassador was filled with flowers and Dimple sat in the back with Ah Fong, Mr. Lee's old friend and customer, who had to be helped into the car.

"He always said he is first to die," said Ah Fong, "I always say, wait, you see, I die first."

Everybody dies, thought Dimple. Losing your family is like dying, which means I've died twice. At the Chinese shop they had shown her a black button she could pin to her sari, the salesman telling her it was the latest thing on the mainland. Instead of an armband you wore a button, silk, very stylish. She wanted the armband, she told him, and she wore it over her sari blouse, an old-fashioned one that Mr. Lee had liked, elbow-length red cotton. She found a framed picture of Mr. Lee in uniform, which she placed on the shrine and she poured a splash of red wine on the ground. There was a plate with sliced meat from a rooster. There was fish and sweet egg cakes. She burned bundles of lucky money in red packets embossed with the symbol for double happiness. His clothes were still in good shape and she couldn't bring herself to burn them, his uniform, the silk padded jackets, the white tunics and black pajamas, his black canvas walking shoes, the stick with the jade dog's head. She put them on a shelf and forgot about them. A week after the funeral, she found Ah Fong waiting at the khana early one morning. He was agitated, talking before she'd even opened the door, and it was strange to see him on the street in the daylight, and to hear the things he was saying.

"I had dream. Ah Lee, standing in front of me, shivering in the cold, naked as day he's born. He said, I have no clothes. Give me your shirt. I wake up, I shout, I was so frighten. Why you don't burn his clothes? This is message, he is sending you message from grave."

It spooked her. She gathered Mr. Lee's things and took a taxi to the cemetery. The cotton garments burned quickly, but the shoes sputtered and black smoke poured from the soles. She asked the attendants for help. They piled everything together in a pit and lit a bonfire. It took an hour for the fire to smolder down to ash and she waited, alone on a bench, and then she felt it, felt his spirit lighten, or was it her own spirit?, lifting like a balloon into the sky. She had done as he wanted in every detail except one: she didn't take his ashes home with her and find a way to return them to China. She'd left him in Sewri. Years later she would be given the opportunity to correct her mistake, but by then it would be beyond her. And by then she would understand that when she felt his spirit leave the cemetery and ascend into the sky, she had been partially right; what she had gotten wrong was the direction in which Mr. Lee moved and the element in which he settled. He went downward, where he waited in water for the chance to speak to her again.

9.

The Pipe Comes
to Rashid's

She wrapped the pipes in muslin and took them to Rashid's. It was early in the day. The screen doors were open to the light and the radio played a song from *Pyaasa*, Geeta Dutt singing of heartache. It made her think of the movies she watched growing up, secret excursions to Tardeo Talkies for Raj Kapoor and Guru Dutt, all that sepia longing and Government of India footage of war and industry. The room was from the same black-and-white era. She came in with the pipes and Rashid was reading an Urdu newspaper. He was islanded, barricaded by a bottle and glasses, cigarettes, pipes, dirty dishes, discarded clothing. He didn't seem surprised to see her. The first thing he did, he asked if she wanted tea. I can call for it from the balcony, he said. I'll put on a shirt and call for tea.

She said, "I don't want tea, Mr. Rashid, thank you."

"Okay, no problem, no problem. What can I do for you?"

"Actually, I've brought something for you."

She unwrapped the pipes and placed them on the floor and picked up the longer one, three feet something from tip to tip.

"At least five hundred years old. Made by a Chinese pipe master, much superior to our local pipes because of the quality of the wood and the seasoning."

"Is it too long?"

"No, sir, it's constructed on the same principle as a hookah. The length is very important, it cools the smoke as it travels from the bowl to the mouthpiece."

"You've been practicing this speech."

"Yes, sir, a little."

He liked her manner, her conservative clothes, the way she spoke Hindi mixed with English. He watched her as she assembled the lamp and oil and chandu and he liked that too, the sight of a woman calmly making a pipe, because an Indian woman in a chandu khana was a rare sighting. She tapped the stem when the pipe was ready and it took him a moment, an awkward moment of grapple, to adjust to the big mouthpiece. But she was right: the pipe was a work of art. The wood was stained reddish brown and there was old brass work at the mouthpiece and bowl. Maybe he was imagining it, but the smoke tasted better and you could take deeper drags and a single pyali went a long way.

"How much do you want for it? Maybe I'll take both."

"I don't want to sell the pipes, Mr. Rashid."

"You call me Rashidbhai or bhai, not Mr. Rashid, this is not America."

"Bhai, let me work for you. I can make pyalis and take care of the pipes."

He said he would not be able to pay her. She would get three pyalis a day and tips. She could eat in the khana but she couldn't sleep there.

"I have a place to sleep, but I smoke four pyalis a day—of good opium."

"Mine is the best on the street. Where do you smoke?"

He was surprised to learn that Mr. Lee was real. Like everyone else, he'd heard the story about a Chinese khana somewhere
on Shuklaji Street and he'd dismissed it as fiction. But he knew the
value of old stories and he incorporated Mr. Lee's into his own.
Rashid told everyone he'd bought the pipes from the old Chini himself. He told the story so many times that eventually he came to
believe it and with each telling he added new details. Mr. Lee was on
his deathbed when he sent for Rashid; it was the second last thing
he did before he died, he handed over the pipes; the last thing he
did was to smoke; he didn't want anyone else to have the pipes, only
Rashid, because he wanted them to go where they would be best
used; the pipes had originally belonged to the emperor of China
and had fallen into the hands of the nationalist army; and so on.

TO MATCH THE QUALITY of Mr. Lee's pipes he put less water in
the cooking mix. Soon the place was packed with regulars and tourists and all kinds of unlikely people who came just to visit. He raised
the price of a pyali to three rupees from two but the opium was so
much better than anywhere else that no one complained; if anything, business improved. A tall Australian turned up. He smoked
all day and drew pictures in a small notebook and spent a lot of
money. He was generous: he bought pyalis for everyone. He came
back the next day and the next and for a week he was a regular at the
khana. He communicated mostly with his hands, because no one
could understand him though he was speaking English. Months
after he left, after he'd taken off for Sydney or Melbourne or wherever, someone said he was a famous musician whose tunes were
played on the radio in the West, and that he'd written a song about

his experience at Rashid's, that there was something in it about "lying in a den in Bombay." Then the son of a well-known director came around. He was making his first movie and he wanted to get the atmosphere right for a scene set in an opium den. He sat at the entrance near the washing area and he didn't try a pipe. He dropped the names of actors and directors, all of whom were close family friends, or so he said. It wasn't his patter that irritated Rashid, but his laughter, high-pitched and smelling of insanity. He wore a straw hat that he held in his lap. He took notes. He took a photograph of Dimple that would appear many years later in a book about Bombay's opium dens (in the picture, a young woman holds a pipe to a lamp, her face intent, and in a corner of the frame is a book, the title partly obscured, *OWERS OF EVIL*). After much deliberation he decided to try a pyali, smoked half, and ran down the stairs to vomit. But it was his smoking technique that was most remarked on. He wiped the mouthpiece with a handkerchief soaked in Dettol, wiped it each time he took a drag and the pipe smelled for days of antiseptic. When he returned from the toilet he asked if he could take more pictures and Rashid said, yes, of course he could, but then he would have to break the director's son's legs and cut off his hands to ensure he never left the khana, which riposte Rashid delivered with a smile, as if he were sharing a joke.

THE BROTHEL KEEPER, Dimple's tai, paid Rashid a formal visit. She was full of complaints. She said Dimple was spending too much time at the khana, she'd become a full-time professional drug addict, she was no longer earning her keep. The other girls brought in more money, said the tai, addressing only Rashid. Not once during the visit did the tai and Dimple speak or look at each other.

Dimple made Rashid's pipe the way she always did, calm and silent, her hands steady, while the tai drank her tea, made her speech, and left. That afternoon, Rashid took Dimple to a room on a half land-ing between the khana and the first floor, where his family lived. There was a wooden cot, a chair and washstand, a window with a soiled curtain. She knew what he wanted. She took off her salvaar and folded it on the back of the chair. She lay on the cot and pulled her kameez up to her shoulders to show him her breasts. Her legs were open, the ridged skin stretched like a ghost vagina.

He said, you're like a woman. She said, I am a woman, see for yourself. She didn't want him on top of her because he was too heavy for her back. She told him to sit on the cot while she faced him, her arms around his neck and her ankles locked on his hips. It took a long time, the drugs working in opposition to his blood, but she didn't stop until he was finished, shuddering with effort, his hands angled on the bed, his eyes looking into hers.

He said, "What about you, what do you feel?"

"Fine."

"No. What I want to know, do you feel pleasure or not?"

"Not like you do and not the way a woman does."

"You don't feel anything."

"Oh, bilkul, I do. I feel pleasure but not, what's the word?, relief."

He studied her face as she arranged her kameez and tidied her hair. He said, I want you to move here, into this room. I'll send someone with you to collect your things.

HER LIFE at the brothel was coming to an end, she knew. She was treated better than some of the others but she worked three or four giraks a day. She was in her twenties and already she felt middle-aged. She'd lived and worked at Number 007 for more than fifteen years. The work was fast. The giraks didn't take off their clothes. They unzipped, they finished in minutes, and they were gone. Their desire for her, for sex, was theoretical. It had no reality. It was the idea of a eunuch in a filthy brothel in Shuklaji Street, this was what they paid for. Dimple thought: they like the dirtiness of it. Nothing else gets their dicks so hard. They don't think of themselves as homosexuals. They have wives and children and they're always making jokes about gandus and chakkas. It's all about money: they think eunuchs give better value than women. Eunuchs know what men want in a way other randis don't, they know men like it dirty.

Lakshmi's way of putting it: what dogs we are when we are men. Lakshmi worked the street, getting shop owners and pedestrians to part with money, doing this with nothing more than a clap of her man's hands. She did it now, a gunshot clap designed to cut through heavy Bombay traffic. A customer in the main room turned around in alarm. He was trying to persuade the tai to give him a discount rate for two prostitutes. Lakshmi said, men are dogs. We know and they know. Only women don't know. Isn't that right, darling? she told the customer. Aren't you a dog sniffing around my ass for a free fuck?

AFTER THE CUSTOMER left in search of a brothel with better rates, Dimple stood on the balcony of 007 and looked down into the street at the cook fires and crowds of pedestrians. Then she put on her sandals and went out. The paanwallah was listening to AIR and he smiled at her when she stepped into his cubicle. She ordered a Calcutta meetha and watched as he assembled it. He was listening to cricket commentary, a match between India and the West Indies. They talked for a while about Indian versus West Indian batsmen. The Indians were skilled but they were no match for the blacks, said the paanwallah. Dimple asked him what he thought about Gavaskar. The paanwallah said Gavaskar was okay but he lacked something. No killer instinct, and that was the problem with Indians. Dimple asked if killer instinct was all you needed to play a good game, and the paanwallah laughed and said he knew what Dimple was leading up to but he'd been in the game for a while himself and he knew a couple of things. Dimple said she was only passing the time of day and then she asked if he put enough supari in the Calcutta. The paanwallah said there was enough supari to make a horse kick and he told her to come back if she wasn't satisfied and he would give her a free one. He said Gavaskar was a good man and a technically sound player, but he was not accustomed to the taste of blood. It didn't excite him. Indians were too mild, said the paanwallah, and it was Gandhi's fault. The old man had taken a race of bloodthirsty warriors, taught them nonviolence, and made them into saints and grass eaters. Dimple laughed. She told the paanwallah to take a look around. Indians are as violent and bloodthirsty as ever, and they would always be looking for an excuse to hack or burn or gouge each other. The paanwallah laughed too. Back in her room, she chewed the paan and watched herself in the hand mirror hanging on a nail above the sink. She watched the shape her mouth made and she looked at her eyes and skin and hair and made a critical assessment: not bad. As she got older it took more work to look good. The more difficult it became, the more she smoked. The more she smoked, the more difficult it became. She thought, if I lose my looks I don't want to live. I don't want to be like the tai whose only joy in life is money. Dimple was the tai's chela, the tai-in-waiting. When she was old and no longer able to work, she'd take care of the business and oversee the other randis. She'd handle money all day long. She would know no other life. It was an inevitability that needed correction and she was correcting her life. So she asked Rashid to wait while she moved her things in small consignments, relocating herself a piece at a time. There was no question of taking her earnings with her. The tai would say that Dimple owed her for food and board, and besides, it was probably a fair exchange: she was trading money (her earnings) for pleasure (her freedom). Variations of this transaction occurred on the street a thousand times a day.

SHE TOLD ONLY one girak that she was leaving, a pocket maar who always smoked at her station. He'd smoke and talk, softly, so the other customers wouldn't hear him. Rashid made jokes, calling him her new boyfriend. Then the pocket maar came to see her at the brothel. He sold cocaine and whisky for one of the Lalas. He was tall and skinny, his thin legs and bony knees out of proportion to his big belly and chest, and he wore his hair long, down to his collar like a hippie. He gave her different amounts each time, two or three or four hundred rupees in small bills, but it was double the amount he was expected to pay and she was always happy to see him. He ordered strong beer, Cannon or Khajuraho, and he sprawled on the bed, drinking from the bottle. He gossiped about the private lives of Raj Kapoor and Nargis, Shashi Kapoor and Shabana Azmi, and his favorite topic, Amitabh Bachchan and Rekha. He kissed Dimple on the lips. She'd wipe her mouth and he'd kiss her again. He took his time, locking the door and staying so long the tai pounded on the partition, shouting, Salim. Finished. Time finished. Dimple, open up, did he die inside you or what?

One night he asked if she would look after a bag for him, a nylon Air India shoulder bag that was zipped but unlocked. He handed it over and disappeared. Inside she found bundles of hundred-rupee notes and, rolled in a T-shirt, two pistols, large six-guns like the fire-arms brandished by Clint Eastwood in English movies. She put the bag into a steel Godrej almirah and carried the key on a chain she attached to the waistband of her salvaar. Salim was gone for three weeks. He came back shrunken, with new bruises on the soles of his feet and on his back. He said: chitchat with the police, friendly gupshup, yaar, with the brown crows. She opened a bottle of white flower oil from a box that Mr. Lee had given her and rubbed it into the discolorations on his skin. The oil's cold burn helped him heal. After this Salim brought her little gifts, plastic hair clips, a keychain, a tiny handbag, a black leather diary with the phone codes of all the world's cities and special pockets for business cards and photos. Sometimes he expected not sex but conversation. He wanted her to tell him what was in the book she was reading, and she would try to encapsulate it for him, encapsulate in a few sentences a three-hundred-page novel by a Latin American or European author. He would ask about her health, about her day, and it would irritate her. What was there to say? Her day was always the same. She worked at 007 and she worked at Rashid's and when she was not working she taught herself to read, there was nothing more to it. His questions were useless but comforting. She wondered if this was what it meant to be married, to be a wife. You were bored and irritated and comforted, all at the same time.

"Why are you leaving?"

"Because I have a chance to."

"What if I offered you a chance?"

"I'd think about it, but you haven't made an offer yet."

"I will, you can put money on it. I'll do it very soon."

But he didn't, and one morning she put her things into a taxi: Mr. Lee's tin trunks, four or five cloth-wrapped parcels, and a many-tiered makeup kit, the kind carried by Air India stewardesses. It was a little after eight in the morning on Christmas Day. Nobody was awake. Nobody saw her go except Lakshmi, who said, bitch, whatever you do, don't come back.

BOOK THREE

THE
INTOXICATED

I.

A Walk on
Shuklaji Street

His older son, Jamal, was waiting by the door. How long had he been there? The boy had a way of appearing without making a sound, materializing from nowhere with his eyes wide and his hand extended. He was six years old and already a businessman, all he wanted from his father was cash. Depending on his mood, Rashid handed over some small amount or he didn't. Today he was opium sick and fearful and god's words were bubbling in his head. No, he told his son. Out, out. Jamal retreated, eyes sullen, and Rashid banged down the wooden stairs, struggling to put on his shirt, his arms and stomach so meaty that it took some mindfulness, some extra push and twist of effort. He thought: I am a fat businessman. When did this happen? Not so long ago I was a skinny criminal trying to make a name and now here I am, an entrepreneur, with cash in my pocket and the shortest commute in the world—out the door and down a flight of stairs—and none of it gives me a moment of peace in my head. How did this happen?

Shuklaji Street was a fever grid of rooms, boom-boom rooms, family rooms, god rooms, secret rooms that contracted in the daytime and expanded at night. It wasn't much of a street. It was narrow and congested, and there was an endless stream of cars and trucks and handcarts and bicycles. But it stretched roughly from Grant Road to Bombay Central and to walk along it was to tour the city's fleshiest parts, the long rooms of sex and nasha. In the midst of it, Rashid's opium room was becoming a local landmark. Trained staff. Genuine Chinese opium pipes. Credit if you're good for it. Best-quality O. He was getting opium tourists who heard about the khana from a friend on a beach somewhere in Spain, or a café in Rome, and they'd come all the way to Shuklaji Street to see for themselves. They'd smoke a pipe or two, because that was the point, and then they'd sit around for hours, drinking tea and taking pictures, collecting souvenirs to show off back home. Like the couple from Amsterdam who asked to visit his living quarters. He took them upstairs where his family lived in rooms that ran the length of the building, where his wives made big meals and his children skulked about and he was a mostly absent father and husband. The Dutch couple wanted to see everything, examine each room as if they were on a guided tour, a bonus to their opium adventure. They shook hands with his family and asked endless questions. How many children did he have? How many wives? Had he always lived in Bombay? Why was his English so good? Did his children go to school?

Then the woman asked: what is a typical morning like? And he had no answer. How to tell her that he got up late and went straight down to the khana, his system stunned from six or seven hours without drugs, his head reeling with visions of hellfire and the annihilation of the godless world; that it took an hour with the pipe before things came up the right way around? And then, sometime in the late afternoon, after a bath and a meal, he'd step out on the street and say a few words to the punters. Okay? Good? Yes. One-word greet-ings, or not even that, a nod maybe, a smile if he felt up to it. Just to be there, taking a constitutional among the horse cabs, the black and yellow taxis, men and women yelling to be heard above the honk and bustle of Shuklaji Street: he'd watch the heads bob on their way to some cash-and-carry transaction, criminal apostles to the great god Enterprise, and it gave him a veiny jolt of pleasure to dawdle, to slow down and take it in.

HE HAD the shortest commute on the street but not today. He stepped out of the building and walked quickly to the corner, duck-ing from the sudden glare. It was a holiday of some kind, a Hindu holiday, because the temple was full of people and he could see the priest, threaded, shirtless, his orange dhoti a flash in the sun. On the street, the punters were out in numbers, the respectable fathers and grandfathers and uncles, the solid citizens on furlough from their lives. He heard snatches of Gujarati, Malayalam, even English as they headed to the numbered rooms above the street. Uncontrol-lable prayer phrases rose to his lips as he walked past the temple. When he was high it was never like this, but when he was opium sick and sober—yes, then, then god was always close. He whispered, guide thou us on the straight path, thou who are round about the infidels. Thy lightning snatches their eyes. He stepped around a small group on the sidewalk, a trio of cripples in white pajamas and skullcaps, arguing about money, their crutches propped against the wall. They worked together every day, begging arm in arm, and now they were throwing accusations at each other. He thought: the idea of Muslims fighting each other over a few rupees, it goes against the grain of the Prophet's word. Or it proves the truth of it. When a storm cloud cometh out of the heaven, big with darkness and black thunder, they thrust their fingers into their ears for fear of death.

HE TURNED INTO Foras Road and entered Timely Watch Show-room, ringing the bell on his way in, the shop empty, as it usually was. Salim was in the office in the back and he got up when he saw Rashid, came around the desk with the city's newest fashion accessory clipped to his belt, the headphones pumping a tinny beat into his skull, some disco beat, *Saturday Night Fever*, what else? Salim's models were John Travolta and Amitabh Bachchan, and he picked up most of his style and language from the two tough-guy actors, or so said Rashid's wife. Today he was wearing light blue bell-bottoms and platform shoes, his shirt the same shade of blue as his trousers. His hair, parted on the side, fell to his shoulders in untidy bunches. Rashid went to Salim's side of the desk, to the leather executive chair with the fancy headrest, and he pulled an envelope from his pocket and slammed it down for the pleasure of hearing that cash money bang. And for the pleasure of seeing Salim jump to attention and take a mirror out of the desk drawer and, tenderly, a bundle of vials. Rashid had a hundred-rupee note already rolled. He spilled the contents of a vial on the mirror and snorted it before Salim had a chair pulled up to the other side of the desk. Salim was being respectful, properly so: he didn't touch the envelope.

"Did you get the whisky?"

"Of course, Rashidbhai."

"Of course, Rashidbhai, so polite, like I'm your uncle. Did you get Red or Black?"

"Black Label, your choice. Not so easy to find these days."

He made himself comfortable in Salim's chair, the seat tilting backwards in tiny clicks, some special mechanism that made minute adjustments for his weight and let him lean all the way back without any danger of tipping over.

"Nice chair, yaar, you must be doing well."

"Doing okay, bhai. I work hard, I make money. I stop working, I'm on the street."

Rashid knew this was the truth. There wasn't much of a margin in Salim's line of work, selling cocaine and black-market whisky for the Lala. He did some pocket-maar business on the side, risky work with questionable results, and he spent the day at his boss's watch shop taking care of nonexistent customers. He'd been with the Lala for less than a year and already it was showing on his face, the shadows scored like leather under his eyes. The Lala picked his boys young and put them to work when they got too old for his tastes. The old gangster liked to quote the Baburnama: "Women for procreation, boys for pleasure, melons for delight."

Salim handed two bottles of Johnnie Walker to Rashid, who checked that the seals hadn't been tampered with and there were no punctures in the caps. He held the bottles up to the light to examine the color and Salim asked if he'd seen the new Amitabh Bachchan movie, *Polyester Khadi*, in which Bachchan played a policeman's son who becomes a criminal because he sees how hard his father's life is. Rashid said no, he hadn't seen it and he wasn't planning to, he had better things to do than watch Amitabh fucking Bachchan. Salim said the best scene in the film was the showdown between policeman father and gangster son.

"You know what he tells his father, played by the veteran Sanjeev Kumar?"

In response, Rashid spilled a small mountain of powder on the mirror and looked up, the hundred-rupee note aloft in his hand.

Salim stood up to say the line, delivering it in a bored baritone very much like the tall actor's. "Are you a man or a pajama?"

Rashid said, "And what is Sanjeev fucking Kumar's reply?"

Salim got up again.

"If I am a pajama at least I am cent percent Indian khadi, not American polyester."

RASHID BENT to the mirror and he was startled by the sight of his face up close, blue veins swollen at the temple, skin the color of clotted milk, a sickly sap of green stubble on the jaw. His hair was too long, almost as long as Salim's, he needed a cut and shampoo. Paan had stained his mouth a permanent red. Worst were his eyes, bloody and clouded at the same time. Then he felt the back of his throat go numb. There was a close thump in his ears. He rubbed a bit of powder into his gums and a wave of nausea hit him and he looked away from his degraded image. But there was half a line still left on the mirror. He snorted it up. His heart beat so erratically and so fast he was sure it would leap out of his chest and land on the glass-topped desk.

"Bhai, that chanduli at your khana, Dimple, who makes pipes."

"What?"

"Dimple."

"What about her?"

"She makes pipes in your khana."

"I know what she does, she works for me."

"She's a hijra, right? She was a man once?"

"Long ago. Her dick was probably bigger than yours."

"So what I was wondering, bhai, is why she looks so feminine. I mean, if you didn't know she was a hijra you'd think she was fully a woman."

"Listen, Salim, you're so interested, you should ask her yourself, take her out to a movie, introduce her to your family. She likes boys like you."

RASHID WALKED BACK to the khana with the bundle of vials and the bottles of Johnnie in his hands. He was calmer now. Even the heat seemed milder, the sun directly overhead but not uncomfortable; and the noise in his head had settled into a hum, steady and controlled, like paper burning in a tray. His white shirt lay open to the sternum and his pants were hitched low on his belly. He wore only white. He spotted the color on the mannequins in store windows and people on the street and to him the figures in white were as distinctive as angels among the earthbound.

He was thinking of Salim's line, "Are you a man or a pajama?" He wanted more options than just the two. His father said they were descended from the Mughals, from a Beg who'd ridden with Humayun. There was a branch of the family in Delhi that had owned sixteenth-century buildings and gardens. It was a family legend that he mistrusted, but every now and then he would catch himself thinking of the Mughals and the majoun they liked to eat, swallowed with a glass of milk like medicine, and he'd see himself as a new Mughal, mixing it up, juggling the booze with the coke and charas and chandu. This morning he was planning to take it easy. He'd keep the whisky down to manageable quantities, a half bottle, no more, and then the rest of it would be manageable too: line of White first thing to get his eyes open, pyali of Black at regular intervals to keep

his nerves easy and his ideas oiled, and, around the time the muez-
zin sent out the evening call, a bit of Brown chased on foil or smoked
in a cigarette, the powder caked so heavy the joint would have to be
lit and relit. This is the new thing, brown powder, garad heroin with
the compliments of the Pakistani government, something sweet for
the mouth from our Muslim brothers; the question being, what kind
of government would see anything in heroin but poison? Which
god would welcome such a drug? Not the Hindu gods and not even
the god of the Christians. So what did it mean that the Pakistanis,
who worshipped the same god as he, were sending garad to India?
It meant that politics, or economics, overrode every other thing in
the world. They shared the same faith, but in other ways they were
enemies. Above all, the Pakistanis were sworn enemies.

Guide thou us, thou, who are round about the infidels.

He had been a believer for most of his life, had observed the
five prayer times and followed the dietary strictures. Then he'd
exchanged one habit for another, he'd given up god and accepted
O. With heroin he'd opened himself to the ungodly and for this he
would pay, he knew. He would be seized by the feet and flung into
the fire. Because the powder was a new thing, the devil's own nasha.
Rashid knew it the first time he saw street junkies bent over strips of
tin foil, the way they sucked at the smoke, the instantaneous effect
of it, how it closed their eyes and shut them off from their own bodies and the world. He saw them and thought: this is it, the future,
coming too fast to duck. And now he was doing the same. And he
was helpless against god's great wrath.

HE ROUNDED the alley to the khana and there was his son at the
beedi shop buying cigarettes. Jamal saw the speed at which his

father approached and he looked wildly around the alley. Rashid grabbed the boy by the wrist and squeezed until he dropped the cigarettes. The cigarettewallah said, bhai, he didn't have money so I gave him on credit, I thought it was for you. Rashid looked at his son's face, the stupidity and stubbornness of it, and rage filled his chest with carbon.

"Six years old and you're on the street, fucking smoking."

He crushed the cigarettes in his hands and let the debris fall to the ground. He caught his son by the neck and propelled him into the building. When the boy stumbled, he wanted him to fall and break something. He wanted to hear something break inside his son. Jamal was terrified but his fright only made Rashid angrier.

"Get up those stairs. Go on or I'll kill you."

He looked at his hands and was surprised to see he was still carrying the bottles of whisky and the cocaine. He put the bottles on the ground, carefully, giving his entire attention to the action but he was unable to clear his head. He heard his son make small sounds that seemed to come from far away, or from a tunnel, a narrow tunnel that smelled of fresh mutton. Then Rashid heard crows, sudden caws from directly above him though there were no birds in the building or even in the sky outside. He made a fist around the vials in his hand and hit the boy on the head and Jamal sat in the dust of the stairwell, his sobs audible in the street. Rashid stood over him, shoulders heaving, and hit him again. Then he saw the beediwallah and his customers staring at him from the doorway. What? he said to them, his rage now mixed with shame, and when the men disappeared, he put the cocaine in his pocket, picked up the whisky, and used his free hand to drag the boy up the stairs.

2.

Bengali

It was too early for customers. When Rashid arrived, agitated and muttering to himself, only Dimple and Bengali were in the khana. The old man kept his accounts and looked after the shop, and had been with him since the early days, when Rashid was a tapori selling charas near Grant Road Station. Bengali spent most of his time locking and unlocking a tin box that served as the register, putting in money, paying it out. He'd been working for Rashid for many years, and no one knew anything about his life before he came to Shuklaji Street, except that he'd once been a clerk in a government office in Calcutta. He was between fifty and seventy, wrinkled skin on bone, and he spoke English with an affected British accent.

"Syzygy," he said one afternoon and he repeated the word in case the student had not heard him. "That is the reason the world has gone mad."

"What?"

"Syzygy. It has never happened before and it won't happen again."

"No, probably not. It's a once-in-a-lifetime occurrence."

"How can it not affect everything? Nine planets, lined up on the same side of the sun. Does it mean the end of the world as some people think?"

"It's tempting to see it that way, I suppose, kind of like a unified theory of apocalypse."

"You understand, all the planets in a row, like sitting ducks. I say it's an important question, the question of syzygy. Maybe the most important question of all."

Bengali was in his usual position, sitting on his haunches with his head between his bony knees. He seemed to be smiling but it was difficult to tell, because his face was so thin and his skin shone with a papery yellow light. He told the student not to worry. Chandulis and charasis were like cockroaches, he said, they would survive anything, including the end of the world. He quoted a Punjabi proverb or poem or limerick:

Charasi, khadi na marsi.
Gar marsi, tho chaalis admi agay karsi.

And he talked about the historical tradition of the apocalypse myth and other matters, for ten minutes, very slowly, like a scholar, and the student listened openmouthed. What Bengali was doing, Rashid thought, was making up big what-ifs, making them up out of thin air. Bengali was a what-if. He talked about mythological, religious, and political figures as if he knew them well, knew their numerous personal failings and feet of clay. He was on first-name terms with Jesus, Nehru and Gandhi, Cassius Clay, Winston Churchill, Gina Lollobrigida, and Jean-Paul Sartre. "Would Orpheus's story have been different if he'd chosen another, slightly more cheerful song?" Bengali asked the student. "Perhaps, in his distraction, he made a mistake, an error of judgment, and he chose the wrong tune.

If you're singing for the Furies, I personally would choose something to please them. What if he had chosen wisely? What would have happened? Would he have kept his wife and his head? And purely as an aside, mind you, I'll point out that the real interest of the tale is the psychological portrait of a person in grief. Because, if you know anything about grief, you know that its main outward manifestation is a deep distraction, like absentmindedness without the insouciance."

From Orpheus or Icarus or Stephen Dedalus he turned to Bengali cultural heroes, Tagore and Satyajit Ray and the Dutts, Guru, Toru, and Michael Madhusudan. He shared the regional affliction that Bengalis were prone to, the conviction that they were the most artistic and talented people in the world. But Bengali was a maverick Bengali and some of his views were a kind of blasphemy. "What if Tagore had not won the Nobel when he did," Bengali asked, "how would it have affected his work? I suspect it would have made him more open to experimentation and more interesting in every way, especially in his poetry, which, I have to say, is not very good. And why shouldn't I say so? The point about Tagore is that the whole was far greater than the sum of the parts. It is the composite figure that matters. But Tagore the mystic and poet? Tagore the painter? Tagore the composer? Not one of those Tagores is worth very much."

THE OLD MAN was sitting by the cook pot, imbibing fumes by a system of osmosis. When he saw Rashid he got up to prepare his boss's pyali. Outside, the day was bright with noonday sun and Rashid could see the balcony of Khalid's place next door, the ancient iron railing and the flaking green paint on the walls. They were meeting today, Khalid and he, after lunch, which could mean anytime before the evening prayer. Rashid picked up the newspaper and put his glasses on, but he couldn't focus on the words. He was still rattled by the anger that had swept him up. He put the paper aside and prepared a hit of coke. The room got busy all of a sudden, two lamps lit, the pot bubbling in the tiled washing area near the entrance, and Dimple fixing his pipe while Bengali placed his pyalis on a tray.

Rashid said, chal, chal, hurry up, don't be doing your randi baazi when my pipe's waiting to be made. Dimple didn't seem to hear him; she dipped a knitting needle into a pyali and cooked the opium into a soft black bubble. Then she tapped the stem and Rashid ducked to the pipe. He smoked cross-legged, never mind the popular version, on your back with your knees bent and your legs triangulated. He was a businessman, a father. He wasn't going to lie there with his legs open to the world. He took a long pull of the pipe and a stream of smoke ascended from his nostrils and veiled his face. He took another pull and this time there was no smoke: he ate it down. It was just short of noon and already the khana was dark, in a kind of permanent half shade. The room made people talk in whispers, as if they were in a place of worship, which, the way he saw it, they were. Already now there were times he could feel it slipping away, a way of life vanishing as he watched, the pipes, the oil lamps layered with years of black residue, the conversations that a man would begin and lose interest in, all the rituals that he revered and obeyed, all of it disappearing.

3.

Business Practices Among the Criminal Class: An Offer

When Khalid arrived, Rashid was having lunch, scooping it up from stainless steel dabbas spread on the floor. The food, sent hot from upstairs, was backed up with a fish delivery from Delhi Darbar and a stack of tandoori rotis and bheja fry and lassi, thick, no froth, a slab of hard cream on top. He had had a craving for bheja and fish, the bheja with its texture like scrambled eggs and that odd resistance when it burst in the mouth. His older wife, Dariya, had tried to make it at home but she couldn't manage the flavor that Delhi Darbar's cook seemed to get every time, without effort. She'd sent biryani, the mutton cooked with the rice, not layered separately, and plates of fresh onion and cucumber, and daal fry with garlic, a film of oil floating on top. He ate no biryani but mutton, bought the meat himself three times a week. Because he could afford it, he ate meat every day, sometimes twice a day, sometimes mutton and chicken. He was sitting cross-legged, hands smeared with rice and masala, working on his second plate of biryani, and he invited his neighbor to join him but Khalid declined, as he always did, declined even to taste the meal. Which was an un-Muslim thing to do, never mind that it was rude. Rashid thought: this is what we do: we eat together from the same dish. This is how we remember we're brothers. He motioned to Khalid to sit. He wasn't eager to share his lunch in any case and he wanted to take his time with the lassi, which he would have last, like dessert. But Khalid's presence in the khana had lessened his pleasure in the meal. It took some effort to ignore the man, who was leaning over, putting his mouth near Rashid's ear, saying he wanted to talk in private, as if Bengali and Dimple were not to be trusted. Rashid continued to eat, methodically working his way through the food. We are in private, he said, when he was washing his hands at the tap. Then they went through the formalities. Salaam alaikum. Alaikum as-salaam. How are you? How's business? Your family? Your health? And they went through the ordering and serving of tea, paani kum from the restaurant downstairs, brought up double fast by a freelance pipeman. The khana was filling with customers and still Khalid wouldn't talk, so Rashid suggested they stand on the balcony for a moment, sip from their glasses of milky chai, and only then did he get to it.

"Much better, Rashidbhai, some privacy in your balcony where I can tell you my news."

"Tell me. One minute," and Rashid said a few words to Bengali, something about getting the cook pot started for the day's second batch of chandu, which was an unnecessary order: Bengali had never forgotten it.

"Okay."

"I've been approached by Sam Biryani. You've heard of him, he's always in the papers."

"He's too much in the papers."

"He made an offer, very good terms to open a garad pipeline from Tardeo to Nagpada."

"If it's a good offer take it up."

"That's why I'm here. I've brought this up with you before but you never give me a proper reply. My suggestion is we do it together. Garad is the future of the business."

"Your topi is fur, isn't it? Doesn't it get warm in this weather?"

"It's insulation, bhai, in winter and summer, that's why we Kashmiris wear them."

"That's why you Kashmiris are so hotheaded. Take it off once in a while, miya, it might lighten your outlook. Meanwhile, listen to me: I won't sell powder here."

"You use it but you won't sell it."

"I use it carefully."

"Everybody says that. What about the Pathan, Kader Khan? I'm trying to remember how soon he was finished. Six months? Or less? Such a dada and look at him now, khatarnak junkie."

"This is what you want to talk about? Give me a lecture about the evils of drugs?"

"You're an educated man. You have your way of seeing things."

"You mean I'm not seeing something."

"I mean you should be thinking of diversifying, expanding your business."

"Garad separates the strong from the weak; it brings out the worst in a man and the best. That's why the Pathan gave up so quickly; inside he was nothing."

"And you?"

RASHID WAS LOOKING at the street. A beggar woman squatted over a puddle by the garbage pit on the intersection of Shuklaji Street and Arab Gully. She was dark and plump and she wore a

fitted kameez that she held up around her waist. Emptying. The correct word for what she was doing. He noticed that her hair had been
very stylishly cut, cropped short over the ears, with pointed side-
burns and a little tail in the back. The puddle under her expanded
and the people on the street stepped over it without comment. Then
the woman's head came up and her eyes met Rashid's and there was
no embarrassment in her face, only intelligence. From the balcony,
he could see into Khalid's khana next door. It was a smaller room,
with a single pipe and no customers, no one there at all except for
the pipe maker. Rashid's was already busy, a group of Spanish-
speaking hippies around one pipe and students from Wilson College around the other. Waiting their turn were Dawood Chikna, an
up-and-coming businessman and gangster, and Bachpan, a pimp,
with his friend and associate, the pocket maar Pasina. Last in line
was a fellow called Spiderman for the way he crawled on all fours.
Salim was there too, in a new shirt, a starched yellow number with
flap pockets and large collars. He was at Dimple's station, deep in
conversation with the kaamwali. Rashid wanted to know what they
were talking about but all he could hear was Khalid, who was saying
that a businessman should never sample his own merchandise, particularly if his business was drugs, and that a Mussalman did not put
his habits before his duty to god, that only Kafirs did such a thing.
Rashid watched the beggar woman who was tidying up the garbage
on the sidewalk and he thought about his system. A man's reputation depended on never seeming intoxicated. So, in the afternoons,
he read *Inquilab*, squinting at the editorials, some article on the
Muslim Brotherhood's travails in Syria or the Jews' latest incursions
into Lebanon, and he stole a few quick nods. Then he'd give an order
to Bengali, whatever order it didn't matter, a shout for a pipe or for
lunch, a summons for the malishwallah, for whisky or cocaine, an

audible order to an employee to reestablish the chain of command. In the evening if he'd been drinking a lot he went upstairs for an hour or two to nap. He was always mindful of his reputation, but here was this Khalid, this Kashmiri, casting aspersions. Just then, Rashid noticed something odd. All sound and activity had frozen, as if a giant wave was about to hit the street and this was the split second of calm before the chaos. The beggar woman was completely still, a black marble statue listening intently to the decades as they passed through her: the Salt March to freedom; the years of upheaval and bloodletting and so-called Independence; the years of the Pakistan wars when headlights were painted black to keep automobiles safe from enemy jets; the years of regulation and control and planned socialism; the years of failure. Everything was frozen, even the traffic and the sunlight and the slight still breeze, and then the woman went back to her work and the street too resumed its normal pace and Rashid realized he'd been holding his breath.

WHAT IS SHE DOING, the beggar woman, what is she doing? he asked Khalid.

"It's already a thing of the past, chandu," Khalid said, "like these pipes."

"Like everything, like us."

"That is the nasha talking, not you. Listen, very soon all the khanas will be closed, ours included. Last month, they closed six. In one month. Padlocks and chains courtesy Customs Excise."

"There are too many on this street. Let them close."

"And then? What will you do for business?"

"This, that."

"You're a BA pass, educated man, but you're talking like you don't know how to read-write."

Rashid brushed the hair off his face with his hands, letting the thought take shape in his head before he spoke. He said, it's a funny thing, only the uneducated set so much stock by education. When you go to school you realize how little it means, because the street belongs to whoever takes it. Today it's ours; tomorrow someone else will take our place. My problem, I don't like garad heroin. Garadulis put their foot on the accelerator and push all the way to the floor. The car was going five miles an hour and suddenly it's up to fifty-five. Super fast, then crash. A chanduli can smoke for years and be healthy; garadulis are impatient, they want to die quickly. You say we're businessmen and we should provide what people want. What kind of a businessman would I be if I supplied heroin to chandu customers? I would be a chooth businessman. I'd be shooting myself in the foot. Why I'm telling you this, it's my way of saying don't ask me again to join you in business.

Salim, Pasina, and Dimple were not looking in his direction, but some of the others were. Even Bengali, unflappable as the old man was, had forgotten himself and was staring. Khalid lit a cigarette and regarded Rashid as he smoked. His shirt was tucked into pleated trousers and the Kashmiri topi was tilted at an angle on his head. He was a drug dealer but he looked like a shopkeeper.

Finally he said, "The crazy woman? She's mending a salvaar, she's stitching, that's why she's half dressed. She's crazy but she keeps quiet. Your kaamwali, the hijra Dimple, why do you let her talk so much?"

"The customers like to hear her talk."

"Our scripture says women must be silent in the assemblies of men. It isn't permitted for them to speak. This is a chandu khana but it is also an assembly of men. Tell her that."

"Tell her yourself, there she is."

But Khalid would not look in her direction.

"*Kaam*," said Bengali, as if to himself, "is work in Hindi, but desire or lust in Sanskrit. So *kaamwali* has a double meaning, which this gentleman is doubtless aware of."

RASHID ASKED FOR TEA and Marie biscuits to be sent to the beggar woman with the haircut who was still stitching, seated on the sidewalk on the junction of Shuklaji Street and Arab Gully. She was not, at the moment, reclining on the garbage. It occurred to him that she used the garbage dump as a toilet and the sidewalk as a living area. He heard Khalid say something about tapping new sources of income and the need to expand one's consumer base if one wished to stay on top of the business. He was talking to save face. Rashid watched a boy from the tea shop downstairs hand the woman a glass of milky tea and a plate of biscuits. She sat on a metal awning from Delite Restaurant, the restaurant out of business, the awning lying on the street for months now, its tin warped. She sipped at the tea, her little finger raised in the air. She ate the biscuits one by one, daintily, dipping each one in the tea before putting it in her mouth. She was smiling.

4.

The Sari and the Burka

She moved into the room halfway up the landing from Rashid's khana. She never went to the floor above, where his family lived. But from time to time she met them on the staircase or on the street and she understood that Rashid's eldest, Jamal, was her enemy. Rashid's wives were friendlier, even if they didn't speak. Only Rashid seemed unaffected. To mark her new situation, he gave her a new name, Zeenat, and he brought her a burka. He sat in the only chair, sipping his morning whisky and peering at her through the smoke from his cigarette. No good, he said, see how lumpy it is? Take off the kameez and leave the salvaar. She took off the printed top and slipped back into the burka. He watched her, his arm propped on the back of the chair. Then he nodded and took her to the mirror. She saw how the shiny black fabric clung to her. How revealing it is, she thought, and looked at herself and whispered, Zeenat. After a while Rashid asked her to take off the salvaar too and now the burka was silk against her skin. He liked it so much he wanted to take her for a ride in a taxi, to sit in the back and watch the sights, and only they would know she was naked under the burka. No, she said, no, never. But she was enjoying herself.

SHE DIDN'T STOP wearing saris, which covered the legs and exposed the belly, exposed the intimate part that should be seen only by a lover or husband. She'd learned how to wear the petticoat low on the hips, how to lean forward accidentally on purpose and let the pallu slip just a little. She admired the uses to which women put the sari, how they wore it without underwear, slept in it, bathed in it, used it as a towel and comforter, and the convenience, to simply lift it up if you wanted to pee or if there was a customer. But she looked at herself in the burka and understood that this was something very different. The tools were fewer. Only the face was visible, only the feet and hands, and because everything else was covered, a glimpse of eye or mouth became tremendous and powerful. And the blackness of it, the gradation, the way the fall of the fabric was different on her breasts and hips. She wondered at the men who designed such a garment. How much they must have feared their own desire. To want a woman to wear this thing you had to know the danger that lay in looking. You knew it and you knew your powerlessness and you dreamed up a costume to conceal the cause of your shame. But the costume only served to punish you further. It made you want to pluck out your eye, pluck it out and hold it, pulsing and sinewy in your hand, and offer it as some inadequate token.

She went out in the burka and she saw the way the men looked at the lipstick on her mouth and the kaajal around her eyes. The men looked at her, Hindus, Muslims, Christians, they all looked. She stopped outside Grant Road Bazaar where the handbags were stacked in piles on the sidewalk. The vendor was a young guy in bell-bottoms, whose eyes lingered on her feet. She bought a clutch purse and paid him in small notes, grubby one- and two- and five-rupee notes that she dug out of her bra. The vendor took the notes with a smile, making sure their fingers touched. She walked on and now the vendors all seemed to be speaking at once, speaking only to her, offering special deals—hello, madam, low price for you—not because they wanted her to buy something but because they wanted her to stop so they could get a look at her.

SHE DIDN'T give up saris. She varied her costume depending on who she wanted to be, Dimple or Zeenat, Hindu or Muslim. Each name had its own set of adornments. Then Bengali told her about a shop in Tardeo that sold saris from the entire subcontinent. She went there one afternoon in the mango season to buy the begum bahar. It was fine see-through gauze. Bengali told her that women painted their buttocks and their feet when they wore the begum bahar, so she tried it too, painted herself with red shellac dye and then took a look in the mirror. She wore no skirt under the sari and the effect was subtle. You could see the shape of the ass and thighs, but the work on the sheer fabric obscured her figure just enough. She knew some of her giraks would pay a lot to see her in the begum bahar. Bengali said, now you look like a lady of the merchant class, an indolent Bania woman with many admirers. No, she said, looking at the semicircles under her eyes, so dark they were like bruises. No, I'm like a woman whose only admirer hanged himself so long ago that she can't remember his name or why he killed himself or whether she misses him, all she's sure of is her own solitude and regret and, above all, her anger. Bengali said, you're wrong, your admirers are numerous and I'm proud to count myself among them. And he left the room so quickly that she knew he'd embarrassed himself. She changed out of the sari and put on a salvaar. She never wore burkas while working; Rashid said it was out of the question. His customers were pimps and chandulis, yes, but they were conservative about some things and they would not take kindly to a woman in a burka making the pipe. In any case, said Rashid, salvaars were more convenient. She changed and took up her spot at the main pipe and after she made Rashid's first pyalis of the day she served those who waited, Rumi usually among them. He came to talk as much as to smoke. He lent her his headphones and played music she had never heard, in particular, jazz, for which he had developed not a liking exactly but a taste, he said, like a taste for anchovies or bitter chocolate, an unexpected appreciation that comes upon a man late in his life. He told her about his work or his domestic situation, and he talked about his life, which, it seemed to her, was nothing if not a disaster.

THE NIGHT BEFORE, he said, he'd come home from work at the usual time, around ten, because the commute by train and bus took an hour and a half. He walked in the door and the television was blaring in the bedroom. His wife wouldn't get up and say hello. She was always tired, so tired she woke up exhausted, which wasn't surprising, since she spent most of her time watching Doordarshan. He was the one who worked all day and she was tired, Rumi told Dimple, his voice thick with smoke and anguish. He put his briefcase down, he said, and he went into the bathroom to wash the grime off his hands and face. Then he pulled on a pair of jeans and a Pink Floyd T-shirt and immediately he felt a little less like an office clerk. In the kitchen he looked at the mess of plates in the sink and checked for roaches. None so far but they'd be out in force when the lights went out. His dinner was on the stove, still warm. She'd already eaten, his wife, whose main pleasure in life was food. She'd eat lunch, really pig out, and right away be talking about dinner. Like there was nothing else worth staying awake for. No, what was he saying? Of course there was: television. Food and television, in that order but preferably together. He heated yellow daal and a dish of dry green peppers and put the bowls on a plate and took some rotlis and carried the food into the bedroom where he sat on a chair in front of the television with the plate balanced on his knees. His wife wore the same nightie she'd been wearing when he left that morning. She was on the phone to her aunt in Delhi. Right through his meal she talked in Gujarati and stared at the television. The conversation was an ever-expanding menu of rotlis and rotlas, bakhris, theplas, undhiyu and chaas. Every topic eventually came back to food. By now, he understood enough of the language to get a sense of the conversation. His wife was telling her aunt how much she missed the mango ras her aunt used to make and there was a shine in her eyes when she said the word *ras*. She might have been talking about sex or god. After a while she covered the receiver with her hand and whispered that there was ice cream in the fridge. His wife was a Jain: there were many foods her family didn't eat, a tremendous array of perfectly harmless items. Ice cream was out of the question because it was made with eggs. If her parents were visiting, she scoured the kitchen to find and hide potatoes, garlic, and onions. As far as her family was concerned non-Jains were polluted, contaminated, damned, and there was only a difference of degree between such a person and an untouchable. He and his wife had met as students at Elphinstone College and when they decided to get married, on his return to Bombay after a year in the States, there had been tears and threats from her parents, their opposition based on the single unalterable fact that he was not of their community. There was no point telling them he was a Brahmin, no point mentioning that he was descended from the Rishis, which he was, he was pure Aryan, one of the elect. What more could a wife want? he asked Dimple. After dinner, he put his dishes in the sink and said he was going out for a walk. And he got out of there before he got into it with his wife, told her to bathe once in a while and change her clothes and act like a human being. But then she'd get into it too, tell him she'd act more like a wife if he acted more like a husband and took her out sometimes, if he brought money home instead of spending hers. In the car, to clear his head, he punched in Band of Gypsys and turned the volume up and drove badly, which fact he admitted with pride, it seemed to Dimple, because he grinned and pretended to change gears. He opened a window when he saw the sea and made the turn at Otters Club and took the Carter Road promenade, where the model citizens had their evening constitutional. He parked at an angle so no cop would spot him and emptied two pudis into a cigarette. Then he took a moment to digress, telling Dimple that he knew the one thousand and one names of god and he knew the one thousand and one names of heroin and if sometimes he mixed them up, at an arti, say, if for example he said Satyam, Sharam, Sundaram—Truth is Heroin is Beauty—he knew it was allowed, because no one was listening anyway, not to him. What he wanted to know was this: who put the words in his head? How did they arrive, these sentences, so fully formed they seemed to be uttered by a divine voice? Why did he say, as he did one evening at a Mahim NA meeting, the room brightly lit, a red neon cross glowing over the decayed beachfront: Our Father, who art in Scag, hallowed be thy Scag, thy Scag is clean, thy Scag is good, thy Scag will be done, now and at the hour of our deaths. Ah men. Ah women too. And to say it so solemnly that nobody took offense, not even the Catlicks, because he folded his hands and let a pious smarmy lilt enter his voice. And of course: he'd smoked before the meeting. And of course: it was the heroin that filled him with warmth and fellow feeling for the collection of self-serving egomaniacs that made up the ranks of the narcotically fucking anonymous. And finally of course: it was the heroin, said Rumi, looking unblinkingly into Dimple's eyes, looking at her so steadily that she had to look back. She noted the unusual length of his lashes, like a girl's, though she could not say what color his eyes were because smoke was seeping from his ears and collecting in pools around his skin. It was heavy smoke that fell from his pores to the floor of the room and filled the corners and pushed inwards. When the smoke level touched her mouth with the taste of sewage, she got up and went to the door and rushed blindly downstairs, but it was thicker there, so she reversed her flight, went up past her own door, past Rashid's and up to the roof, from where she saw that the street and the city and possibly the world in its unimaginable entirety was submerged, and though she shouted to the dim shapes discernible below, shouted until she was hoarse, no one was able to hear her, because the smoke was in her own mouth now, in her own nostrils, filling her with its white living vapor.

5.

"Dum Maro Dum"

Rashid took her out one day. He said he wanted to do what poor people do, eat the air on Chowpatty, eat the air and drink the breeze and enjoy. She thought to herself, such a filmi dialogue. But she liked the mood-setting tone of the words and she put on a black-and-white chiffon polka dot that was the happiest thing she owned. They took a taxi to the beach and kept it waiting while they strolled on the sand. Rashid lit a cigarette from a pack of 555s and from the butt he lit another. He smoked the entire time they were on the beach, not more than twenty minutes, and then he wanted to stop somewhere for a drink, he said, get some Scotch or honeydew brandy, good for you, no, a drop of brandy? She suggested a lassi instead. They went to Rajasthan Lassi but chikkus were out of season. The lassi was so thick it was like ice cream, only better, and served in a glass, with a spoon that stood upright in the thick cream. They sat in the back of the cab and had two each, one after the other, and the taxi driver had one too. Then they went to Opera House to watch Rashid's all-time number one favorite movie,

Hare Rama Hare Krishna. It was at least ten years old, no need to wait in line and buy tickets in black. He'd seen it many times and knew the words of all the songs and long exchanges of dialogue that he said aloud, usually Dev Anand's bits, though he disliked the actor.

"He's a chooth, look at him, flopping around like a faggot."

His favorite song was "Dum Maro Dum," in which a bunch of homegrown hippies smoked endless chillums and the lead actress lip-synched to Asha Bhosle's voice, Asha sounding like she'd been up three nights straight, smoking too much opium and drinking dirty whisky. Dimple liked it too, the stoned lilt of it.

> *Duniya ne hum ko diya kya?*
> *Duniya se hum ne liya kya?*
> *Hum sub ki parva kare kyun?*
> *Sub ne humara kiya kya?*

The song stayed in her head for days, but the message meant nothing to her. All she saw was a group of rich kids smoking charas in the mountains. She saw their beauty and she heard their laughter. They didn't work and yet they had plenty of money and friends and fashionable clothes and families who worried about them. Why were they so full of self-pity? What were they rebelling against? Why didn't they just admit it, that they liked to get high?

SHE DIDN'T GET IT, but she knew why *Hare Rama Hare Krishna* was Rashid's favorite movie: Zeenat Aman, the bronze-skinned miniskirted actress he'd named her after. She was everywhere, on movie posters, on billboards two stories high. She was on the cover of *Stardust* magazine, smiling like she knew a secret no one else did: she knew why you were standing there with the magazine in your hands, gazing at her image with awe, maybe, or desire mixed with dazzlement. The magazine had its own name for her, Zeenie Baby. There were gossipy items about Zeenie's boyfriends in London, New York, and Bombay, about the grasping mother who managed her career and love life. The magazine had names for its articles: tear-jerkers, exclusive scoops, bombshell exposés. She read—fast, very fast, though sometimes she said a sentence aloud to get the sense of it—about Zeenie's love for her father, a writer who died young, and she looked at pictures of the modest homes Zeenie grew up in and glamorous stills from the movies that had made her famous. She's pure romance, thought Dimple, like Meena Kumari and Madhubala and Begum Akhtar, the female legends beloved of eunuchs, prostitutes, and poets.

Rashid took her to a beauty parlor in Colaba, where he asked the hairdresser to straighten her hair. "Make it fall like a curtain, like Zeenat's, see here," he said, pointing to *Stardust*. It took hours of work with a hot iron, sitting in a chair reading a magazine, music on the radio, Lata, who else?, singing "Yeh Mausam." But afterwards she had a taste of what it was to be Zeenie, beautiful, famous, desired by everyone, the thing that happened when she took a walk on the street on some routine chore, and the men turned to stare, or they followed her, or attempted to start a conversation, any conversation, as if she were emitting some kind of bio-radar, some hormone ray that magnetized male animals. A Spaniard at the khana called the actress Zeenat A Man—he had to explain the joke—

because he said there was something drag-queen glamorous about her. She was making his second pipe when the man said: you look like her.

"You're the fourth person who said that."

"The fourth person today?" He was smiling.

She said, "No, not today. But I'm prettier."

He said, "Much, much."

It wasn't true, not at all, but she could pretend.

DIMPLE, sitting in the movie theater with Rashid, looked up at Zeenie's moonlike face, her round milk white face that had absorbed every injustice in the world, and Dimple wished for a sister, an older sister she could talk to. The theater was very cold: cold air was blowing in from the sides, and she wished she'd brought a shawl. It was the AC, Rashid said. What is AC? she asked. He said something in reply, something she forgot instantly, because she was watching the screen so carefully. Zeenie was playing a woman who runs away from a broken home and renames herself Janice. When she and her brother meet as adults she cannot remember him.

JANICE'S BROTHER (trying to jog her memory): Look at this flower. You used to like flowers.

(Janice accepts the flower and smiles a smile of such sweetness you know, if you're at all knowledgeable about such things, that she will die very soon.)

JANICE: Beauty is in the mind, in the eyes.

(They are among a crowd of flower children. Someone passes Janice a chillum and she takes an impossible, elegant

puff and hands it to her brother, though she doesn't know
him yet.)

JANICE'S BROTHER: No, I have a cough.

JANICE (**scolding**): If you want to sit with us, be like us. Joy,
intoxication, peace—these are the things we believe in. Do
you believe in joy?

JANICE'S BROTHER: Is it only by smoking that you can
believe in joy?

(Rashid knew the line and didn't think much of it. He
shouted it out anyway, only slightly out of sync with Dev
Anand, laughing thickly as he mimicked the actor. A man
sitting ahead of them turned to say something, took a look
at Rashid, and changed his mind.)

JANICE'S BROTHER: Are you happy? Janice, are you happy?

(Janice is quiet for a time, a light in her eyes, an ancient
light like the light from a long-dead moon, and when she
speaks it is in a whisper, and everybody in the theater leans
forward to hear.)

JANICE: Yes, I've never been so happy. It's good to run away
from home when nobody needs you and you have so much
love to share with the world.

Dimple imagined Janice was talking only to her, ignoring the others
in the theater and tilting her moon face so her beautiful dying eyes
were looking into Dimple's. She wished Rashid had named her Janice instead of Zeenat, Janice, who didn't remember her mother or
father, who was strumming a guitar, saying, oh, I know this song, it's
on the tip of my tongue, make me another chillum and I'll remember. What is this song? So high she was like an alien from a glori-
ous superior species. And later, lying on the grass, lost, mountains

around her, this lovely girl looks at the audience and says, parents, why do they have us? A moment of pleasure and they're saddled for life. They don't really want us.

Dimple understood the exact nature of Janice's suffering. To know you were unloved by your parents, it was a wound that would never heal. Nothing Dimple did to forget her early life could change this fundamental fact. She was always under the sway of it. It never went away. She'd think she was okay, but she wasn't. If she wasn't sleeping enough or if she was anxious, it would catch up with her, as fresh and wet and red as it had ever been. In the scene when brother and sister are finally reunited in a village in Kathmandu, Dimple made no effort to hide her tears. Others were crying too, men and women, entire families weeping together as they munched their popcorn and sucked noisily at bottles of Thums Up and Fanta.

THE MOVIE HAD a tremendous effect on Rashid, though he'd seen it many times. He didn't speak until they were in a cab heading back to Shuklaji Street. Number eight, he told her, holding up seven fingers. And I'll see it again. This is the movie that got me into drugs. This is why I opened my first adda and became a hippie. The only thing I can't stand is that Dev Anand. He wouldn't last three minutes on Shuklaji Street. Then he sang the song so forcefully that the melody lost its haunting quality and became an anthem. He lingered on the chorus, on its famous first couplet,

> *Dum maro dum,*
> *Mit jaaye hum.*
> *Bolo subah sham.*

But there he stopped. He would not sing the final line, "Hare Krishna, Hare Ram." It was too Hindu for him. Instead, thinking about dinner, he sang the verse again, changing the words.

Dum aloo dum,
Mit jaaye hum.
Bolo subah sham,
Dum aloo dum.

6.

Stinking Asafetida

When he started the car again he was feeling better, a miracle actually, the way his mood lifted, Rumi told Dimple. He drove towards Khar with "Machine Gun" turned up loud, the smack kicking in like Buddy Miles's big bass drum, never mind the shitty car's shitty speakers; and the feedback and weird radio interference, some kind of helicopter noise, GIs in Vietnam maybe, then Jimi again, doing his voodoo shit, the spaces between notes liquefied into scratchy slow-mo sound grabs, the guitar loud, beyond loud, like a car crash in slow motion, metal and flesh fused: gave him the shivers every time, made him want to crash the car, or drink till he died, or tattoo a motto on his chest with a rusty nail and industrial dye, Kill You Quick. And that, said Rumi, was when he saw the woman. She was standing at the turn from Khar Danda to the main Juhu Road. She turned into the headlights when she heard the car slow. Her dark skin was scarred with old smallpox and her hair was held in place with pins and she carried one of those striped shopping bags, like a housewife. She was looking right at him. He stopped the car and she put her head at the window. He saw a bunch of keys on an ornate silver ring hooked to the waist of her sari. Maybe she really was a housewife, doing some quick freelance on the side to supplement the family income. Should I get in? she said. He fixed the price and drove until he found a street that was dark enough and then he parked between two cars, backed into the space, and turned the engine off. He told her to move to the backseat and climbed in beside her, already conscious of her stink, what was it, garlic? Asafetida? She'd been cooking recently and she had a powerful body odor, which excited him. She smelled of food and sweat and faintly of cologne and she was rubbing two fingers against her thumb. He dug into his jeans and gave her a hundred-rupee note, telling her to use her mouth on him. She gave him a look, like she didn't do that, like she was out on the street selling sex but only on her terms. No water in my mouth, okay? she said, and her voice was pure business: she could have been a hooker on Shuk-laji Street. And when she'd been at it for a while, head bouncing like a toy, a spray of bobby pins holding the hair in place above her ears, and he maybe nodded off a little, a tiny teeny little bit, she goes, you slept off or what? Then she muttered something in Bambayya Hindi that he didn't catch and she started to gather her things. Fin-ish, he told her, his voice loud in the small car. She put her shopping bag down and shot him a look and went back to work. He was half erect, when all of a sudden she stopped. Her jaws hurt, she said. She asked him to fuck her, which he did, reluctantly, because this was not part of the deal: fucking was work. He slapped her lightly and she moaned. She liked it; she fucked him back. Then he hit her again. She grabbed his hand and he punched her on the head, fuck-ing her hard, and when he came, for the first time in weeks, he did what he always did, he screamed words he didn't know, and by now she was screaming too, in fear, and so, to shut her up, he hit her in the mouth, drawing blood, and the sight of it pushed him over and he came again. He pulled out, still dripping, and opened the door. She was moaning but unconscious. He put her on the ground by an abandoned handcart, small piles of shit nearby, human, by the smell of it, and as an afterthought he put his hand into her blouse, realizing that he hadn't touched her breasts until then, a pity, because they were swollen and wet at the nipples. He fondled her briefly and took the wad of notes folded into the whore's bra and drove away as slowly as he could.

And this was when Dimple tried not to show her surprise. She said: you should have asked me. I have a friend who would have given you much better service.

RUMI TOLD HER he drove home after his adventure with the housewife hooker, and walked in the door to a full-scale family celebration, his wife's relatives, wandering around the house half naked. First thing they do, these people, walk in the door and take off their clothes because of the heat, which wasn't any worse than usual. There were five of them, a man in shorts and no shirt, his wife, fully dressed, unfortunately, two small half-naked children, and an older woman, stopping by on their way home to Ahmedabad. Rumi sat on a couch in the front room, flipping through a magazine while the travelers repacked their bags and made phone calls. The older woman was bragging about her son's new car. He caught the word *Maruti*, as he was meant to. And in case he didn't, she repeated it for him in English. Darshan bought a new car, she said, Maruti, such a nice car. His partner bought a new model Ambassador, but Maruti's mileage is better. At least Darshan had the sense to be embarrassed by his mother's propaganda: he looked shamefaced. Just

then the older child came in from the kitchen. He wore only underwear and he made a low *whooo* sound as he ran across the room.
At the last moment, just as he was about to crash into the couch, he
made a sharp turn into a new flight path parallel with the wall; his
whoop became higher-pitched. The other child staggered around
the room like an old drunk, bumping into furniture and babbling
with happiness. An instant later her face crumpled and there was a
long exhalation. She stopped breathing. Her arms hung by her side
and only her feet moved, in rhythm, walking in place. There was
silence for a long excruciating moment, everyone waiting for the
child to breathe. Then: a telescoping wail so loud it shook Rumi out
of his half nod. Here Rumi digressed for a moment. He told Dimple
that childhood was a kind of affliction, certainly physical and possibly mental. Children were at a hopeless disadvantage; they were
unsuited for the world. They were short and ungainly and stupid,
half people, dwarf bundles of ectoplasm and shit, stunted organ-
isms incapable of finding food or keeping their asses clean. They
needed constant attention and they couldn't communicate their
needs. All they could do was wait for it to pass, years of waiting until
the blight was gone. It would make anybody bawl for no reason, he
said. Soon he heard his wife ask her cousin about his business. Her
cousin and his partner had set up the company eight years earlier
to provide technical support for office computer networks. It hadn't
begun well, had begun so badly in fact that they thought of packing
it in. Then the economy opened up and they started to get orders
from all over the place, and now there was so much business he'd
bought his mother an apartment. Everybody, it seemed to Rumi,
was making money except for him. After her relatives left, his wife
went to sleep. Rumi thought of the time immediately after his return from LA, when he had a job in advertising and was earning

better, and his wife was the one who had initiated sex. She'd been insatiable; it was all they did. He'd come home from work and she would pull him into the bedroom first thing. It was hard to believe this was the same woman. If he were bringing more money home, would it make a difference? Of course it would, he was sure of it. Her manner had changed almost to the month and day that he'd lost the job at the agency and taken up employment at her father's brokerage. In that case, if money was the lubricant that made her agree to sex, what was the difference between her and the woman he'd paid earlier in the evening? If there was a difference, it was the prostitute who came out of it in a better light. At least she was true to her profession and her station in life. His wife was true to neither. If she were, she would understand that her duty was to serve him and make him happy. He was her pati, her husband and lord, and his happiness was her need. This is what he thought about as he lay beside his sleeping wife, Rumi told Dimple, and it gave him pleasure to remember the adventure with the prostitute, to relive it while his wife lay beside him and to smell again the street woman's kitchen sweat. He sniffed his hands and smiled in the dark.

7.

Business Practices Among the Criminal Class: C & E

There was a Godrej padlock on the door. People came up the stairs and it was the first thing they saw. Then they saw the Customs and Excise notice tacked to the wall and understood that Rashid's was shut indefinitely. They went elsewhere. That morning, Rashid, Dimple, and Bengali were in Gilass Palass, a tea shop and falooda parlor near Grant Road Station. Only Bengali noticed the mirrors on the walls and ceiling and, on smoked-glass shelving that ran the length of the premises, a collection of figurines in the likeness of swans and androgynous, possibly female angels. Rashid drank masala chai, and he held an unlit triple five in his hand.

"It's nothing," he said, "temporary, tell everybody we'll be back very soon."

"How soon?"

"Very soon."

"You already said that."

"Eat your khari biscuit."

"I told you something was wrong. The use."

"You didn't."

"Noticing things, telling you. And then you forget. What's the use?"

"You didn't tell me."

"Bilkul, I did, bhai, told you there was something wrong when that Customs and Excise came round asking for five lakhs instead of fifty thousand. He's been taking money from you for years, same amount every time, like tax, and suddenly he adds a zero. Something was wrong."

"When did you tell me? You think I'd forget?"

"Why not? You forget everything else."

She was using the formal *aap* though her words were not formal at all. Bengali's thoughts were in his face: look at this woman, until yesterday she was a prostitute in a hijra's brothel and listen to her now, talking as if she's Rashid's equal. He was dismayed by her manner around his boss and by the way she said whatever came to her mind, whether respectful or not. She talks as if she is his wife and Rashid listens like a husband, he thought. But she's more than a wife, more than both his wives put together: she's his business partner and she's better at it than he is. If she was in charge, we'd be rich and the competition would be mincemeat.

"So that's why you're here, to remind me."

"And meanwhile."

"Meanwhile, we have a temporary shop and we keep going."

"Sounds like this meanwhile will be a long meanwhile. And you'll do what?"

"Something, I'm thinking."

"Bhai, the khana won't reopen by itself."

Rashid lit his cigarette and blew a ring and then he blew another through the first.

"I know who's behind it, the bhadwa. He came to see me, made an offer to buy my khana, such a low price I knew he was the one who put the C & E lock on the door."

"Khalid. He fixed it to put you out of business."

"Or take it over."

They paid the bill and went to the new shop Rashid was renting in Arab Gully. It was in a side street off a side street. They'd settled in and set up a pipe (the place was so small there was room for only one) and Rashid was already comfortable, too comfortable, according to Dimple. She complained to Bengali that he had accepted the unacceptable. He was doing what he'd always done. He smoked the pipes she made. He drank his Black Label and chased garad. He got his meals delivered from Delhi Darbar. He didn't seem worried by the loss of the khana, or by the fact that he'd been put out of business by a man like Khalid. Get it back, she told Rashid. Whatever it takes. Maro him if you have to, just get it back.

BENGALI NOTICED that her hair had started to thin, and her body had lost its roundness. There were new lines around her mouth and her skin was darker. He wondered if this was why she'd taken to wearing a burka. He wanted to tell her not to worry, that, dark or fair, she was a striking woman. Then, one night, on his way to get dinner for Rashid, he saw something that frightened him. He saw her standing under the streetlamp outside Mr. Lee's, though the Chinaman's khana had been long gone by then. It was early, around eleven, but the street was dark and there were few pedestrians and he didn't see Dimple until he was a few feet away. She was dressed all in black and in the darkness the only thing visible was her face. She stood frozen, her eyes turned up to the white light of the lamp, very still, except for her lips, which seemed to be moving, though he could not hear what she was saying. Her eyes were wide, as if she was begging for something, imploring someone implacable or merciless, someone who would never forgive or let her forget her errors. His first instinct was to apologize, for what he didn't know. In the fluorescent light she seemed to be raw bone and skin wrapped in black fabric and she billowed like the sails of a ship. What kind of ship? An Arab ship, thought Bengali, a dhow, a ghost ship whose inhabitants rarely came on deck because they had to toil twice as hard as the living. Her skin had a bluish tint and her features were set in stone. She stared upwards without blinking and the thing he would remember later was the look in her eyes, there was no light in them, not even the reflected light of the streetlamp. He thought: this is a woman who understands death. She has tasted the meat of it and it pleases her. The thought frightened him and he walked past her without stopping.

DIMPLE FIXED the Khalid problem herself, without meaning to or knowing she had. Salim found her in the room on Arab Gully, a space so tiny it could not be called a khana. It was a cupboard, smaller than the rooms at 007, and there was barely enough space to stretch out for a smoke. There was only one pipe, which Rashid was using. Salim had to wait with two other men, wait on the street with his O sickness building. Inside, he couldn't speak freely to Dimple, because everything was overheard and there was only one topic of conversation that day. Salim listened without seeming to and he asked how they knew that it was Khalid who had shut down the khana. Was there a chance the customs people had done it for their own reasons? Rashid put his pipe down and took a deep breath, as if he was about to address a public gathering. Salim, I'm a businessman, it's my skill. Yours is lifting wallets in such a way that a man will never know he has been robbed. Khalid has always wanted my business. I know this. I know it as surely as you know how much to charge for the Lala's cocaine. Then Dimple said: of course it's Khalid. I've seen him with that bhadwa, the Customs and Excise, going bhai-bhai. He won't be happy until he owns your business and he'll charge twice the price and dilute the opium so it won't do shit.

LATER, they put together the details from sources on the street, reliable and not. Salim was seen arriving at Khalid's with two friends, Kaanya the informer and Pasina the genius pocket maar. They waited until Khalid was alone, then put him on the floor and tied his hands with twine. They force-fed him two pyalis of opium mixed with hot water. Khalid was not a smoker and the drink worked very quickly.

"What we do, someone like you, we take a walk," Salim said.

"Take a long walk, to Pydhonie or Dongri or even a make-it-fast walk to Grant Road Junction," said Kaanya.

"We leave you on the pavement," said Pasina, laughing with his mouth open, his gums and lips bright red against the dark grain of his skin.

"This is late at night, right, nobody around," Salim said.

"Late at night, yes. We let you lie there for a while, look up, enjoy the stars, examine the cloud formations, see if it's going to rain. Isn't that right?" said Pasina.

"Bilkul. Cent percent correct," said Kaanya.

"Then, when you're nice and comfortable, we pick up a stone, lots of them under the Grant Road Bridge, and put it on your head," Salim said.

"Don't worry, miya, it's halal," said Pasina.

"More merciful than halal, my yaar, this is quicker," said Kaanya.

"And the patrakars will make some smart headlines about the Pathar Maar, stone killer this and stone killer that," said Salim.

"Everybody's happy, even the patharwallah," said Pasina.

Then, laughing redly, he added, "I think this fellow is nice and relaxed now. You should get high more often, miya, it suits you."

THEY LEFT HIM tied up, retching dry when there was nothing left to vomit. They left him on the floor with the door open and they went to Shuklaji Street, stopping for jalebis, which they wolfed from newspapers, the jalebis unusually yellow today, egg yellow and very sweet, hot from the deep fry. They stood in the crowd, three happy men working their jaws, saying nothing while they ate. Salim ate his from the outside in, saving for the end the knotted bits at the center, where the sugar syrup was thickest. After the jalebis, they had a glass each of masala tea, and they were ready. They borrowed a cab from Kaanya's brother and drove to Khalid's house. They waited until his son came home in his blue shorts and shirt, his big school bag full of books. They picked him up and put him in the car and—this was Pasina's idea—they left the school bag on the sidewalk in front of the house.

Salim's friends drove the boy, nine years old, asthmatic, too well behaved to be frightened, to Pune, about six or seven hours away on the national highway. They checked into a guesthouse on MG Road and for the next few days they went to the movies, two, sometimes three screenings a day. They saw *Star* with Kumar Gaurav, music by Biddu. No good, Pasina told Salim on the phone. Budhu should stick to what he knows, Tina Charles and disco. He's useless when it comes to Hindi. The songs are pure dinchak, no heart, yaar. Even the bachcha was bored.

"Biddu."

"Arre, yaar, Sallu, I know his name. Budhu, Biddu, he's still a fool."

They saw *Desh Premee*, with Kaanya's favorite actor, and Salim's: Amitabh Bachchan. Amitji with a meesha and what a meesha, said Pasina, like a skinny dead caterpillar on his upper lip, even Kaanya was disappointed. Pasina's one-line review was categorical: believe it, total flop it will be because of the choothiya mustache. They saw *Namak Halaal* and *Shakti*, both starring Amitabh with Smita Patil, whom Pasina called a "dusky up-and-comer," a phrase he'd found in a film magazine. The two movies received good reviews from the kidnappers. Even the bachcha liked, Pasina said. Still a kid, can't stand up straight and piss, but you should have seen him looking at Smitaji: his eyes were like headlights.

Salim called Khalid a day or two after his son had been taken, called him a few times a day, at strange hours, with updates about the boy. "Bachcha has asthma, poor fellow, he needs constant care." "Looks like your boy takes after you, stubborn as hell." "Eats a lot, too much, you ask me." Khalid said in reply: please. It was all he had time for before Salim ended the call. So when, five days after the boy had been taken, the kidnappers gave him a chance to talk, Khalid had a lot to say, and it took a little less than a week for Rashid to reopen his shop.

8.

A Chemical
Understanding

At first she continued to smoke opium, using garad only occasionally, but very soon—she was surprised how soon—she was smoking only garad. She made the pipe for customers and she lost interest in smoking it herself. Suddenly it seemed as if everybody had switched to powder, the customers, the pipemen, even Rashid, who hated it but smoked all the same. Then Salim brought her maal from a new source. It had a new name, Chemical. The first time she tried it, she felt something shut down, her nervous system, maybe, or her brain, some motor somewhere. She felt herself slipping through the mat into the floor. Below was a thick layer of cotton wool and below that were the blue pools of her nightmares. She was awake but removed from her body and she could no more have lifted her hand than fly. The deeper she sank into the water, the easier it was to sink; it was very easy, it took no effort at all. She settled heavily to the bottom of the pool, where she lay inert and comfortable, like the creatures that stirred around her. The nearest had an old man's head, Mr. Lee's head, which turned or swiveled to her and said, I've been waiting for you. Do you know why I'm at the bottom of this pool? She knew, of course she did, but she couldn't speak. Because you broke your promise, Mr. Lee said, because you lied to me. You said you were my daughter but you didn't act as a daughter should. You abandoned me. You know that, don't you? Dimple nodded her head. You said you would take my ashes to China but you didn't. Do you even know where they are? No, Father Lee, I don't, she said at last. She noticed that his face was not wet exactly but covered in tiny bubbles and she noticed that the water was getting colder. Do you know why I'm here? To remind me, she said, to make sure I never forget. You're right about that. Oh yes, this time you've got it. Which was when she realized that he was speaking perfect English and she wondered if he had always had the ability to do so and had simply chosen not to. I'm here because my spirit has not been able to travel to its rightful place, he said. I've left my body or my body has left me, which is the first death. The second death occurs when those who love us and are loved by us also die, or forget, and our names are no longer spoken. Spirits such as mine must wait—it could be we have unfinished business, or we died violently, or were not given a proper burial, or our clothes were not burned with us—for whatever reason, we must wait, and the only way we can exist is in water. Otherwise we would disappear. I don't like it. I smoke Chinese opium, the best opium in the world: of course I hate water. But I must live here if I am to live. Can you imagine what a trial it is? Can you imagine how infuriating? Of course you can't, you're one of the living, said Mr. Lee with such contempt that Dimple flinched. Okay, enough for now, I'll stop talking. Good, said Dimple, because you've said a lot, you really have. She noticed that the water was icy and she could no longer feel her limbs. But Mr. Lee hadn't finished. One last thing: you have to carry me, take me on your back because my leg's still broken. Nothing changes when you die, except you can't do half the things you used to and the other half you no longer have any interest in. Oh, and you have to live in this cold, cold water. She put him on her back, he weighed nothing, and they floated to the surface, where he bobbed and breathed but refused to let her go. He grabbed her face and whispered into her ear. Come back to see me and I'll give you a chance to unbreak your promise. And then he swam agilely away. It was at this moment, as she felt herself sinking again, that her lungs began to fill with water and she knew she must wake up or die.

IT WAS DIFFICULT to buy fruits and vegetables, but garad was available in plenty. Someone told her not to go out. A mob had set fire to the police station and there were armed gangs hunting for people to burn and rape. The man told her how the riots started, because of a rumor that a Hindu family of six had been burned alive, and the killers were Muslim, and the children's screams could be heard far away. It was only a rumor but now there were real fires all over the city, though Shuklaji Street was so far untouched. When Dimple went out, she noticed that the only people walking around in numbers were the garadulis, as if they'd been touched by the hands of a god more powerful than the gods who were on fire, and because they'd been touched by a great god they were untouchable by the hands of men. At Salim's she smoked Chemical, very little, because she knew how to use it now, she knew to respect it. She asked Salim, why is it so strong? They put rat poison in it, he told her, and the strychnine gives the maal its kick. He said, don't worry, it won't kill us, we're not rats. But looking at him, she was not sure this was true. He had lost weight. His teeth protruded and his whiskers were short and bristly, like fresh stitches on his face. She thought: how quickly he's aged. And: I have too. The window was open and she caught the smell of petrol and burning rubber. Who are they killing, she asked him, Muslims or Hindus?

He said, "They're killing themselves, the fuckers, let's hope they do it right this time."

She put the vials in her purse and left the shop. It was a short walk to the khana, but today the route seemed unfamiliar. Nothing moved on the street except for a man pushing a long cart. He was far away and at that distance all she could see was his dirty white kurta and bare feet. In the cart were long objects, sticks or swords, she couldn't tell. She took a detour through Kamathipura Third Lane. The lane was usually difficult to walk in: people put their cots on the road and spent all day lounging in the narrow shade. But the cots were gone, the randi's cages shuttered, the shops closed. Nothing was open except a raddiwallah's, where an old man sat behind a pair of scales and small mountains of used books and magazines. She reached out and took the first thing that came to hand, because she was reading now and had not gotten over the habit of reading at random.

SOME USES OF REINCARNATION

By S. T. Pande

Head of Department, Theology
& Symmetry, Haryana University

She recognized the author's name and took another look at the book. It was slim and in good condition, a school textbook with illustrations. The raddiwallah gave it to her for one rupee. She walked quickly to the khana and banged on the door a few times and shouted Bengali's name. She banged some more. She said, come on, open, I know you're there, the door's locked from the inside. Go home, Bengali told her. Go home and don't come out. She went up. As she dug in her purse for the key she had the sudden feeling that she was being watched, but when she turned around there was no one there.

IT WASN'T VANITY as much as its opposite. Why show her face if she didn't want to be seen? She was grateful for the refuge of the burka. It simplified things, made her day-to-day life manageable, which, she knew, was no easy thing. She put kaajal on her eyes and painted her nails and put on a pair of sandals and she was ready to go. Under the veil she could have been anyone. She took the veil off at the khana, but she worked in the burka and Rashid made no objection. At home she spot smoked: a little powder on the foil, a match under it, a quick drag at the straw and she was done. Because they were tiny drags, she took a hit as often as she could.

One afternoon Rashid came by with a bag of fresh vegetables and a dabba of mutton masala and rotis still warm from his kitchen. There was no food in the markets. Don't go out, the mobs have taken over, he told her. They've appointed themselves our executioners. Then he saw her spot smoking Chemical and he wanted to try it too. Dimple told him what had happened the first time she smoked. She told him the entire sequence of her nightmares, starting with the house of blue pools and ending with her last conversation with Mr. Lee. She had a fear of water now, she said, even a puddle made her fearful. This is strong maal, it does something to your head. But the warning only made Rashid impatient. He said, if it's as strong as you say I'll have to pace myself. First sex, then smoke. Dimple bent over her foil and he got on his knees behind her. He saw how bony her ass had become. He used spit to wet her and he thought about the beggar woman with the haircut whose body had been found on the street, the Pathar Maar's latest victim, according to the newspapers. Or was she a victim of the Hindu-Muslim wars? What community had she belonged to? Did she know? No one did, he thought, not even the man who killed her for sport; and he fucked Dimple as the Chemical pulled her into a nod. Rashid saw her head go down and he closed his own eyes to concentrate on his orgasm but a disembodied head floated past him on a tide of ink. When the old Chinaman swiveled around to smile, Rashid cried out a name. He pulled out of Dimple and sat on the floor, taking big gulps of air. What was the name he cried? He didn't know. What he did remember, what he'd never forget, was the revelation that followed immediately afterwards: dreams leak.

THEY DO, thought Rashid, sitting on the floor of Dimple's living room, as the crows went quiet and the street turned red from the glow of a timber warehouse that was burning nearby. Dreams leak from head to head; they travel between those who face in the same direction, that is to say, lovers, and those who share the bonds of intoxication and death. That's why the old Chini's head is in mine. I'm dreaming Dimple's dream and I want to stop but I don't know how. The beggar woman is dead and Dimple too is dead and I deserve to die for fucking the dead. He smelled the smoke from the burning warehouse as the sweat broke on his face and the room turned red. I deserve to be here in hell, he thought, as he reached down and squeezed his dick with his hand, squeezed as hard as he could, squeezed until he was shouting and he saw a vision of himself in the future, sitting in a room while the evening gathered, still dreaming her dream, except the dream was not of Mr. Lee but of himself, years after Dimple's death, when he was old and pious and waiting for her ghost, and he heard her future words, the lovely words with which she would greet him: dreams leak and the dead return, but only if you love us. Of the dozen words she would speak in the future, he'd be struck by the word *love*, because it had never before been uttered between them, not in all their time together. By then, Rashid would know the truth of the words, though he'd be glad to hear them from her; and by then he'd be grateful, bewildered but grateful that she'd come back to pay him this compliment.

SHE HAD THOUGHT about what to say, she'd prepared herself. When Mr. Lee thanked her for coming back, she said: it's nothing. How could I not come? I owe you this much. Now tell me what you were going to say the last time. He blinked at her, his impassive face flickering in the blue. She noticed tiny bubbles in the corners of his mouth. In his newly acquired accentless English, he said, when my father died our lives changed forever. My mother was sent away and I had to start working. My father lost interest in being a man. The only thing he was interested in was opium. Then he died, in that way he let us down, but I always honored him. I attended to his rites as long as I was able. I fulfilled my duties as a son. When I became a father I was always afraid I would become like him, become a slave to opium and forget how to be a man. So I took care, I took the utmost care to fulfill my responsibilities. When I died, what did you do? Were you not my daughter? Wasn't I a better father to you than your real father? I left you only when I had no choice. Until then I gave you my protection and shared my life and all my possessions with you. In return I asked for one thing. When you said you would do it, did you know you would not? This is the question I wanted to ask you. This is why I asked you to come back. Her reply was so soft even she could barely hear it. No, Father Lee, when I said I would do it, I meant it. You didn't: you lied then and you're lying now. You made a fool of a sick man. Dimple's tears were of a slightly different color than the water, less transparent, of a lighter blue. Old Father Lee, she said, forgive me. Please, I'm so sorry. What must I do to earn your forgiveness? And it was when she heard Mr. Lee's reply that she knew she would never be able to appease him, that he ill-wished her, that he would never forgive her and she would never forgive herself, and that grievances did not disappear with death, if anything they became more pronounced.

Mr. Lee said: smoke more Chemical.

9.

The Intoxicated Entity

It was 1992, which meant that she'd been living in the apartment on the half landing between Rashid's khana and his home for almost ten years, and though she'd come across his family on the stairs or in the neighborhood—a cause of apparent distress to his wives, who lowered their eyes and walked on without a word—she had never been to his home and knew nothing about his family life. He rarely mentioned his wives, and if he did, it was to complain about some trivial domestic matter, as if they were employees and he was disappointed with the quality of their service. She wondered if he spoke about her in the same way, and if he spoke about her at all. His wives kept his home running, laundered his white shirts, and made his food the way he wanted. She on the other hand had no official standing. She could not bear children or cook; all she could provide was sex and conversation. The sex at least he couldn't complain about, she knew, because that had once been her job and she'd been good at it. He didn't have complaints, but she did, though she had no one to tell them to. He had an aversion to touch, to any kind of friendly touching, and cuddling was out of the question. He didn't like to be seen with her in public. He took too long to come. Sometimes, when they were fucking, she thought of a story she'd read in which the plague arrived to a town in Europe. You sneezed for a few days and died, just like that. As soon as people were identified as sick, they were bundled into carts and taken to the cemetery, where they were dumped, alive, to await burial. In the carts, the men and women fell on each other like animals, not stopping even when they were seized by the handlers and flung onto the cemetery grounds. It seemed to her that they, Rashid and she, fucked in the same way that the plague-stricken couples did, in a frenzy, to the death.

SHE SAID, tell me about your life upstairs, what is it like to have a family and never be lonely? But Rashid only shook his head. He was smoking a joint loaded with Chemical. He was happy, he said, why complicate things? Besides, talking about something is a way of jinxing it. She said, in fact talking about something is a way of not jinxing it, because if you say it, it won't happen. He didn't know this basic fact because he was still an amateur when it came to superstitions and she on the other hand was a master of the science, and that was were they left it. She went to the door to see him out and it seemed to her then, as she watched him climb the stairs, that he was her only contact with the living. She had seen no one else that day. The khana was closed and there was a curfew in the city and if she looked out at the empty streets she felt as if she was the only survivor of a terrible planetary mishap. She stood in the landing after Rashid's footsteps had faded. There was a film of perspiration on her face and she let the air cool her. She sniffed herself and thought:

I smell of sex. And then she became aware of someone crouched in the dark of the stairwell leading to the street below. She took a few steps forward but saw nothing. The Chemical, she thought, it's rotting my mind. I have conversations with a dead man and I think I'm being spied on.

SHE SAT ON the floor and opened the book she'd found at the rad-diwallah's. She was sure it was the author she'd read a long time ago, S. T. Pande, but previously he'd described himself as a professor of history, not theology and symmetry, and he'd been affiliated with some other university. How could there be two professors with identical names writing textbooks for schoolchildren? It had to be the same man, and yet, how was he an expert in so many disciplines? Was symmetry a discipline at all? She opened a page at random, which was the way she liked to read, and started from the first line:

> "what use, then, the machinations of desire? Since God cre-ated each felicity of body with a concomitant object of grati-fication, the desire for immortality is in itself the evidence of immortality, as is the existence of its sister state, immutability. Cf. the Katha Upanishad: 'When that self who dwells in the body is torn away and freed from the body, what remains? This is that.'"

She flipped back to the beginning of the book and it struck her that *Some Uses of Reincarnation* was not part of the school examination syllabus. The title page, page iii, had only the name of the book and the author's name: it said nothing about being a textbook. Facing it, on page ii, were printing details: This edition published 1987 by STP Enterprises. New Delhi*Madras*Bhubaneshwar. Page iv gave a Haryana address for STP Enterprises and at the bottom of the page India Educational Services was listed as the publisher. On the facing page were the title and author's name, this time in an old-fashioned woodcut design, and overleaf, the contents. Pande had divided the book into two sections, "An Introduction to Aggressive Reincarnation" and "The Algebra of Being." The first section listed "active reincarnation practices" in the case of those who died strange, violent, or painful deaths and it began with a prologue, which had a précis of each of the sections to follow:

1. Immortality
2. Guilt & Consequence
[sections 3–6 are omitted]
7. Premonition
8. Revenge
9. Tonguelessness

She started at the beginning and read slowly all the way through.

IMMORTALITY. In which the author posits the idea that reincarnation, as a way of prolonging indefinitely an entity's earthly existence, is nothing short of a curse. The author contends that only intoxicated entities, forgetful of god, wish for unlimited lifetimes in which to prolong their pleasures. The author suggests that such entities should actively take their afterlife into their own hands and seek out the shape in which they wish to return. If they want to eat and drink to their heart's content, they should ask to be given the body of a pig;

if they wish to lie in the sun and move very little, they should ask for the body of a lizard; and if they wish to copulate all day and all night, they should ask for the body of a monkey. The author is by no means contending that these three body types are the limits of the intoxicated entity's available choices, certainly not, as there are manifold conditions, for example: inward envy, sleepiness, prideful urination, aversion to heights, devotion to heights, aversion to water, devotion to water, & etc. (See Fig. 8.)

FIG. 8

GUILT & CONSEQUENCE. In which the author posits the idea that there are no innocents and no bystanders, because all living things play an active role in their incarnations, reincarnations, and subsequent existences; that each entity is born carrying sins and memories from its previous existence, and the stronger the memories, the more dynamic the play of hope and power in its early life; that these memories fade as we grow into adolescence, a loss that occurs despite our own best efforts, because we are encouraged to do so by our families and the society we find ourselves struggling to fit into; that those who die painfully, through no apparent fault of their own, are in fact paying for past errors; that the question therefore of god's cruelty is moot, for god has no hand in the way we conduct our births on our upward or downward trajectories, as is our course and our curse; and that there is no action without its immediate or delayed consequence.

PREMONITION: In which the author provides an example from his own life. Days before her death, his dear wife was engaged in a strenuous discussion with the author, the details of which he is unable to recall at the present moment. It had something to do with the author's work habits, which his wife termed obsessive and isolating. She said she felt lonely and cut off both from her husband and the world. The author, irate at the intrusion and the time he was wasting, time that could profitably have been spent at his desk, was about to tell his wife in the strongest language that she had to find her own obsession and could not look to him for happiness, harsh words he had flung at her before, when he became aware of a figure standing immediately behind her. The figure, dressed in stereotypical loose white cotton, told the author, or he didn't speak exactly, but managed somehow to communicate very clearly that the author should not say the words that were already positioned in his mouth, aimed and ready for launching. The figure said his wife was not long for the world, and that he, the author, should be as kind to her as possible or he would be guilty for the rest of his life. At this moment, his wife moved to the window, where she lit a cigarette, and her invisible companion moved too, so he was always immediately behind and above her, like some kind of broken shadow. As the reader has correctly anticipated, the author did not follow the white-robed figure's advice. The author uses this anecdote to consider the question of premonition in reincarnative episodes.

REVENGE: In which the author provides a procedural for thwarted entities who wish to exact satisfaction from those who tormented them during their most recent lifetimes. The author makes special mention of brides set on fire by their husbands' families as a punishment for bringing inadequate dowries. The author enumerates the steps by which such women can be reincarnated within the very families that destroyed them, so as to decimate said family from within its own bosom. First, the author recommends that reincarnation be delayed until such time as the husband's new wife is pregnant, usually a period of around nine or ten months, because the husband's remarriage most often occurs immediately after the death of his previous wife; second, the reincarnating entity enters the womb in question and assumes the fetal shape, a process that requires deft maneuvering and practice; third, she must focus on her task throughout her subsequent childhood, as there will be many forces working to undermine her resolve; and last, she must take pains to disguise any physical signs, for example scorched birthmarks on the skin and a marked aversion to fire, that may signal to an astute enemy that she is the prodigal wife returned. The author contends that will is the paramount faculty to ensure successful reincarnation, particularly when the purpose is revenge. The techniques described in this section can be applied by any entity, i.e., it is not the sole prerogative of murdered housewives.

TONGUELESSNESS: In which the author explains the phenomenon known as partial reincarnation, and contends that partially reincarnated entities, also referred to as ghosts and spirits, are an example not of reincarnation but of delayed departure. The delay is usually caused by an abnormality in the transition of an entity from the world of the living to other worlds. The author posits the possibility of engineering the delay, so as to ensure that there is a chance to say good-bye to the departing entity. Again, the author provides an example from his own experience. When his wife died, suddenly and tragically, he carried out a ritual experiment in an attempt to communicate with her. The author removed his tongue by means of a minor surgical procedure. He is not at liberty to divulge the details of said procedure, because its legality may be open to interpretation; but he will go on record as saying, so to speak, that he was extremely pleased by its efficacy. As a result of his mutilation, the author was vouchsafed several conversations with his wife, who appeared not the least bit daunted by his tonguelessness. Indeed, the author suggests that far from hampering their ensuing interactions, the lack of a tongue may in fact have enhanced them. While he does not recommend such a course to his readers, he offers it as one possible answer to the question: why do you write? And also: why do you never answer your phone? He suggests too that headlessness be considered, but only by advanced entities skilled in self-decapitation. (See Fig. 9.)

CHAMPAKLAI AND CHAMPAKALI   FIG. 9

Dimple flipped to the back of the book hoping to find a picture of Pande, but where the author photo should have been there was a line drawing, a self-portrait. The book was very slim and in the middle was a glossy insert section with more line drawings that corresponded very loosely to the passages they were supposed to illustrate. Figure 8, for example, which was meant to be an illustration of the section on immortality, had nothing to do with anything in the book, as far as she could see, other than the fact that the words "devotion to water" appeared as a sort of caption. She realized at that moment that Pande was a fraud, that he had printed the book himself (STP was his company, named with his initials), and she knew too that the only part of the book that was not fraudulent was the cross around the author's neck in the self-portrait at the back. He believed in a Christian god, that much was plain to see, and as she looked at the drawing she realized she did too and she wanted, for the first time in her life, to go to church.

THE KHANA was back in business the next day. Late in the afternoon, she put on a dress and went to Salim's to buy Chemical. Bits of rubble and the shell of a burned taxi lay strewn on the street. She noticed there were no dogs to be seen, not a single one. Where had they gone? There were no cattle or birds either. Salim told her he was out of cocaine and to give Rashid his apologies and to tell him that garad was available and would continue to be available. Chemical, in particular, was available in plenty. Why was that, she asked him, where did it come from that it wasn't affected by what was going on in the city? Salim smiled at her with sudden affection. It had been a long time since he'd had sex with anyone, he thought, much less a woman and a hijra-woman at that. What the Lala did to him wasn't sex, it was payment. The Lala took his ass in return for the job opportunity he provided and the pleasure in the exchange was entirely one-sided. Salim could barely remember what an erection felt like, but at that moment he felt affection for Dimple and he would have liked to fuck her, a friendly or nostalgic or tender fuck. Sit down, he said, and I'll explain it to you. Garad comes from Pakistan. Garad, you know what it means in Urdu? Waste. This is the unrefined shit they throw away when they make good-quality maal for junkies in rich countries. Even the worst junkie in America-Shamerica wouldn't touch garad. That's why the Pakis send it here. We buy it happily and ask for more. And to give it a special kick we add more shit to it and call it Chemical. Now you might say this is some kind of special ingenuity, a skill, to take bad shit and make it worse. But I'll tell you what it really is, we're khatarnak sisterfuckers, all of us on Shuklaji Street, we deserve to die, we're only happy when our heads are touching the floor and we're praying to the god of garad. We deserve to die. Dimple told him to speak for himself. I don't want to die, she said, not today. I've got things to do. Tell me why Chemical is freely available when there are no tomatoes in the market. Because, Dimpy dear, the city belongs to the politicians and the crooks and some of the politicians are more crooked than the most crooked of the crooks. Garad sales are protected, it doesn't matter that it comes from Pakistan. They'll make speeches about Mussalmans and burn our homes and shops but this is a multi-crore business and in Bumbai money is the only religion. They're not stupid. Now you tell me something, what are you doing here? Dimple nodded. The world is ending, she said, anything can happen to anyone at anytime.

FROM SALIM'S she went toward Novelty Cinema. All along Grant Road, the shops were closed. There were groups of men, always men and always in groups, who stared at her as she walked and she felt a difference in their attention. It wasn't the usual staring; it was more businesslike, as if they were weighing her for meat, guessing how much she would fetch in the market. Everywhere was rubble and the smoke of recent fires. She saw smoldering taxicabs and trucks.

She saw a woman's slipper, one slipper, in the exact center of the road. It was in good condition, imitation leather with blue and yellow flowers on the straps. She saw two men who were armed for medieval warfare; one carried a sword and the other a trident. They held their hands to their mouths and kissed the tips of their fingers. White smoke lifted from their cupped palms. They watched her without speaking until she turned the corner. She wasn't sure where the church was and she hurried down the street until she found it, hidden between a police station and an electrical store. The police station was closed. Why wouldn't it be, on a day when the city was burning? The police and the dogs, it seemed to her, were always the first to smell trouble and disappear. As she went up the stairs to the church, she had the feeling she was being spied upon. But it was so recurrent these days, the feeling of being watched, that it no longer bothered her. The doors were closed but unbolted and she pushed them open and went into a small room with metal chairs and a statue of Christ Jesus. The only light came from a bulb burning in a cage above the statue, which seemed to float in the air above her, one hand pointed at the ceiling. She smoothed her dress, a long one that hung to her calves. It was the first time in months that she'd worn something other than a burka. She smoothed the dress and curtsied to the figure. Where had she learned to curtsy? Then she pushed a chair in front of Christ Jesus and took off her shoes and climbed up. By standing on her toes she was just able to reach his hand and place her forehead to his index finger. She noted that his lips were pink and blue, strange lips, like those of someone who had died and been inappropriately made up for viewing. His hair was unwashed and his eyes were tired. There was no hint of a smile on his face, no suggestion that his life was anything other than a

titanic struggle, against what?, against himself, his own coward-
ice and unworthiness, and, above all, against his shame. She knew
his life was a trial from the moment he woke to his last thoughts
before sleep, if he slept at all, because there were small bruises under
his eyes and it didn't look like he got much rest. His wounds were
dramatic and glossy, movie star wounds that would not heal, that
would stay forever raw, and the circle of thorns on his head dripped
blood into his eyes and colorful lips. She felt a sudden gratitude that
made her sit down and cover her face with her hands. Then, when
she looked up again, she saw the words leave his mouth though his
dead lips didn't move, and the words appeared to her like smoke
writing, English words she had no trouble deciphering: love me
because I'm poor and alone like you.

WHEN DIMPLE LEFT, Salim shut the watch shop and went to give
his boss the day's accounts. The Lala's house was in an alley among
a maze of alleys off the main road and it was guarded by young men
armed with country revolvers. Salim was thinking about freedom
and fear. The city was burning; maybe Dimple was right, maybe it
was the end of the world, which meant there was nothing to be afraid
of. Nothing mattered. He thought about Dimple and was overcome
once more by a wave of affection and melancholy. When he got to
the Lala's room, his boss was in a meeting with other bosses, the
men sitting around in their Pathan suits and drinking whisky and
tea. He placed the bag of money next to the Lala's chair and waited
until the older man had the bag put away. The Lala was telling his
friends about Chemical, telling them it was so strong that his guinea
pig, the German junkie Eckhardt, had died while sampling it. The

men laughed. "The pig deserved it," someone said. "He wanted to die," said the Lala, also laughing. Salim had known Eckhardt and liked him. He was always surprised by the German's fixing technique: he poked the needle into his thigh, right through his jeans, and he used the same needle for as long as he could. The German seemed to like it that people were horrified, even other junkies, though they all watched and they all asked why he did it. His reply was always the same: "Come on, isn't it obvious? Because I cannot find a fucking vein." Eckhardt had a marijuana leaf tattooed on his calf and one day he sliced it off with a barber's razor because, he said, the tattoo was a satanic symbol placed there by god to torment him, Eckhardt. The German may have been crazy but to Salim he was always courteous and he was sorry to hear the man was dead. He went back to the watch shop and made himself a smoke, chasing a long line of Chemical on a clean piece of foil. He lit a Four Square and chased the heroin with a hit of tobacco. He was thinking of locking up for the day when the Lala walked into the back office and, without a word, bent Salim over the desk and pulled down his pajamas. "There's coconut oil on the desk," Salim said. In response, the Lala rammed harder and Salim felt something tear in his ass. The Lala's hands were on his neck pressing him down, giant hands that made it hard for Salim to breathe. Then he saw his pocket-maar knife on the desk, a few inches away. He opened it and reached behind him and sliced off the Lala's dick with two or threes quick saws of the blade. At first there was no blood, just shreds of red and white meat, and then a fountain spilled to the floor. The Lala stared at the stump of his penis for a moment before he began to bellow. Salim stabbed the knife into the big man's neck but nothing happened, the Lala continued to scream. It was only when Salim picked up the strongbox and smashed it on his head that the gangster shut his mouth. Salim smashed until the Lala's head was pulp. Then he dragged the body into the alley behind the shop. He cleaned the office floor, locked up, and went home.

IT WAS THE TERRIBLE January of 1993; the Lala's body was one of many lying unattended on the streets of the city. Salim knew it was common knowledge, what had happened to the Lala, because he, Salim, was seen walking away from the shop in bloodstained clothes. He expected a visit from the police but it never came. Four months later, after the city had returned to some normalcy, he was arrested for a robbery he knew nothing about. During the interrogation, which lasted a day and a half, Salim confessed to the murder of the Lala and the contract killing of a movie producer. Then he committed suicide by hanging himself with his belt, all this according to the police report. Though his corpse bore bruises that did not appear to be self-inflicted, he had no family and the body went unclaimed. The policemen who conducted the inter-rogation were friends and business partners of the Lala. After the interrogation, they didn't bother to conceal their marked fists and shoes, and later that night, at Topaz, a beer bar frequented by cops, many glasses were raised to the Lala and to the brave men who avenged him.

ON CHRISTMAS DAY, Dimple had gone back to the church. There was a small crowd, poor people from the neighborhood looking for somewhere to rest without having to worry about being attacked.

They looked exhausted. Dimple wanted to pray, but the only prayer she knew was for Mother Mary, which she repeated though it didn't seem like the right thing to do. On her way home, past empty rubbled streets, she spotted a loose group of men. For some reason they were all on one side of the road, as if there was a line they would not cross. She stopped only when a man stepped in her way, a drunk with a bandanna worn low on his eyes. He was chewing paan and he had a slight smile on his lips. His eyes were so bloodshot she wondered if he had conjunctivitis. He said one word. "Naam?" It was a signal for the others to gather around her, to examine her the way they would a rare bird, a bird with human hands and a woman's breasts. "Dimple," she said, looking the drunk man in the eyes. "Christian?" Without hesitating she said, "Yes." The man spat a stream of juice at her feet and a few red drops hit her sandals. "Nikaal," he told her with a jerk of his head, and she hurried on. She thought: if I'd been wearing a burka they would not have spared me, the dress saved my life. But before she reached the corner of Shuklaji Street she heard a shout and stopped and felt the hair on her arms stiffen. They've changed their minds, she thought. But they were shouting at a boy on a bicycle. It was Jamal; she understood then that he'd been following her and had been following her for a long time. One of the men took hold of the bicycle and another grabbed him by his kurta. She couldn't hear what they were saying, but she saw the look on the boy's face and she saw that he was trying to pull himself free. Then she heard herself shouting. She was only a foot or two away from the safety of Shuklaji Street but she might as well have been in another country. She shouted: "Stop!" The men looked in her direction. Jamal pointed at her and said something, something decisive, because they let him go. He ran straight to her.

"Don't run," she told him, "whatever you do, don't run." She took his hand and walked slowly towards home.

What had he said to the men? Jamal wouldn't tell her. But from then on he always greeted her when they met on the street or the staircase, which to her was a great thing, an achievement, something, finally, to be proud of.

10.

Confessional

I t was around this time, while the city killed itself and the smell of charred flesh hung in the air, that Rumi told her he'd killed someone, or almost killed someone. He had had to drop his uncle to the airport and on the way, in Bandra East, he was stopped for running a red light, he said. It was the first time he'd been stopped in years. The cop asked for his driver's license and of course he wasn't carrying it, that day of all days he'd left it at home. Instead of objecting or arguing, he simply handed over a note and thanked the man in Marathi. It was like paying a fine. His uncle stayed silent through this. But when Rumi started the car, Angre went into a tirade. He said, paying a bribe is the worst thing an Indian can do. You are perpetuating a system of negativity by condoning a corrupt model that has brought this country to its knees. His uncle was the CEO of the business, a veteran public speaker, who could bullshit for hours into a microphone in front of a roomful of people. He was skilled at this kind of thing. He said: "Your generation is reaping the rewards that your elders sweated and sacrificed for. I was a young man during the freedom struggle and I know the sacrifices my parents made,

I know how simply and frugally we lived. Above all we believed in truth and I am deeply saddened to see the way you took those notes out of your pocket and gave them to that man, as if you were buying a ticket to the cinema." For the rest of the ride, a good forty minutes, there was silence in the car. At the airport, his uncle took his case and walked away without saying thank you or good-bye. There would be hell to pay. His father, who was the poor relative in the business, would go on about how Rumi had jeopardized the family's future by bribing a cop in his uncle's presence. Here Rumi paused for a moment and asked a number of questions that were not addressed solely to Dimple. And what about his own future? he asked. He was on the rebound. His marriage was over. Leaving his wife meant leaving her family business. Which meant going back to his father's company, where he was given plum assignments such as driving his uncle to the fucking airport. Only a question of time before the shit hit. What would happen to him? He'd be fired, of course. And then? Where would he go? What would he do for money?

IT WAS LATE, past ten, but the traffic was still heavy on the road from the airport back into the city. The day's emissions had settled into nighttime mode, a toxic dust cloud that sat on the tarmac and flavored the air with the taste of industrial effluents. He wound the window down and took a deep breath, filling his lungs with the usual acrid metal of Bombay. He drove fast all the way to Bandra, where, stopped at the traffic light, he saw a man sleeping under the flyover, his head and body wrapped in a sheet. He looked like a corpse ready for burning, or a pile of rags ready for the incinerator. Beside him were his possessions, bundled in bedsheets, and nearby a fire had been lit. Rumi didn't notice the man in office clothes until he was at the passenger-side window, saying something about a flat tire. When Rumi looked down at his tires, the man reached into the car, snatched his wallet from the dashboard, and ran the other way. Rumi left the car where it was, unlocked, and took off after the guy. "It was all reflex, yaar," he told Dimple. He ran easily, in time to the music in his head, *wah-wah* and echoey vocals, If I don't see you in this life, I'll see you in the next one, don't be late. His vision and smell were so acute he could smell the thief's breath and the heavy odor of his sweat. His peripheral vision was tremendous. He saw a cockroach on the wall of the flyover. He saw the sleeping man, his cooking utensils and the bricks on which he'd made a meal. He knew the bricks were still hot, knew it without touching. He was moving, no, he was being moved: he was pure body. He stopped running and moved sideways, silently, in a crouch, with his hands hanging. The thief squatted in an unlit area under the flyover. He was going through Rumi's wallet and putting things into his pocket when Rumi poked his shoe into the man's side, poked hard, and said, "Up, sisterfucker." The man jumped, his hair wild, a construction worker or a homeless guy in ill-fitting office clothes, not defending himself until he was kicked in the stomach. Then he was punching wildly in the air because Rumi kicked him again, well-aimed kicks to the stomach and chest. And then, he told Dimple, he took the hammer out of his waistband and held it in the two-handed grip he'd practiced many times. He already knew the sound it would make, the exact sound of metal sinking into the man's cheek, the sound of bones breaking. All this he knew; what he was unprepared for was the joy that shuddered up from his hands into his brain and, as he turned, the first thrilling glimpse of the sleeping man's face, who was awake now and burbling in fear, begging Rumi not to hurt him.

II

Flight

O n that last day—a day of deluge, water stacked in green and brown layers under a floating membrane of debris, the streets and houses flooded and the neighborhood returned to its original aspect of swamp fed by pestilential rain, a place for mangroves and undersea life, not human habitation; when the city's network of supply and demand had broken down, and it was impossible to find eggs and coffee, much less the drugs I wanted; when everything had at last been arranged, I was leaving the neighborhood, the apartment, the habit, I was leaving and I wouldn't return—on that last day, in parting, the city was revealed as the true image of my canceled self: an object of dereliction, deserving only of pity, closed, in all ways, to the world.

THE CITY CLAIMED seven islands from the sea. In the rainy season, the sea claimed them back. For two days the sky was iron and on the third the rain poured itself into every crevice. It didn't let up for a week. I looked for the black kites that lived in the coconut tree near my fourth-floor window. I put both hands on the ledge and leaned out until I saw them, two big birds, huddling, miserable in the downpour. I went from room to room. There was a stain on the bedroom wall, a waist-high discoloration where water had seeped into the brickwork and though the floor was clear of everything except dust, I sat in the exact spot where my armchair had been. This is what I did, I leaned out and hunkered in and waited for a call from the airline. But the phone didn't ring and I went out into streets that were bright with water. I'm leaving, I thought, and this is my last time. I wanted to be generous to the city because I was leaving it and I thought I heard a wind blowing through the broken streets, a clean wind unimaginable in the midst of such decay. I felt a heaviness settle in my chest and just then I was sure I'd never be free of that chaotic obsolete Bombay, and I'd never be free of my beloved lie, that heroin was an aberration, a last time. I thought: how close I am to happiness and how far in understanding.

At Bandra Station, stranded commuters were playing card games on their briefcases. The weighing machine was silent and on its base a small boy slept with his mouth open. I saw a fight break out among a group of boys who couldn't have been more than ten years of age. It didn't stop until a cop came along and clubbed them with his lathi, clubbed them repeatedly. Not even the sight of their own blood pulled them off each other. I saw a woman with her leg in a cast bang her crutch against the weighing machine to wake up the boy sleeping on its base. She shooed him off, sat, and lit a beedi. I saw three small children set up a stone under the eaves to chop onions for lunch. They were focused on their task, oblivious to everything, like practitioners of a great and dying art. It might have been there that I saw Rumi, or if not there then not far away, under the eaves on platform 1, or he might have been facing the

other way, looking towards the sea and the road to Bandstand, I
don't remember now, but there he was in the drowned light, with
his pleated trousers and white shirt, his ballpoint aligned with the
vertical, no color on his person except for the saffron tilak near his
shaved hairline. He yawned like an old man and fixed his watery
gaze on me and said, crazy fucking city. Then he said the dealers
were out of maal and we would have to go to Bombay Central. But
he didn't move from his spot. He lit a Charminar and offered one to
me. "Try this," he said, "no filter, no menthol: compared to Charmi-
nars, Camels are crap and Gauloises are for homos."

THE RAIN HAMMERED down and I saw or I thought I saw Rumi's
tall figure in front of me and I splashed after it. After a while of
this, I lost track of time, I could have been anyone, I lost myself,
which is the reason people like me get into drugs in the first place.
Just then, a man splashed past astride an oil drum, paddling with
his hands, riding the drum like a water scooter. The rain streamed
into my glasses and I lost sight of him, but I was affected by the joy
on his face. A red double-decker stopped and we got on. Water ran
in sheets down its rusted metal sides. From the bus's upper deck
the view was legendary, like footage from a documentary. The sky
was the color of someone's black eye. Cows stood in the water, too
bewildered to move. Snapped power lines sputtered near a movie
theater. People stepped carefully on the dividers in the middle of
the road. They walked in a long broken line and they carried boxes
and dead umbrellas and plastic bags filled with flotsam. When they
saw the bus some of them tried to run after it but the others stood
where they were. We got off at Grant Road and made our way to
Hijde ki Galli. The shops and restaurants were open, but under the

bridge where the crowd of shoppers was usually too thick to negotiate, there were no people, just bamboo scaffolding standing in the floodwater, tethered to nothing.

THE PLAYHOUSE LODGE had once been a theater, three stories, peaked roof, gothic parapets and arches, and a grand colonial name. But English fell out of use and the playhouse came to be known by a phonetic variation, Pilahouse, with a nonsensical bilingual meaning, yellowhouse. Now it was a lodge in name only, there were no rooms and nobody lived there who expected room service or clean sheets. It was where Rashid had set up shop after his opium room on Shuklaji Street finally closed. The staircase that led to the Pilahouse was made of rough wood, its planks warped, the lower steps lost in water. Half a dozen men stood huddled near the top. The air was heavy with flies and the smell from a public toilet next door. Rumi wanted to cut the line but the man at the top of the staircase wouldn't give up his spot. He was huddled in a Mandrax stoop and he mumbled baby talk. He said: "Hold on, wait, his sheeting, understand?" He said: "You want, you wait, like." Rumi reached around him to bang on the door. There was a conversation, Rumi's words rapid, monotone, the Mandrax man hoarse and slow.

"So we're waiting for the African to shit, that's what you're telling me?"

"Yes," said the Mandrax man, and he laughed without making a sound. "He brought the garad in his ass and he's been trying all day to shit."

"That's completely fucking disgusting."

Rumi made a face but he made no move to leave.

"The shit's in his shit, that's why we're waiting?"

"That's how it gets here. Mules, like."

"African donkey, more like."

"You want government-controlled health warnings? Everything neat and organized, nutrition information on the side and best-before dates, stuff doesn't get you off take it to the consumer protection bureau, petition the dealer?"

It was a long speech for the Mandrax man and it silenced Rumi, but only for a moment. He coughed into his fist and rubbed his hands together. He said, I saw a Negro once when I was a kid. In my school, he was an exchange student from Nigeria. He looked so dirty, like a monkey. The shock made me puke. Then, when I was living in LA, I saw lots of them and I learned not to puke. I learned to be a man of the world. But not even in LA, where, believe me, weird things happen on a daily basis, not even there did I wait in line for a Negro to shit.

THIS CHOOTH COUNTRY, cunt country, how the fuck are you supposed to live here without drugs? Look at the Gujaratis, chooths, we all know this, kem cho choothiyas. Human calculators, you can't even talk to them without giving them cash, they're such accomplished chooths. And the Kashmiris, complete chooths, offer them your hand, they'll take your ass. It's their nature; they can't help it. And what about the Madrasis, all those Keralites and Kannadigas and so on? Chooths, undu gundu choothiyas, idli dosa choothiyas, nothing personal, but it's true, you know it and I know it. And Punjabis, do I even have to mention Punjabis? Number one chooths, the Punjus. They'll eat and drink with you and all the while they're measuring you for a coffin. Bengalis? Bengalis are beyond your average category of choothiyadom, they're chooths of the highest order, first-quality bhadralok choothiyas, who invent new levels of choothiyaness daily. Followed closely, as in everything, by the Oriyas, who are more in the league of chooth wannabes. But none of them approach the level of choothiyahood perfected by the Sindhis, who are the world's most sophisticated chooths, inventors and tweakers of the choothiya's guidebook, in short, chooth perfectionists, true masters of the genre. As for the Christians, the Anglos, and Goans, chooths, as you know, unquestionably chooths, though they'll act as if the word has never left their lips or entered their brains. And the UPites and APites, they're criminals to a man, born criminals, you can't trust them with a pencil. Then there are the chooths-in-waiting and the chooths by association, such as the Parsis and the tribals. Now that may seem like an odd chooth combo, but it's not. They are exactly alike in at least one way, they act like they aren't chooths, but they are, deep inside they are utter chooths. The only non-chooths in the entire country are Maharashtrians. I grant you there's been some degrading of the rule in recent times but at least with Maharashtrians what you see is what you get: islands of sanity in a sea of chooths. But even here, in the only non-choothiya place in the whole choothiya country, I challenge you to live here without turning to grade-A narcotics, said Rumi, leaning across the staircase to knock on the door in rapid frustrated bursts.

HE WAS STILL knocking when the door opened and we were motioned inside by a hijra in a cotton sari stained with mud and water. The room was small, bare except for a few sleeping pallets and oil lamps and a poster, a picture of a yellow-haired girl in a wide-brimmed hat and the words "Gather ye rosebuds while ye may." In a corner, Rashid was filling a cigarette with powder. When he lit up, the joint gave off a tang of derangement and for a moment I smelled the color of it, acid green, like the barium of firework displays.

"I get a commission, but I tell people to stay away from this shit."

He used the English word. Sheet.

"Afeem's different."

"Afeem."

"The old word for opium. You lie back, someone makes your pipe, you take your time, you enjoy."

"Until the world changes and everything goes to hell," I said, pointing. "A beautiful piece."

"At least five hundred years old and it will last another five hundred, longer than all of us. I bought it on Shuklaji Street from a Chini refugee who escaped to Bombay. He demanded a lot of money, as much as you'd pay for an antique in a shop on Colaba Causeway, but look at the carvings and the teak. I bought two for ten thousand rupees around twenty years ago. They must be worth lakhs today."

He was looking at the pipe but he had a heroin joint burning in his fingers. And I wasn't interested in opium: I wanted to be kicked in the head.

Rumi whispered, "Yaar, something get you?"

"What's that?"

"Everybody here's a Muslim except you and me. You see this?"

I didn't respond: garad had a way of putting things in perspective and socio-theology went to the bottom of the pile. But we were overheard. I was waiting my turn to go inside when Rashid said, "Sit here. Tell me why you think Muslims cannot be trusted."

"I didn't say that."

"You don't have to say what's written on your face."

"There's nothing on my face except boredom, Rashidbhai. Boredom and more boredom. I came to your shop for so many years but what do you know about me?"

"I know you're a garaduli. Isn't that the important thing?" He laughed loudly at his own joke. Then he said, "You switched from chandu to garad when you moved to Bandra, you talk English when you're high, and you're a Nasrani. Now tell me why you don't trust Muslims. We are all smokers here, nashe ki aulad, there's nothing to fear."

"It's not that you're not to be trusted."

"Then?"

"Then why not talk about it, the thing we don't talk about? Is that what you mean?"

"Yes."

"My religion is no way of knowing me."

"Mine is a way of knowing me. When I pray I feel I'm doing something clean."

"But why pray so the whole neighborhood hears your prayers? Why use microphones? And drums and music in the middle of the night."

Just then the Mandrax man said, "There's a town in Kerala, like, the main road has a temple, a mosque, and a church, all using loudspeakers, loudest street in the world."

Rashid said, "The city has changed, people wear their religion on their faces. As a Muslim I feel unwanted in many places, you should feel it too."

"I feel it. Who doesn't?"

"As a Nasrani, you should feel it as much as me. Okay, all Muslims cannot be trusted but what about the Hindus?"

Rumi said, "What about the Hindus, Rashidbhai?"

"Arre, you, with the hammer in your briefcase, you're just waiting for another war."

"Hammer?"

"Chootiya, the whole street knows about your hammer."

"It's a precaution."

"Must be, there are no nails here."

Some of the men sitting against the wall laughed, but Jamal, Rashid's son, did not smile. He was in his teens then and he was serious and self-absorbed.

"Tell me why you have the name of a great Muslim poet if you are a Hindu?"

"It's a nickname."

"Rumi is a mighty name for a mighty sha'ir."

"Rumi is a Muslim name?"

"Jalal al-Din Rumi. Bhadwas who never read a book will recite a ghazal by him as if they wrote it themselves."

Right then, a pimp said, "'Everybody's dying, even he, even she. / Knowing this, how can you not feel pity?'"

Rashid rolled his eyes and took a pull of the pipe and a suck at the joint.

"There used to be thirty-six chandu khanas on Shuklaji Street," he said, "now mine is the last one here, perhaps the last one in the whole city. If you stand on the balcony and look out some night, you'll think it's the last chandu khana on earth. And it too will soon be gone. What else will be gone? The words we said and the people we knew, and you and me, all of us will be sucked away like smoke in the wind. Do you know what will come in our place? New business, and if you want to do new business you'll have to pray to the same god as your client." He licked his finger and wet the joint's burning tip. "Nasrani," he said, "are you listening?"

Before I could reply the hijra in the stained sari reappeared and it was our turn. Rumi and I jumped up and went inside.

THE HIJRA LED US behind a partition to a back room where the Nigerian sat at a desk. A plastic jug of water stood on a side table, with a saucer of used tea bags and a collection of small bottles. There were several brands of laxatives and a bottle of cough syrup. On a room service tray were a dozen or so latex eggs, washed, but large enough that I wondered how he'd managed to put them in his ass. He wore a fresh skullcap and a striped business shirt and his shoes had a deep shine. There was a prayer bruise on his forehead and behind gold-rimmed spectacles his eyes were clear. He introduced himself as Pepsi and apologized for the delay. It was difficult to shit knowing a crowd of people was waiting, he said. Then he cut two uneven lines of dirty white powder on the cover of a movie magazine. He handed Rumi a hundred-rupee note rolled very tight. The twin lines ran diagonally across the famous mouth and vertiginous cleavage of the actress on the magazine's cover. Rumi bent over the currency note and snorted up a line and closed his eyes and put his fingers in his ears. I broke my line in two, one for each nostril. The powder hit the back of my nose with a hard chemical burn, and, in an instant, my knees dissolved in the anhydride rush that disconnects neurons from nerve endings, obliterates bone and tissue, and removes anxiety by removing all possibility of pain. I thought: if pain is the thing shared by all living creatures, then I'm no longer human or animal or vegetal; I am unplugged from the tick of metabolism; I am mineral.

RUMI AND PEPSI were on the couch, smoking a joint of heavy Bombay black, afloat on the smoke and conversation. The Mandrax man was there too, bent, his eyes wide with understanding or stupidity. The hijra, on the floor, smoked tiny bits of powder on a strip of tin foil. She cut an empty Gold Flake packet into long tapers that she lit from a candle and held to the foil, and when the powder melted and a coil of smoke appeared she sucked it through a foil-lined straw. She held the drag deep in her lungs until it disappeared into her cells, where it mutated and multiplied. Her hair was cut very short and there was a wound on her chin, a deep excavation filled with mucus. I was watching her, I couldn't look away, and when she caught me looking her eyes filled with water and that was when I realized it was Dimple and I was ashamed that it had taken me so long to recognize her. She pointed at the hole in her chin but she didn't speak. I'd seen her last about ten years earlier, when she'd been Rashid's personal pipe maker and known for her beauty. There was no trace of it now in the white stubble on her cheeks and the thin honey-colored hair. We had once been friends, but I'd never thought of coming to see her or to ask after her. There was always some sort of crisis, a crisis every day, and heroin trumped friendship every time. Now I did the easy thing: I took the money out of my pockets, kept some for a taxi home, and what was left I put on the floor beside her. It amounted to a little over six hundred rupees. I wanted to do something more but the truth of it was I was too high to care. In a corner a television flickered: mute images of healthy men and women, white, running in slow motion on a beach. There was clean sand and sunshine, the water clear, the color so vivid it seemed as unreal as the people running in their tight swimsuits.

I said something, I don't remember what, and Dimple tried to look up but she couldn't, the nod was too heavy.

I THOUGHT: for every happiness there is an equal and opposite unhappiness. Then I took a drag of charas and the room filled with light. Everything was transparent. The skin on my arms was as thin as paper. I looked into my flesh and saw the moving bones wrapped in pink translucent sheets, and all the while the rain fell in great washes against the roof, sheets of water that streamed from the windows and gathered in the corners of the room. We smoked that dirty hash, Bombay black charas, with the color and texture of goat shit, and we chased heroin on strips of foil. We spoke those words, the beautiful ones without meaning or consequence. We laughed for no reason and interrupted our laughter with silence. Pepsi spread a prayer mat and prayed and we waited in the room where the television flickered like firelight and the rain gurgled and crashed. We smoked. People came and went. We spoke the beautiful words and we called heroin by its joyful name. I didn't sleep but I was full of dreams and when I made my way outside it was dawn. The rain had thinned. Everything was lit with meaning. Water lapped against the city's ruined buildings, dirty water strewn with petals and garbage and smelling of attar. People waded on the street, soaked to the skin, their faces ecstatic in the charcoal light. I knew them as my brothers as I stood in the rain. I spread my pitiful, deluded arms wide. I wanted to hold the city, each woman and child and animal and man. I wanted to save them. And then I saw Dimple on the balcony reading a book, squinting as if her life depended on the words. When she saw me she stood up. There was a piece of sticking plaster on her chin and she said something I didn't understand, or maybe I did understand but I don't remember. I went to say good-bye and she whispered something in my ear, repeated what she'd said earlier or said something else, though I still didn't understand until I saw the Air India carry case in her hands. She had packed her belongings and she'd been waiting for me on the balcony. It was still raining and below us the floodwater suddenly seemed very deep, though I knew it wasn't. Dimple watched a puddle form on the balcony. She said, take me with you. I'll die if I stay here.

WHAT EXCUSE COULD I have made, other than the fact that I was leaving and I had nowhere to take her? And then it occurred to me that it wasn't true, there was a place she could go. We set off as if it was the most natural thing to do, set off together, I carrying her case, Dimple looking straight ahead, concentrated on the task of climbing down the flimsy wooden staircase, and only I looked behind to see if anyone had noticed that we were leaving, Rashid maybe, or one of his minions, lumbering after us, but no one was there. The water had receded a little and we found a taxi on the main road. Dimple was silent until we passed the waterfront near Worli and then she recalled something someone once told her, that the only beautiful thing about Bombay was the sea. She said it wasn't true, there were other things that were beautiful, though at the moment she couldn't think of a single one. After a while, she asked when we would be passing Chowpatty Beach and I told her that it was behind us, but she looked so stricken at this that I asked the cabbie to turn around and take us back. We parked on the road and walked a little way onto the beach, which was deserted at that time. The sea was swollen with waves and rain. There were no birds in the sky, or there were fluorescent birds that piped harsh melodies, birds that revealed themselves to be kites, and moments later revealed themselves to be not fluorescent at all but transparent, and not kites but crows, transparent albino crows barking dissonance, not melody, and Dimple crouched under the terrible sky wheeling with luminous birds and asked me if I could see the lights of a ship where the horizon was. I followed where her finger pointed but saw nothing, because the sea was full of chop and rain. I don't remember what I said in reply, or whether I replied at all, but just then I experienced a moment of clairsentience, a feeling of longing and anxiety, Dimple's, and for a moment I saw what she saw, a lost junk with tattered sails that seemed to have traveled a great distance of time, from the past into the future, with too few stops for refueling and repairs. And I knew that she wanted the ship to send a boat to collect her and take her away, take her somewhere calm and clean, where she could rest and repair her own wounds, and just then, just as I felt her sadness settle in my chest, she got up and went back to the taxi.

I HEARD the phone ringing when we got out of the elevator at my apartment. It was the airline calling to say my flight had at last been rescheduled and I would be leaving that day. I hung up and looked around the apartment and suddenly it seemed I was leaving too soon. In a suitcase I found a pair of jeans and a shirt and Dimple changed out of her sari. We sat on the floor and she talked of many things. She said garad no longer got her high, she smoked just to be okay, to be not sick. She'd been to a doctor who said she had a problem with her stomach and she might need an operation. The thing that gave her pleasure, perhaps the only thing, was reading and more than anything she liked to read about the sea. At the moment, she said, she was reading a book that had a hundred words for the sea, words she had never seen before and other words, better words, words that were more helpful because they were common. She said she liked the book because the men in it were as obsessed and insane as the people she knew, and though it was a big book the chapters were short, like poems, short and mystifying, and there were songs—sea shanties and lullabies and drinking songs and strange chants to make men brave. She looked at the stained walls of the empty apartment and asked if she could have some tea, but the kitchen had been dismantled and in a while I picked up her case and we took a rickshaw to a stall where the tea was strong and served with bread and butter. I heard bells and realized it was Sunday. The rain had stopped. There was even a hint of sun. I took Dimple to Safer, the rehab center where I'd taken my most recent unsuccessful cure. The center operated out of a church on Chapel Road and was usually open by six in the morning, when the inmates took yoga classes before breakfast. They were making morning tea when we got there and in an hour she was processed and settled. When it was time for me to leave we shook hands like a couple of guys.

And though I'd been waiting a week, packed and ready to leave, I arrived at the airport with only minutes to spare. I rushed through immigration, down the flaking corridors and water-stained halls that were empty except for the security detail who watched as I ran past, my pupils tiny pinpoints filled with heaven's white light. On the plane, I threw my carry-on into the overhead bin, but my suede jacket I handled very gently, holding it in my lap for the duration of the flight. In its inner pocket was a hole in which I'd hidden a bag of heroin. While the plane was still on the tarmac I made my first trip to the bathroom and cut a line on the back of my wallet. I returned to my seat and sat with my head tilted back and let the heroin dissolve into the back of my throat. I was nodding out when the plane lifted into the air and through half-closed eyes I thought I saw the rusted corrugated roofs of the Bandra slum where I'd bought drugs for so many years, the one-room dwellings that housed entire families, the broken-down shops selling cigarettes, batteries, and lightbulbs, the open sewage-clogged drains and crowds of people walking in single file; and in a moment I saw the streets of Bombay Central and the staircase at the back of the Pilahouse Lodge, still flooded though the rain had stopped; and then, the faces of the people I knew blurred and reassembled into a face that seemed very familiar to me, though I couldn't say why, the face of a sister I'd lost, or a son I'd never known, or the face of someone loved, who'd died.

12.

Rehab, Relapse

Rumi was at Shakoor's not Rashid's, because Shakoor laid on complimentary lines of cocaine and his heroin was cheaper and stronger and anyway Rumi didn't want opium so what would be the point of going to Rashid's? He was in the inside room with a couple of guys, a dealer and a pimp, and the dealer was saying to the pimp, listen to me, are you listening to me? Have I got your attention? The pimp was spot smoking with a short plastic straw. He took the straw out of his mouth and looked at the dealer. Well, said the dealer, if you're sure you can spare a minute of your precious time, I'll tell you something you want to hear. The pimp kept looking at the dealer, who was younger than him but similar in build and complexion. In fact, thought Rumi, they could be brothers, or cousins; even their mustaches are similar. Bring a woman with you, said the dealer. Haven't you learned anything? Shakoor sees a woman, any woman, even one of your street whores, and he'll lay on the lines like they're free. The pimp said something inaudible, then his eyes closed and he dropped into a nod. The dealer looked at the pimp for a while and turned to Rumi and said in English, fucking pimps, no ambition except for pussy. Rumi said, say cunt, don't say pussy. Only pussies say pussy. The dealer said, what? You think I don't know the difference between cunt and pussy? Rumi said: I ever tell you about my days in LA? Yes, said the dealer, you did. You're from a good family and you went to school in the States and you drove a limousine. You weren't always a garaduli. I ever tell you about the singer? Rumi asked. Not sure, said the dealer. What singer? Well, listen, said Rumi, let me tell you about the singer.

I DROVE A LIMO, and not just any limo, a stretch custom job, Rumi told the coke dealer whose name he didn't know though they'd had business dealings several times. Sometimes I took movie producers or music industry guys to the airport and they'd lay out cocaine and cognac and I'd think, yeah, these guys are living the life. Or I took party girls out for the night, strung-out chicks who'd crash in the car, so stoned they'd fuck anybody. Sometimes I'd be on the road for days, running on speed. Change of clothes in the trunk, drive around from fare to fare, sleep at the airport parking lot and stay high all the time. It was school, man. No, said the pimp, it was better than school, you got fucked and you got fucked up. You're right, said Rumi, for once in your life you are a hundred percent fucking correct: it was better than school. One time I picked up a fare from the airport, older woman, maybe thirty. We get to her place and she changes her mind. She says she doesn't want to go home, she wants to drive around some more. She'd just flown in from a concert in New York and she was still wired. She wanted to wind down. Are you a performer? I ask. Yes, she says, I'm a soprano, a coloratura soprano. I sing opera. I drove some, thinking: opera. Then I say, listen, I know this is asking a lot, but maybe you could sing something.

I mean, I've never been to the opera. I could see her in the rear-view and I saw the look on her face, pure pity, because she couldn't believe there were people in the world who had never heard opera. She puts her drink down and does some breathing exercises and she says, no, she's not going to do it because she can't sing sitting down. So I say, no problem, and I open up the sunroof. But she needs a pick-me-up, that's what she called it, a pick-me-up for her nose. I take her to this place I know in East Venice and we walk into a house with no furniture, one broke couch, pit bulls in the yard, the works, and the singer sits down and does everything that comes her way, smoke, toot, shots of malt. Late in the night she asks me, do you believe in ghosts? She says she didn't either, until recently, when she came to believe that ghosts are a source of comfort, perhaps the only source of comfort for the bereaved. And then she reaches for my dick and sucks me on the couch, with these kids crashed everywhere, sucks me like it's the first time she's sucked dick and she can't believe how good it tastes. Or like she's sucking someone who just died, someone who hasn't fully departed, and she's trying with all her might to keep him in the land of the living. Or like she's sucking the future, sucking it down one day at a time, the days she never expected to see, the days that would vanish in a gust of wind if she didn't suck with all her tenderness and talent and ambition. You ever been sucked like that? he asked the pimp. The pimp laughed. What about you? Rumi asked the dealer. You ever been sucked like that? The dealer said nothing and Rumi called for a Thums Up, in a glass, with lots of ice. He said, at dawn, she woke me up. We do a couple quick lines and get into the limousine. I'm driving past the beach and it's still dark, the street all quiet and pretty before the freaks and the fuckups start their daily shit, right?, the ocean on my right, and that's when she tells me to open the sunroof and she starts to sing, so loud you'd never believe that big voice was coming out of this small woman, and all of a sudden I got it, you know? The words were in German, but I got it, the function of opera, I understood that it was the true expression of grief. I understood why she needed to stand and turn her face up as if she was expressing her sadness to god, who was the author of it. And for a moment I understood what it was to be god, to take someone's life and ash it like a beedi. I thought of her life, her useful life, and I wanted to take it from her for no reason at all. And I drove that big car better than I ever had, the sky lightening, the clean water close by, and her voice carrying up to heaven. I wanted her to sing forever. I thought, as long as she keeps singing, I'll keep driving.

RUMI TOLD THE STORY the way he drove on the freeways of California, on autopilot, his mind half elsewhere. Where exactly? What was he thinking about when he talked about the opera singer? His mind was not in the air with the high voice that was trying to reach the ears of god, but down to earth below, on a pair of cowboy boots, to be specific, a pair of ostrich Tony Lamas, the most beautiful pair he'd owned and he'd owned a few. The opera singer asked him to stop at a diner, she needed food or her blood sugar would spike. They stopped at a twenty-four-hour place, toast, eggs, and beer for him, poached eggs for her, with bacon and coffee. The restaurant had framed photos of dead musicians on the walls, but only if they died when they were young; musicians who died of natural causes at a ripe old age were not similarly honored. Rumi was surprised at how many photos there were, how many musicians in how many genres. After breakfast, she got in front with him and curled up on the bench seat and put her head on his shoulder. He took her to Mulholland Drive, where she told him to wait in the car. He couldn't come up. He waited, he found news on the radio, then a rock station, except the music wasn't rock exactly, it was some kind of chant, a robotic voice saying something about corpses rotting in the red alleys of the moon, giving up their flesh to the cat-sized rats that came out to feed when the dog-sized cats had fed their fill and gone. When the song ended, the singer put her head in the window and gave him the boots. Whose are they? he asked. A friend's, she said, a friend who died. I want you to have them. Rumi didn't want a dead man's boots, but when he tried them on they fit like they'd been handcrafted specially for him. He never mentioned this part when he told the story about driving the opera singer around the hills of Los Angeles: he kept the boots to himself.

DIMPLE'S NEW LIFE at Safer was governed by the clock. They gave her a complete medical at Holy Family Hospital. The hole in her chin was not dangerous, the doctors told her, at least not at the moment. It was better to wait and see what happened, but first she had to detox. The staff at Safer put her on chlorpromazine, available on the street under the brand name of Largactil, and it was months later that she discovered how controversial the drug was, and dangerous, because it was still experimental. But she did what she was told, she took the pills they gave her and tried to live through detox. The chlorpromazine made her hallucinate so heavily that she wasn't aware of the torment her body was enduring, the pain, the panic and diarrhea, because she was tripping. Four or five days after she started on the drug, when the worst of the withdrawals had passed, they took her off. For two weeks her bowels were loose and for a month she didn't sleep, not at all, she lay awake on the turkey mattress and waited for dawn. The center was on the top floor of the church premises and from the roof she heard the birds at four in the morning. Then the sky lightened and the others woke and the day began. At six there was a yoga class. All turkeys had to attend, one of the other inmates told her; it was compulsory. Yoga was followed by breakfast: two fried eggs, two pieces of toast, jam, butter, and milk tea. Then the morning's physical therapy session began, an hour and a half of sweeping and swabbing. Once a week they swept out the church in which the center was located, Mount Carmel's, where the yearly Feast of Our Lady of Infinite Sorrow was held. Afterwards, the turkeys showered, or most of them did. The new turkeys who couldn't stand the touch of water went straight into the morning meeting. There were two house meetings a day, run by those inmates who'd been sober longest. At her first meeting, the guy who was in charge, an older Catholic fellow named Carl, asked her a question. She was still feeling the effects of the chloro- promazine, which made it difficult to lie. The only lie she could keep straight in her head was the lie of her name and gender. So when Carl said, why do you take drugs?, she told him what she thought, told him the truth because the least such a question deserved was a real answer. She said, oh, who knows, there are so many good rea- sons and nobody mentions them and the main thing nobody men- tions is the comfort of it, how good it is to be a slave to something, the regularity and the habit of addiction, the fact that it's an antidote to loneliness, and the way it becomes your family, gives you mother love and protection and keeps you safe. Carl, trying to keep to the moral high ground, trying to protect his position as the meeting's architect, said: but there are good habits and there are bad habits. Drugs are a bad habit, so why do it? Because, said Dimple, it isn't the heroin that we're addicted to, it's the drama of the life, the chaos of it, that's the real addiction and we never get over it; and because, when you come down to it, the high life, that is, the intoxicated life, is the best of the limited options we are offered—why would we choose anything else? When she looked up she found Carl gazing at her with narrowed eyes, and when he asked her to continue, in a tone of voice that suggested animosity or at least reluctance, she said she was feeling sick and she had nothing more to say.

YOU TELL ME, the dealer told Rumi, what was she, the singer, pussy or cunt? Cunt, said Rumi, they're all cunts, and that was when someone rushed into the room, a man so black he could have been African, with a red mouth that smelled of sweat and sewage, and for a moment Rumi thought it was the devil in his natural state, blackened and sooty and looking for company, or the devil freshly returned from the flames of hell, his red mouth about to burst into laughter, but it was Shakoor. He was offering trial hits of some new maal. Free, he said, who wants to go first? The pimp opened his eyes and said, me, I want to go, and he cooked up and tied off before Rumi had said a word. The pimp stuck the syringe into his ruined veins but couldn't find any blood and the deeper he dug the more frustrated he became. Shakoor gave Rumi a vial and he spilled a little of the powder on the tabletop and snorted it up and felt his body go limp and his heart wind down, actually felt his heart expand and seize up and start again. He staggered to the bathroom and put water into his nose and spit out as much of the powder as he could. He threw up and he threw up again and his legs wouldn't obey him and it was a while before he felt well enough to walk back to the room. Shakoor and the dealer were standing up, close in the small space, looking intently at the unconscious pimp. Get him out of here, said Shakoor. The dealer pulled a gun from under his shirt, a country-made pistol that would almost certainly misfire, though there was a chance it would not, and he pointed it at Rumi and said, go on fuckface, get this sisterfucker motherfucker out of here. He followed as Rumi dragged the pimp, first by the arms and then the feet, dragged him out of the khana and onto the road in broad daylight. See you, cunt, said the dealer as he walked back to Shakoor's. Rumi, dry heaving and sick, put the pimp on the road and passed out or fell asleep. He was woken by a skinny constable, low caste or no caste, probably a chamar, who put him in a van and told him the pimp was dead and he could be dead too. And the low-caste cop also told him something he knew: he was in a lot of trouble.

CARL ASKED if she would take a session at the center the following week. She could do whatever she liked, pick a topic like pride, say, or faith, or she could discuss a book, Anthony de Mello's great work *Prayer of the Frog*, for example, or hold a study class of some sort. She was still shaky from the withdrawal medications, the chlorpromazine and Avil; she felt like she was shedding skin, not dead skin but living skin, and her flesh felt raw and chafed. Then Carl asked what kind of class she would take, what subject?, and the answer popped into her head almost as soon as she heard his question: she would teach history, she said, a history of evil as suggested by certain individuals, obscure and not, including but not limited to poets, priests, and prostitutes. Carl started to shake his head before she had finished speaking. Inappropriate, misdirected, and overcompensation were some of the words he used, and there were others too, but they were not as interesting. Carl thought the kind of session she had in mind was more suited to a university or some kind of arty lecture series. There was nothing uplifting about it, so how would it benefit a group of recovering addicts whose hold on sobriety, not to mention reality, was shaky enough to begin with? She agreed that there was nothing uplifting about the subject, or nothing obviously uplifting, but it would certainly benefit those in recovery, since addiction was one of the fringe topics that fell under the general heading of evil, and she wanted to talk about the ideas of Burroughs, Baudelaire, Cocteau, and De Quincey, to name only four historians of evil, though the last named was a cusp case. Who are they, Carl asked, poets and prostitutes? Writers, said Dimple. Carl asked if they all took drugs. Yes, said Dimple, they did, opiates mostly. Well, then, they're junkies plain and simple, fuckups who got lucky, they were not to be trusted. And besides, said Carl, they're not the kind of positive thinkers we prefer to focus on at the center. This program is aimed at getting people off heroin, not glamorizing it.

HE GOT THE SHITS when the garad wore off. The toilet was a hole in the floor that was impossible to locate because there was so much shit around it, weeks and months and years of shit. He stood in his shoes, pulled his pants down, and added to the pile, trying not to breathe through his nose. Then he went back to his spot on the floor and yawned and shivered through his withdrawal. There were bodies all around him, silent men with their hands on their valuables, if they had any, and he lay in his spot, his eyes and nose streaming, until one of the bodies appeared beside him, a tall pig-nosed Iraqi who materialized from a puff of beedi smoke and asked if he had money and if he wanted garad. Rumi bought three pudis and snorted two off his hand and only then did the shits stop. He also bought beedis from the Iraqi and he smoked them carefully, half a beedi at a time, and when he got to the end he untied the string and opened the leaf and saved what little tobacco remained. That night Rumi sat in his sleeping spot, surrounded by the bodies of thieves and faggots and murderers and atheists, and he thought about doubt. He thought: doubt is another word for self-hate, because if you doubt yourself and your position in the world you open yourself to failure. You have no place among men. You are the carrier of a virus and you're contagious and you should be put down, because doubt is the most dangerous indulgence of them all, more dangerous than vanity or greed, because doubt feeds on itself like cancer or tuberculosis, and unlike the sufferers of such ailments, the doubter does not deserve sympathy: doubt is a decision. He told himself, I am unkillable because I am without doubt and the saying of it will make it true. He repeated the words aloud: I am unkillable. He breathed deeply and filled himself with the stale smells of the cell, with the odors and emissions of the criminals around him. Then, aiming carefully, he spat into the corner where the murderers slept, in the best spot, under the window. There were two of them, a man who strangled his wife and two children as they slept and a man who stabbed a friend to whom he owed money, stabbed him thirty-two times and dumped his body in a drainage canal and would eventually (months later, long after the case had fallen off the pages of the local dailies) escape the death penalty on a technicality. The two murderers were unimpressive in the flesh, one was potbellied and asthmatic and the other was a scrawny younger guy with terrible halitosis. But they were treated like movie stars, they didn't wear the prison uniform and they were allowed out for a walk once a day whenever they felt like it. Rumi's gob of spit landed on the bare foot of the man who had strangled his family. He opened his eyes and wiped his foot against the floor, carefully wiped it clean. Then he sat up and looked around him until he saw Rumi. In the dim light the man's eyes were like water. I know what you want, he said. You don't know a thing, Rumi said. Not a single thing that makes a difference in the world. Friend, said the murderer, I'll tell you what I know and you tell me if I'm wrong. You want to hit me and you want to be hit, you want to be beaten almost to death, isn't that right? You want to taste blood because you're bored and pain is preferable to nothing. Isn't that right? I, on the other hand, prefer boredom because it's a comfort to me. What I'm saying is, if you can't sleep ask the Iraqi for Mandrax. I'm not going to fight you. After making the speech, the murderer flung his elbow across his eyes and lay still.

IT WAS HER first dream in weeks, her first sleep since arriving at Safer. She dreamed of a poster that had been on the wall of Rashid's for more years than she could remember, a poster of a blond girl in a sun hat. In the dream she got up from the turkey mattress and went to the window, which gave out onto a lawn that was lush and green, the kind of green that hurt the eyes, it was so bright. She watched the blond girl take off her large, her overlarge hat and place it on the lawn (and here the dream took on a cinematic quality, because she was no longer looking at the scene from a window: the frame became a kind of lens that zoomed in and out with dizzying speed), and she saw that the girl wasn't alone, that she was in fact surrounded by an army of shadows that moved on the lawn's periphery, moved as if their claim on the lawn and the color green, on the sky and the color blue, on the earth and its thousand unknowable colors, was older than hers, was so old that it could be ignored only at her peril. The girl, who was not more than thirteen or fourteen, removed her hat and placed it carefully on the ground. Then she lifted her dress or shift, a light cottony garment with a flowery pattern, and squatted above the hat and filled it with blood or shit, something, at any rate, that was black and crusted on the hat's upturned brim. And then the words began to flicker across the bottom of the screen like subtitles and the shadowy figures who crowded around the edge of the frame moved into the center, towards the girl, whose skin was white and rose. The camera focused on her face, on her petallike lips that mouthed, very clearly, the word *what?* But the subtitles that appeared at the bottom of the window or screen said something very different: "You were nameless and pagan. I gave you context. For two hundred years I gave you context and how did you reward me?" Then the girl's eyebrows took the shape of an inverted V and she mouthed the word *no.* As soon as the word left her lips she was overrun by the shadows, who, as they came into the light, revealed themselves as ethnic ecclesiastical figures in robes of white or saffron, and others in skullcaps, and still others in conical hats and tattered purple. In minutes, one of the figures in purple lifted his cassock to display a great brown belly and black penis surrounded by gray fuzz. He dipped his hand into the hat and smeared himself and soon the other figures were doing the same. The camera fell to the ground as if the person holding it had been attacked or was taking part in the activities he or she had until then been recording, and when the camera was picked up again there was a close-up of a penis penetrating, very slowly, the girl's anus, and then two words began to slide across the screen, words that were repeated with each stroke, the penis now sliding to half its length in the girl's small orifice, and there was a close-up of her face, which looked stupid more than pained, and again the words appeared, in quotes, "Tradition" and "Values," and the camera cut to the priest, whose face was glazed

with spit and sweat and the words he spoke needed no subtitles because they were synced and perfectly audible, "This is India," and
Dimple woke, her heart beating so fast she thought she might die
and the thought of dying was a sudden comfort.

ON THE THIRD DAY, or it might have been the second, they took
him downstairs and put him in a room with a lawyer, a Muslim,
who told him his bail had been arranged and they were going to
try something new, they were giving him a choice between rehab
and jail. Well, now, Mr. Advocate, what a wonderful deal you're
offering me, said Rumi, thank you. He took a matchbox from his
pocket, opened it, and shook out half a beedi. He lit it and took a
deep drag and when he exhaled the Muslim flinched because the
smell was so strong. Thank you, thank you, thank you, for nothing,
Rumi said. Jail or freedom, that's a choice, rehab or garad, that's a
choice, but rehab or jail? That's like choosing between death and
dying. No, I take it back, it's like choosing between syphilis and gon-
orrhea. I know what I would choose, said the Muslim. I know what
you'd choose too, said Rumi, but it's the wrong choice. You want to
know something? When they put me in here I thought it was all
over. I thought I'd be fucked up right away, stabbed or strangled,
something, for being Hindu. I thought jail would be full of Muslims and I'd be at the bottom of the under-trial hierarchy. Well, I
am at the bottom, but not because I'm Hindu. Can you believe it?
The Muslim said nothing. I asked myself, what does it mean that a
garaduli is lowest on the ladder, lower than a ragpicker or a thief?
How can it be? I asked a shooter who was in for the contract killing
of a movie producer. Tell me, I said, I want to know. Why would a
Hindu trust a Muslim over a garaduli? You're a Hindu, you tell me.

The shooter looked me over, as if he was measuring me for a suit or a coffin, and then he said, garadulis will do anything. I said, why single out garadulis? Anybody will do anything. The shooter said, garadulis turn on their own kind—not even a pocket maar will do that. Rumi was silent for a while and then he said, what did you bring me? News, said the Muslim, the best news you can hope for. I mean, did you bring me food and cigarettes and money? No, said the Muslim, I brought you something better, we're getting you out: we've worked out a bargain with the court. Rumi said, just leave me some cash, whatever you have. You can get it back from my father. Look, Ramesh, the Muslim said, you're getting out, it's all been arranged and the money's arranged too, take it cool, don't take so much tension.

Of course it didn't go as easily as the Muslim, whose name was Majid, said it would. It took another week of watery daal and uncleaned rice and watching his back, and then, a trip to court, where Majid the Muslim did most of the talking. Afterwards, a constable put him in a jeep and escorted him to a place recommended by the judge, who said it was the first facility of its kind in India, that it was a program run by former users, that it used both physical and spiritual exercises to help bring about a speedy recovery (which phrase made Rumi smile, because it sounded like the judge was making a paid advertisement, and because if you knew anything at all you knew there was no such thing as a speedy recovery when it came to heroin), and that it was talked about mainly for the sessions, part psychotherapy, part literary criticism, conducted by a former monk and heroin addict named Soporo Onar, who had taken over the running of the center some months earlier. The judge said the doors of the facility were locked though only at night and therefore escape was not impossible, but he was of the opinion that it would be wiser for Rumi to stick out the six months of his sentence than dodge the court for the rest of his life.

WITH THE DREAMS came memories, or perhaps they weren't memories at all but fantasies she imagined were memories. It was as if, by lifting the cloud of garad and chandu that had been her companion for so many years, she had also liberated her recollections of infancy, if they were true recollections at all. It surprised her that she remembered the church her mother had made on the bottom shelf of a steel cupboard, something no one knew about except her mother and herself. She remembered the marigolds her mother placed on the shrine, and the framed image of Swayambhunath's painted eye, and a figurine of a woman in a blue veil. She knew now that the woman in blue was Mother Mary and that her mother had worshipped both Hindu and Christian gods. But how could she possibly remember such things when she'd been separated from her parents at the age of seven and at eight had already come to live with the tai, who had named her Dimple, not because she had any, but because there was an actress of that name who had, for the briefest of moments, captured the nation's excitable imagination? But she did, she remembered with absolute clarity her mother placing her in the hands of the priest. And she remembered too her mother's fits, when she screamed for no reason and tore her hair, and the fights with her father, whom she didn't remember at all because he died young, and she remembered the noose her mother was rescued from, a noose made from a dupatta that had been fastened to a nail on the kitchen wall. Or was it Mr. Lee's mother who was rescued from a noose? Had she stolen the memory? Perhaps she had no memories at all; perhaps she was stealing other people's because she had none of her own.

IN HIS FIRST DAYS at the center, Rumi met only the two inmates who had been told to stay up with him during his withdrawals. The Parsi gave his name as Bull and was the tougher of the two. The Catholic's name was Charlie and he claimed to be an electrician and knife fighter. They took turns sleeping so one of them could keep an eye on Rumi at all times. On his second night, when the drugs they gave him seemed to have little or no effect and he began to pound the wall, first with his fist and then with his head, the Parsi and the Catholic moved his bed to the center of the room and tied him down with nylon rope and cotton wool. He kept asking for stronger drugs but the best they could do was diazepam in useless five-milligram capsules. Bad timing, man, said the Catholic. Since Soporo took over things have changed, otherwise they would have given you the best medication, full-on hallucinations. Soporo thinks cold turkey is the best turkey. Fuck Soporo, said Rumi. The Parsi laughed and hit him in the stomach and the pain was such a relief from the withdrawals that Rumi said it again, fuck Soporo. This time the Parsi only laughed and said, if you had a razor you'd be cutting yourself, wouldn't you? Rumi said, fuck you too, and vomited in his direction. Bull the Parsi danced easily out of the way. He said, at least you have the right attitude.

HE FELT LIKE he'd joined a cult, because all they talked about all day long was Soporo this and Soporo that, stories he didn't want to hear, much less hear again and again: how Soporo exposed the guy who'd been in charge of the center, a cross addict (sex, alcohol, and heroin), who'd been using right under their noses, nodding off during sharing sessions and nobody the wiser because after all this was the session leader; how Soporo went after him at an NA meeting and made him admit it; how, three months after taking over, he persuaded the trustees to put up more funding and leased another floor from the church to build a gym and meeting rooms; how all kinds of people turned up at his talks, including those who'd never done drugs in their lives; and how, if Rumi made a good recovery, he'd be able to attend the talk on Wednesday night, which was titled "The End of Time." I heard a rumor, said Jean-Luc, a French junkie who'd been living in India since the seventies and had graduated from opium to heroin to Tidigesic, a synthetic opiate. You want to hear? The rumor is he will talk about how heroin annihilates the idée of time as a logical or chronological imperative, and he will talk about the Miles Davis album *Kind of Blue*, which he says is an example of heroin time, not musical time, and he's going to prove it by playing some of the tracks. Where's the talk going to be held? Rumi asked. Down the road at the church annex, said Jean-Luc. We need a bigger room than this one because a crowd will turn up, I don't know why. How do we get there? asked Rumi. We walk, what else? Hey, turkey, said Bull the Parsi from across the room, you want to be carried? Is that it? It was Rumi's first time at the lunch table, sitting with everybody, trying to eat. His hands shook so much he couldn't hold a glass and he felt weak and nauseous; the sight of food, in particular, the tongue served for lunch on Sunday, only made him sicker. The tongue had the exact shape and rough texture of a human tongue, except it was four or five times the size, and pinker and thicker and difficult to chew or swallow. He watched the others gobble it down and it seemed to him that they were attempting to swallow their own tongues, to commit suicide in this most ferocious of ways, and he was carried by a wave of white nausea mixed with disgust. He thought, you don't deserve to eat, not with so much appetite, and you don't deserve your good teeth and excellent digestion. You don't deserve to live, he thought, touching his neck surreptitiously to feel for the fever steaming under the skin. Down the road suddenly seemed like an impossible distance and he barely made it from the table to the turkey mattress without assistance.

He got better, or he pretended to get better, and on Wednesday when he saw them showering and shaving he did the same, and when they put on their best clothes he did too, put on the only clothes he owned, a checked shirt and jeans that he'd hand-washed once in prison and once at the center, and when a dozen turkeys and non-turkeys went out, chaperoned by the Parsi and the Catholic, he was among them, walking with a convalescent's hesitant step, a misfit in a company of misfits, stumbling or walking placidly among the normals, while Jean-Luc combed his dirty blond hair with his hands and Walter the obese chain-smoker talked to himself in Oriya and all of them eyed the women on the street. They stopped for tea and cakes, then made another stop for beedis and cigarettes, and between the cigarette shop and the annex where Soporo Onar's talk was to be held, a distance of twenty meters or less, Rumi walked backwards into a crowd of pedestrians and vanished.

BULL DIDN'T REALIZE the new guy was missing until they were seated and he had a chance to do a head count. He did a second count but the result was the same, ten turkeys, where was number eleven? He looked around at the congregation, the usual collection of users and losers and old people, aunties in housedresses, sickly parishioners, and at the very back a group of boys in camos and basketball shoes, looking severely out of place. He asked Charlie, we lost the new turkey, what's his name, Ramesh? Charlie also did a head count. He'll be back, he said, where's he going to go? Bull shook his head because the room was filling up and they couldn't talk without being overheard. But the front row was made up entirely of Safer inmates, all of whom seemed to know that the newest turkey had flown, was out there right now getting wasted, and though no one said anything, some looked to the exit and wished they were on the street, free to do what they pleased, including fuck themselves up, because that was the real meaning of freedom, wasn't it?, choice, the perfect adult liberation of being able to decide for yourself as to right and wrong and to choose wrong if that was what you wanted. Bull experienced it himself when he imagined throwing it away, all the months of odd sobriety, for one last stab at craziness, and he knew Charlie felt it too: a rush of blood that felt like happiness. Is there time for a quick smoke? Jean-Luc asked, and Bull would normally have said yes, but they'd just had a runner and who knew what kind of impulses that had set off in the Frenchman? He hesitated and the hesitation was enough for Jean-Luc to know exactly what was passing through the bulldog's head. Just then Father Fo cleared his throat.

HE WALKED WITH a group of people who were headed to a coffee shop on the corner. It was part of a new chain, with big windows and a burnt orange color scheme designed to make patrons feel warm and fuzzy, and filled him instead with rage. He crossed the street to Nikita Ladies & Gents Beauty Salon, and went in quickly and shut the door behind him and bolted it before the girl had a chance to protest. There was no one else in the shop. He drew the curtains and told her to take off her blouse and she didn't argue. She was young and dark and her breasts were heavy and she lifted them inexpertly from the cups. He pulled down her slacks and let them fall around her ankles and he told her to stay where she was and look at her reflection in the mirror and to touch her nipples and cunt and do nothing else. Don't move, he said, don't move anything except your fingers. Then he went around the small room, opening drawers and taking out herbal massage oils and towels and hair dye and waxing utensils, and dropping them on the floor. A jar of henna shattered, though the bottles of massage oil did not, and Rumi continued his rampage, opening and shutting, throwing shit around. There was a sudden smell, sharp body odor mixed with the unmistakable stink of fear. Ooh, he thought, when he saw that the girl's eyes had filled with tears and a fingernail-sized scar on her forehead had turned dark. She was not pretty; when teary-eyed she was ugly. Tell me where it is, he said. But the girl's eyes rolled up in her head and her hands fell to her sides. Don't stop touching yourself, he told her, and hit her on the ass with his open hand. She was too frightened to speak but she was trying to tell him something, the rolling of the eyes was a message, not a prelude to a fainting fit. He looked to the side and found a shrine. Behind a portrait of Ganesh and a stick of incense was a box with three thousand six hundred rupees. Is this all? There's nothing more, said the girl in Hindi. What about in your pockets? She shook her head. He found a hundred and ninety rupees in the back pocket of her slacks, which he transferred to his wallet. Maybe I'll give you a good-luck tip, he said, but first I want a full-body massage. Put a fresh towel on the cot for me. The order cleared her head because it put his presence in the parlor on a professional footing: he was a client and she the masseuse. She felt she knew what was expected of her, though the knowledge did nothing to lessen her fear. She asked him to change and averted her head as he stripped to his underwear.

She said, "Aapka naam, sir?"

"Rumi, I mean Ramesh."

"Aap Mohammedan hai?"

"No."

"My name is Zoya."

"Zoya."

"Zoya Shaukat Ali, Mohammedan."

"One minute, Zoya, I asked for your name?"

"Ji, nahi."

"Then why tell me? You think I care? Why you asked if I'm Mohammedan?"

"Aapka naam, sir. Sorry."

"My name is Ramesh. Understand?"

"Haan, ji."

"You have coconut oil?"

"Ji, sir."

"Take this off, and this, put oil. Go on, put more, more."

"Ji, sir."

"You smell bad."

"Ji?"

"Your sweat smells bad, in fact it's horrible. Why is that?"

"Nahi, sir."

"Tell me why."

"Nahi."

"Because you eat too much meat."

"I, no, sir, I don't eat too much."

"Not no, sir. Yes, sir."

"Yes, sir."

"Smell me. Go on. You see? No bad odor. Why? Because I eat only pure vegetarian. Use both hands. Don't touch my nipples," said Rumi.

The girl said, "Handshake left hand se hotha hai, right se khana katha hai, sir."

"Right, left, you think you're Hindu? Use the other hand, use both hands."

He stared at her in disbelief and when he finger-fucked her she cried, *ma, ma, ma,* like a small goat.

THE ANNEX was a big room with a high ceiling and folding chairs instead of pews. NA meetings were held there and so was the weekly old people's meeting. It was a large space with nothing in it except faded red matting and a cross on the wall, just the cross, no figure. First there was an introduction by Father Fo, the man who had allowed Safer to open a center in his church. He appeared in the press and on TV because of his work with addicts and the elderly. Each year, during the fair, his name appeared in letters that were only slightly smaller than the letters that announced the festivities. First, Father Fo got up to sing "Lead, Kindly Light" in an unexpected baritone. The boys in camo joined him on harmony. When the hymn came to an end, Father Fo thanked the singers, who went back to their seats. Then he said, it gives me great pleasure to introduce a young man who I hope will grace us with more occasions such as this. Soporo took his time going up to the stage. He waited until there was complete silence. Then he looked around at his audience and said, I have a question for you and a confession and, to end, a lament. There was some scattered applause from the row of Safer boys but Soporo looked down at his hands and it stopped.

He said he had come to the meeting with an outline in his head of a talk concerning music and time, but, as he looked around the room, he realized it was an irrelevant topic that would interest no one, or not for more than five minutes, and later, if they remembered it at all, they would remember it as a kind of silly puzzle. Again he stopped and looked at his hands as if he'd forgotten something. I think we have more important things to talk about today, he said. And then he talked about what freedom meant, that is, the play of free will as opposed to habits of the body, like smoking or injecting heroin. At the word *heroin* there was a slight change in the room, as if every member of the audience had taken a deep breath or shifted in their seats. I want to start with a question. Is it true that taking heroin is an example of free will at its most powerful? I believe there is a good case for this argument. All users know how addictive the drug is, and dangerous. OD, infection, crime, we know we're risking our lives and yet we choose to do it. Here Soporo paused and stared at the boys of Safer, or at a point just behind them, as if he was reading from a teleprompter, and his argument took a sidelong tangent. He mentioned a commentator who said it was the painkilling nature of the drug that made it so addictive, that if scientists were to isolate and neutralize its painkilling element it could be taken with no fear of addiction. But why hasn't a scientist already done this thing, synthesize a version of the drug that would provide only pleasure, that is to say, pleasure with no payback? Because then the scientist would be entering into the realm of ethics, into god's realm, he would remove evil and leave only good, or, to put it another way, he'd remove the devil and leave only god, and this is something no government or religious institution will condone, much less pay for.

The system depends on the idea of consequences for one's actions, and consequences, as most of us know, is simply another word for the devil. But I want to talk a little bit about God. I want to remind you of the shock and fear that God felt when he realized he was not the only god of the world. How do we know he knew? I am a jealous God and there is no other God beside me, he told the angels, and by so doing indicated that there were indeed other gods, or why would he be jealous? And as long as there is jealousy, how can there be freedom? And if God is not free how can man expect to be? Excuse me, Soporo said, and walked slowly to his chair. He took a bottle of water out of his satchel and came back to the stage, which was a clear area in front of the room. There was no pulpit or microphone. He took a drink of water and swallowed carefully and placed the bottle on the ground by his feet. He said it was possible that some day a scientist would take up the good work, but until then heroin would remain utterly addictive. Then he said, the interesting thing is that we choose it, despite everything we choose it and continue to choose it. Is this an example of free will in action?, that's my question. And, secondly: are addicts free? Are they in fact the freest of men?

HE TOOK A CAB to Rajesh Khanna Park and kept it waiting while he went into the Tamil slum known as Murugan Chawl and bought a five-gram pack. The woman who sold him the smack had a baby at her breast and he sat on the floor and snorted a quick line off his wrist and then he made a joint. His ass immediately tightened and he felt better, or better than better, best, infinitely best. The woman was telling him about her brother who used to run the family's heroin trade but had died from TB and drugs. Two of her brothers-in-law were dead from mysterious illnesses that she attributed to garad heroin,

and her husband, also a garaduli, had fallen off a train earlier that
year, leaving her with two kids, etc., etc., etc. The lament slid from
his head like rain and he stared at her breasts, or breast, since only
the single one was visible, one pathetic tit being suckled by the vampire baby leech that was fattening as he watched. It was less than a
year old and its greasy black hair was plastered to its forehead and it
had the face of an old sow, and its future was written on its forehead:
fatherless childhood, adolescence of petty crime, garad or alcohol
in his late teens, more crime, illness, the usual ending. Why did you
have another baby? he asked the woman. You have no money, your
husband was a garaduli, and you already have one mouth to feed,
why another? The woman's face was oily and her oily black hair
was tied with a rubber band. She took the baby from her breast and
held it to him. Hold him and you'll know, she said. He saw a drop
of off-white milk on her black nipple. She smiled shyly and pulled
the blouse down to cover herself and only then did he look at the
thing in his hands. When the baby's eyes met his, it began to cry. He
wanted to shake its misshapen dwarf hand, because the reaction was
the first sign of intelligence he'd seen all day. He held it away from his
body and examined it, the color, untouchable, and the smell, ripe,
a nauseating mix of talcum powder and Parachute coconut oil. He
wanted to take it with him, but how? And what would be a fitting
reward to the mother in lieu of her blighted offspring, how many rupees, a thousand, two? Something of what he was feeling must have
communicated itself to the woman by a kind of aboriginal voodoo.
Give it to me, she said. Give, give. The baby was crying in earnest
now, its mouth wide and its eyes closed tight, and he was impressed
by the amount of noise it produced. He knew the mother was moments away from shouting for help and then, in an instant, the male
members of her criminal clan would be at the door. He gave the

baby back and stepped out of the room and walked along the open gutter to the street. In each of the hovels he passed a woman was cooking while her husband drank country liquor and their children puked or pissed in the approximate vicinity of the gutter. He negotiated small piles of watery shit and imagined a great firebomb that would end the poverty and desolation of Murugan Chawl, a big beautiful explosion that would engulf the entire slum and blow its inhabitants straight into the next world. Smiling now, he felt ready to take on the fuckers at the rehab, but first he had to make one last stop and he'd forgotten all about the cabbie, who was still waiting, pacing near his fucked-up piece-of-caca Fiat. Chalo, he told the man, who got in the car without whining, and he directed him to Bandra East, to the slum near the station, so poor it didn't have a name, where he picked up a gram of Charlie and treated himself to a quick equalizing line—or three.

SOPORO SAID HE WANTED to make a confession. He took a few steps around the stage, distractedly, like a sick man, then he picked up the bottle and took another careful sip. Instead of a confession he made a joke. He said when he looked around the room at the sinners and the saints, the young and the old, he knew that as far as confessions went his was no big one. But here it is anyway, he said, because after all I'm in the right place for it. Then he explained that he was an uneducated man, or, if not exactly uneducated, certainly unschooled. When he was growing up in China he had every opportunity to study but he chose instead to work and eventually came to India with the intention of solving the mystery of what had happened during the last days of his ancestor, a Muslim Chinese admiral who died here. Instead of solving one problem he found another, he became an addict and he got lost in Bombay. But even in the lost years, or decades, he was reading. What did he read? Whatever came his way; he was unsystematic. He had no discipline and he could afford not to, after all he was not aiming to be a scholar. He read because it gave him instant gratification in a way nothing else did, and, as was the case with all addicts, gratification was the important thing. He liked history, travel, anthropology, cookbooks (which he read in the same way he read other books, for pleasure); he liked books with specialized information. At the moment, he was reading about a thirteenth-century poet who invented a particular poetic form, a form that was so difficult, so fiendish, that subsequent poets rarely attempted more than one example in their entire lifetimes, and almost no one wrote three or more, and this was still the case some seven hundred years after it was invented. The poem consisted of five stanzas of twelve lines each and a last stanza of five lines, with a strict, tremendously intricate rhyme scheme in which the rhyme wasn't the sound of a word's ending but the word in its entirety. In each stanza the rhyme words were repeated a certain number of times in a pattern that varied (though even the variations were strict) over the course of the poem. And though there were sixty-five lines there were only five rhyme words, imagine, which meant the poet had to be as inventive as possible beneath the strict framework of the form. For example, said Soporo, writing with his finger on an imaginary blackboard, this is how the rhymes occur in the first stanza:

a

b

a

a

c

a
a
d
d
a
e
e.

In the next stanza the e rhyme takes first place:

e
a
e
e
b
e
e
c
c
e
d
d.

And in the third stanza the d rhyme takes first place and so on until the final stanza, when each of the words occurs once, for the last time. The arrangement and rearrangement of rhyme words allows each to be first among equals, even if it's for one stanza only. It's as ingenious a form as any you can name and certainly more demanding than most. Here, Soporo stopped and raised both hands in the air as if he was placating an angry mob. He said, okay, okay, bear with me for a moment. The point is this: why did the poet invent such a difficult form? Did he have nothing better to do? Was he some kind of curmudgeon who wanted to make a difficult art more difficult still? Or was he simply perverse, which he must have been to some extent, after all he was a poet, and a good one. When asked, the poet said at first that he didn't belong to those who may be asked after their whys. Then he said he wanted to make a form that was akin to wrapping himself in chains, because within the prison of the form it was pure exhilaration and freedom to write such a poem. So, there's freedom and there's freedom. Now, said Soporo, here's my confession. I may take heroin again. I may do it tonight, when you've all gone home and I'm alone in my room, reading a book and drinking tea, or not even reading, just looking out the window at the street and the cars going by. I don't smoke, I don't drink, I don't take drugs, and I live alone. I look at the cars that are full of people and I look at my hands and wonder what to do with them and it's a possibility, it's always a possibility that I'll go out and catch a cab and take it to a place I know. I may do it and I may not. Either way, I'm free to make a choice because it affects no one else in the world except myself, and that, friends, is the happy and unadorned truth of the matter.

SOPORO SAID he was tired. He would have liked to talk for longer but he got tired quickly these days. He said there was just one last thing he wanted to do before they called the meeting to an end. He wanted to say something about planned obsolescence. The first English movie he saw was in 1979 or 1980 at Eros, which at the time was Bombay's grandest movie theater, located near Churchgate Station, as they all knew, and if they didn't they certainly should. The movie was set in Los Angeles in the not distant future, in fact, in the near future. As far as he could remember, it was about a corporation that made highly intelligent fighting machines, human-looking creatures built to self-destruct after a few years, five years, or four, because the corporation, being a corporation, was run by paranoid bureaucrats who didn't want a race of superbeings running around the planet. As the time grows closer to their annihilation, the brilliant killer machines, blessed or cursed with human sweetness and human rage, become desperate. They decide to find the head of the corporation, their creator, the god who made them in his imagined image, though in reality he is nothing like them, he is unbeautiful, intellectual, distant. They dream up a way to enter the fortress in which he lives and persuade him to reverse the death sentence embedded in their cells, the sentence of accelerated decrepitude, as they call it. This is defiance and the viewer sitting in his seat feels some of their exhilaration as the humanoids call their god to task. But even god cannot change their fate; once written it is irreversible. The leader of the renegades speaks softly to his maker. I want more life, father, he says. Then he kisses him and crushes his skull, as sons tend to do to their fathers. The group of beautiful machines dies one by one until only the leader is left, the most beautiful and dangerous of them all, and when it's his time to die he makes an unexpected gesture of mercy. He allows the detective who has been hunting him to live, the venal human detective who has killed his lover and his friends, who has pursued them and shown no mercy, he allows this killer to live, saves him in fact, because at the last moment, as he sees his own life come to a close, he gives in to sentimentality. And which viewer does not feel a little of his torment? Here Soporo paused and his gaze wandered around the room and settled on the cross, as if he had never before seen such a strange object, and he repeated the words *planned obsolescence.* I wonder, said Soporo, if you've heard the phrase before, because I saw it recently and now I don't remember where. But the idea is that companies design products with a short life, like the pretty computers I see these days, with the shiny logos, the biblical half-eaten fruit and so on, pretty objects that are built to self-destruct, so you buy another in a few years, and another and another, and in that way you feed the insect empire, the insects in their insect suits, thinking insect thoughts with their sexed-up insect brains. Yes, and finally, Soporo said, to end, he would make two points. First, nothing he'd said that day was original or new, they were ideas he'd picked up from the air, from things people said or didn't say, from shreds collected long ago or a moment earlier, collective, shared notions or emotions. Second, he wanted to suggest an antidote to obsolescence, planned or not, and to decrepitude, accelerated or otherwise. His idea was a group lament, a gong, which, in China, meant something collective or shared. The lament he had in mind was a short one, and how could it be otherwise?, since no lament could be long enough to express the grief of the world. His suggestion was that each person spend a few minutes thinking about the people they'd lost, those boys and girls and men and women who had been taken by garad heroin, and that they say the names of their dead ones, say them quietly or aloud, it didn't matter, but say the whole name, because that was the way to do it, say the whole name and remember, that was the way to honor the dead.

THERE WAS A TIME, even after he'd moved into two small rooms at the rectory, when he was at Safer almost every day. Now he went only three times a week, for meetings and for housekeeping, to settle accounts, buy provisions, medicine, clothes and linen, and to fix problems when they arose. He was a kind of liaison between Father Fo and whoever was in charge of the day-to-day, which would be Bull. The arrangement left him free to do whatever he felt like, which, lately, wasn't much. He was on the terrace talking to Charlotte the cook, telling her the same things he'd been saying for months, repeating them as if she was a child, which she most decidedly was not. Use less oil, he told her. Don't overcook. When you're cooking prawns put them in last and turn off the flame. Do what the Chinese do, high heat, bite-sized pieces, a couple of minutes of cooking and— Charlotte, are you hearing any of this? And that was when Bull asked to see him. They took a stroll around the terrace while Charlotte chopped the veggies and marinated the meat and washed rice. It's about the new turkey, said Bull. He'd run away the day before, taken off while they were on their way to Soporo's lecture and now he was back asking to be let in. The guy was a hard case, an asshole, part of the prison rehab experiment, Bull said, and he should be taught a lesson. Bull thought they should let him stew, let him spend a couple of days on the street and he'd return a changed man. Otherwise, he was going to be a lot of trouble, he was going to be more trouble than he was worth, Bull could smell it. Soporo grinned suddenly. He said, suppose I'd said that about you when you first turned up here? Do you remember what an asshole you were? Bull said, you can't save everybody, you know. Some souls are beyond saving. They went down to the third floor, where Rumi was waiting on the other side of the staircase gate. He was nodding out on the steps. He opened his eyes when he heard Soporo and Bull, but he didn't get up. I would let you in, said Soporo, but I'm told that it may not be a good idea. Rumi looked Soporo in the eyes and said, please let me in. I give you my word it won't happen again. I don't believe you, said Bull. You're not making the decisions here, said Rumi. You see? Bull told Soporo. You see what I mean? The guy's beyond rehab, we're wasting our time. Rumi said, Mr. Soporo, I give you my word, sir. It won't happen again. This time I won't let you down. Soporo told Bull to open the gate, which was unlocked, and Rumi went up without another word. That day he didn't say much. He ate his meals, did his share of work, slept well. In the following days, too, he seemed changed, as if he'd reconciled to the sober life. Later, after the terrible events that followed had been analyzed and analyzed some more, the inmates remembered how different he'd seemed in those days, how interested he was in everything, in the running of the center, in its history, in Soporo's personal story. It was inspiring, he said, so inspiring that he wanted to know everything about the man. Then, three days later, he did it again, disappeared for a night and a day and returned just as dinner was being served.

BULL CALLED SOPORO at the rectory saying Ramesh was back and demanding to be let in, but this time they couldn't do it. There were rules. A prison intake was only allowed the single slip; two, and they were within their rights to send him back to Arthur Road or Yerawada or Tihar or wherever it was he belonged, because one thing was certain, he had no place at Safer. Also, he'd been asking to see Soporo in person, not asking, demanding, as if he was in a restaurant and he wanted to complain to the manager. Bull hadn't allowed him in and he'd gone to the abandoned yards across the street where he'd walked into one of those drainage pipes and no doubt was getting high at that very moment. Bull suggested they wait until morning, then call the authorities and let them take the guy away. We'll see, Soporo replied, and he put down the phone. His back was acting up, had been acting up for days, and he felt like he was coming down with something, a cold maybe, and he put aside the book he was looking at and went into the kitchen to make a cup of tea. He put water on to boil and cut ginger into long strips and put half a lemon into the squeezer. He poured the hot water into a big cup, dunked and removed a bag of Ceylon tea, added the ginger and lemon and took the cup with him into the living room, where he measured a teaspoon of honey from a small bottle on the dining table. He sat in his chair by the window and looked for the moon above the rooftops and though he couldn't see it he thought he saw its reflection in a building window. He looked around the room as he took a sip of the tea. It was small and unpretentious: on the floor were books stacked against the wall, because he had never gotten around to having shelves made, and there were postcards taped to the mirror and money plants in glass bottles and plenty of light (the apartment faced east) and some air. It was a quiet place; in Father Fo's words, "serene and modest." He took another sip and winced a little, there was too much lemon. He thought: I'll be sorry to leave here.

HE PUT ON his shoes and took a stick with him, because at night the streets belonged to the dogs. As he left the church, walking quickly in the dark, he banged into someone, who fell to the road shouting, aiee, aiee, my foot. Who is it? Devil, devil. Then he recognized Tara or Sitara, who swept and swabbed the church and helped Charlotte in the kitchen. She said, forgive me, Father Onar, I didn't know it was you. Please forgive me. Where are you going at this hour? As he helped her to her feet and assured her he was fine, he told her not to call him father, but he had said this to her many times before and he had no doubt she would forget the words as soon as she heard them. Soporo came out of the church grounds and walked away from the main road towards Bandra East. After a while he saw the drainage pipes, a dozen of them, giant pipes spread haphazardly around the periphery of the yard, and then he heard someone singing and followed the voice. He could make out only some of the words. A man with a beautiful house, a beautiful wife, and a beautiful car wakes up one day and realizes that none of his prized possessions belong to him. The song was disjointed and out of key until Rumi came to what sounded like the chorus, something about living in a big womb. He was sitting at the lip of the pipe with paraphernalia spread around him, a candle, a box of wax matches and a lighter, vials with caps of different colors, half a dozen loose cigarettes, and silver foil. When he saw Soporo he got to his feet, though he continued singing for a minute. After a while, Rumi said, Mr. Soporo, sir, how nice of you to grace my humble abode with your famous presence. Please sit if you can find somewhere that's not too shabby. Oh, I almost forgot, you're no stranger to shab-biness, are you? Then Rumi smiled, or tried to smile. He said, I knew you'd come. I know who you are. Soporo said, no, you don't. I knew as soon as I saw you, said Rumi. And I knew you'd come. I even know what you're going to do next. You're going to let me come back to Safer and stay as long as I want. If I ask for money you're going to give it to me. You're going to let me do whatever in other words the fuck I feel like. You know why? Soporo found a concrete block in the yard's debris. He sat down and sneezed. He said, tell me why. Because you don't judge, you never did. You accept everything without condemnation. Why do you think I told you those things? You were like a doctor or priest, never surprised by anything, least of all what people did. I knew you'd never tell, so I told you. I left out things of course. Then Rumi told Soporo some of the things he'd left out. For instance, he said, he'd left out the story about the insane woman who lived under Grant Road Bridge, the lice-infested crazy woman with her lice-infested baby. So inadequate, he said, everything. I mean, what can you say about such a baby? What can be said about the mother? Then he pretended to think. And who else? Yes, a beggar woman on Arab Gully. She wanted to die, begged me to kill her, and I wouldn't, because I hadn't appointed myself god's executioner. And then I did, because. It was my social service. So, the question is, what's the worst that can be said about me—that I put two or three people out of their misery? By the way, I'd do the same for you, but what would be the point? You're already dead. He sat down and soon he was nodding so low that his head touched the ground. Soporo got up at last and went to him. He saw a rapid pulse beating in Rumi's throat. A crow squawked somewhere nearby; at that time of night it was an unexpected sound. There was a smell of burning, garbage or leaves, and a plane passed overhead, flying incredibly low. Soporo looked at Rumi and thought, how easy it would be.

BOOK FOUR

SOME USES OF
REINCARNATION

A Large Accumulation
of Small Defeats

I returned to the city in stages. I flew into Delhi and, some days later, took a train to Bombay. I spent most of the final leg standing by the door of the Rajdhani Express and watching the countryside fall past. Late in the night, a shape staggered up to me. His face was wet with blood and pockmarked with smallpox scars and though his mouth was moving I heard no words. Then I realized that the stains were paan, long spatters on his chin and shirt. He wiped his mouth and fell backwards into the compartment. There was silence in the corridor but only for a minute. The door opened again and this time he made it all the way to the sink, where he gripped the sides and bent into the small space between the mirror and the drain to retch into the bowl. I went into the compartment and climbed into my bunk. I fell in and out of sleep. I met Rumi in a dead man's bar; I imagined I heard gamblers whisper good-luck theorems, complex prayers for the winning of money; I thought I saw the painter Xavier, drinking Martinis and losing money to Dimple, who wore a gold tooth and eye patch and had an opium pipe dangling between her legs, and to each of the painter's

questions she made the same reply, that the city was a large accumu-
lation of small defeats, nothing more, and each new arrival to the
city brought his own minuscule contribution to the inexhaustible
pile. I could not understand a thing. Much later, when I went into
the corridor, the pockmarked man was still there, still gripping the
sink and examining himself in the mirror. Now I understood what
he was saying. Sick, he said, I'm sick, which he was, unquestionably.

I DREAMED it was twenty years earlier, in 1984, and I was in Colaba.
There was a blackout in the city and I kept hearing the cries of small
children. I went into a restaurant favored by Bombay's Nigerians
and my friend was sitting in the back room drinking vodka shots
and beer. Candles burned in a row on the bar. I took a stool and
said it was good to see him. Where had he been for twenty years?
Rumi laughed for a long time. This is the past, he said, not the present. Then he said, I died. Didn't you hear? He laughed some more,
softly, as if to himself. I said, What happened to you when you died?
He shook his head. I don't know why you bother, he said. It's not
like you'll do anything about it. You'll just go on pretending. You
should ask yourself why: is it because you have no imagination or
because it's the only way you can bear the thought of extinction?
To be honest with you, I have no idea why you do it, but you do, all
of you, pretend this life is forever. His eyes were half closed and in
the candlelight his face was red. He said, but that isn't what I came
here to tell you. He tried to catch the bartender's attention. I asked
him to tell me whatever he wanted to tell me, because I'd come a
long way to hear it. He banged on the bar top and asked for a frozen vodka shot and a beer back. He said: when I was a high-caste

Hindu I beat my wife once or twice a month, did you know that? Sometimes with my slipper and sometimes with my hand; I had to teach her the inevitability of obedience. I knew my duty even if she did not. And what was my duty, my difficult duty, which, to begin with, I performed reluctantly, though not without a certain excitement? To teach those who were born from the belly button of the lord, from the hip and thigh of the lord, from lower down, from the lord's unmentionable parts, from his nether regions, his Africas and South Americas, from his unnamable parts that may not be spoken of without grave risk to the speaker. I tried to teach the lowborn that there is more to the world, immeasurably more than the little they knew. I wanted to teach them radiance and humility, also endurance. I tried to teach my wife and the other women, the lowborn women I favored, the cunts into which I put my wheat-complexioned penis, because I wanted to teach them and also because I liked it. Do you know why I came to this bar? To tell you this, to tell you I beat my wife with my slipper and my open hand. I beat her till she liked it too. Do you hear me? And now that I've told you may I go? I said, wait, why are you telling me this? I don't have a wife. Rumi looked at me and laughed. He said, you don't understand a thing. Then he pulled a stone out of his cowboy boot, a flat black stone that had been sharpened to a dull point. Pathar, he said. But that's not it, or not exactly. Then he drank his shot and finished his beer and walked out of the bar and I sat where I was until I woke up on a train traversing the Indian plains.

LATE IN THE NIGHT, I went to the door and manhandled it open. I watched my shadow in a yellow rectangle of light as it slid past the fields into the early dawn. When the train stopped at Kurla, it was raining and I was ragged with sleeplessness. I broke a rule and accepted the first ride to come my way. On the highway, the driver left the motor running to buy a mouthful of tobacco and white paste. He said, okay, which way do you want to go, the highway or the inner road? It's completely up to you. I understood that it was a way of testing my knowledge of the city. Depending on which route I chose he'd know if I was a first-timer (and he could cheat me a lot) or an old Bombay hand (and he could cheat me only a little). It was early but the streets were full of people. The walkers were out, in their ugly new shoes and branded tracksuits. Men in green overalls swept the street and there was a garbage truck nearby, and it occurred to me that in all the years I'd lived in Bombay this was the first time I'd seen a garbage truck or city workers in overalls. A trio of Jain nuns crossed a bridge on foot, single file, in white robes and head coverings. They carried staffs and small white bundles. With what belongings were the bundles filled? Their slippers and masks were made of thin white cotton and were no protection against the pollution, which was fierce. But it wasn't for protection against the world that the nuns wore their masks; it was to protect the world from their own small mistakes. When I arrived at my address, the rickshawwallah's meter was double and a half what it should have been. The meter was covered in black plastic that was hard to see through and impossible to remove. I paid and picked up my bags and stepped into the city. I was soaked through in minutes. Dom, I said, welcome, welcome to Bombay.

I SUPPOSE it was a homecoming. I found a place to rent and moved in a few weeks later, when the worst of the monsoons had passed, though it continued to rain every day. It was around the corner from the Bandra building in which I'd lived almost a decade earlier. The apartment was the smallest I'd ever seen. It came with a washing machine and no fridge, cooking spices and no dining table. The saucepan was extra small; it held two cups of water, no more. The stove top had two burners. There was a collapsible couch, a bookcase, a steel Godrej almirah, an armchair, a kitchenette, a bathroom, all squeezed into three hundred square feet of space. In a week I was hooked up and settled and it was as if I had never left. The city had changed, but it was still a conglomeration of slums on which high-rises had been built. There were new highways but all they did was speed you from one jam to the next. Everything was noise and frenzy, a constant beat, like house music without the release. One night I took a rickshaw home. Stuck in a jam on Hill Road, I watched a man work the traffic. He was splayed on all fours, his hunchback exaggerated for effect. The spot was a crossroads of bars and restaurants, with shopping arcades on two sides and a hospital. It was incredibly busy, a long snarl of stop and go, and the hunchback worked it calmly, juggling simultaneous bits of information: make of vehicle, type of passenger, access route between scooter and rickshaw, availability of traffic island. He crawled to the window of a new car and I saw his mouth move. Then he held out his hand and a child's fingers appeared holding a note. He took the money and hump-walked away, but instead of trying one of the other cars he came to my rickshaw. When I shook my head, the man smiled. Yaar, long time, he said in Hindi. Remember me from Rashid's? I remembered: on the street they called him Spiderman.

"Shankar, are you okay?"

"Very okay, boss. I got married, bought a house." He looked surprised. Then he said, "I gave up garad."

The lights had changed but the driver made no move to start his rickshaw, he seemed fascinated by the Spiderman. Around us, Bandra honked and stalled. From a rickshaw, the city was all exhaust, face-level and toxic. Shankar asked if I was going to see Rashid. I hadn't thought about it, but all of a sudden the question, so casually spoken, seemed very important. Say hello to him from me, Shankar said. I can't do it in person. I go down there I may not come back. You know how it is.

2.

The Citizen

The driver had a cricket match going on the radio, India vs. Pakistan turned up loud. On the way to Rashid's, for an hour and a half in the lunchtime traffic, I listened to the old Hindu-Muslim sibling anxieties recycled in the guise of expert commentary. I got off at the junction of Shuklaji Street and Arab Gully and caught a quick savor of change. New blocks loomed at the Bombay Central end of the street, short glass-and-steel buildings that seemed to have come up overnight. The brothels and drug dens were gone. In their place were hundreds of tiny cubicles or storefronts, each indistinguishable from the next. The street itself was as cramped and ramshackle as ever, but there was a McDonald's on the corner and a mini mall and supermarkets, and I knew it was only a matter of time before the rest of the neighborhood followed. I walked around the street for many dazed minutes. Then I realized I was standing in front of it. The entryway had been bricked up. You had to go around the side and there it was, Rashid's old khana, now become an office space. There were plywood partitions and desks under tube lighting and young men and women sat at terminals and spoke into headsets. A television in the corner was tuned to a news channel and a boy in a blue uniform went around with tea. The old washing area, with its tin barrels and open drain, had been converted into a kitchenette with two tiny sinks and a miniature fridge. A man sat in a cubicle to the left where the balcony had been. It was the only private space in the room and his was the only desk with a computer and printer. He clicked off his screen and stood up.

"You are?"

"Looking for Rashid, he used to own this place. Do you know where I can find him?"

"Not here. You can leave your number on that pad and I'll ask him to call you."

A small group gathered around us.

"Look, can you tell him an old friend is here to see him? I won't take much of his time."

"You have to give me your name, old friend, some information, otherwise he won't see you."

"Tell him I was a regular here in the old days and I've come a long way to pay my respects."

I saw something flicker, an involuntary something triggered by a word I'd said or a cadence. He motioned to a chair but I stayed where I was. The others dispersed and Jamal and I stood facing each other like cowboys in a chapatti Western. He drew first. Yes, I'm Jamal, he said, and his hand was slack and gripless. I asked if his father still lived upstairs. He hesitated. Then he said, my father is no longer in the drug business. Are you sure you want to see him?

THE OFFICE WORKERS did several things at once, their accents full of the new intonations of cable TV and recognizable anywhere in the world, America via *Friends* and *Seinfeld*. Two women sat at adjoining desks and discussed a client. She has a long-assed name, four syllables, said one. What, said the other, like Gonsalves? No, said the first, four sill-a-bells, like O-Doh-her-tee, and I'm like, shorten it, bitch. The second woman said, call her Doh. Yeah-ah, said the first, I know what to call her. They laughed and looked at me and stopped laughing. I caught a glimpse of myself in a mirror tacked to one of the walls. I carried a red leather bag with a change of clothes. I had keys to a borrowed room in the suburbs. I had a notebook and cell phone and money and I had no reason to be there. When Jamal returned, he'd exchanged his white business shirt for a kurta and skullcap. On his feet were jutis I'd never seen in Bombay, dark camel skin, the tips curled in a huge arc.

He said, "My father is busy, he isn't meeting anyone."

"He'll want to see me. I was a friend."

"You were a customer. He had many customers and they all thought they were his friends. It was business, but he wasn't good at it."

"Jamal, you don't like it, I know, but your father is my friend. Can I see him?"

"Sit down and have tea. We'll discuss, then we'll see."

HE SAID: "You're Dom Ullis. We used to call you Doom or Dum, for 'Dum Maro Dum,'" and he sang the line from the movie. "Sometimes I called you Damned Ullis because of the things you said. I'm older now. People my age don't take our culture lightly. We're not as tolerant as our fathers. But do you remember? You said religion wasn't important." It surprised me that he remembered a conversation from so many years ago, remembered it as clearly as if it had just occurred. He recalled the exact words Rashid and I had exchanged and forgotten. It was as if he was still hearing them in his head. He said: "Do you know what my father told me when I was a child? He said we were descended from the Mughals. I should never forget it and I should carry myself with pride. I did some reading: I studied what the Mughals brought to India, their inventions, the ice and running water and planned gardens to soothe eye and spirit. But what do Indians remember? Only the pyramid of skulls. They say, see how bloodthirsty the Muslims were: even then they liked to kill." I told Jamal there was a difference between him and the Mughals, because the Mughals loved life and poetry and beauty. I said, "What do you love except death?" For some reason, my words pleased him. We moved to his desk, where he took his seat and stared at the computer. The room was full of moisture. I sat in the visitor's chair and wiped my neck with my hands.

"You see what they're doing in Afghanistan?"

"Who doesn't? It's on the news every day."

"But do you see? And Iraq? They take ancient Babylon and they fortify it, they make it a restricted area, and all the time they are excavating, excavating. They find things that belong to history and they destroy them or steal them."

"Yes."

"Think if someone did it in Washington, D.C., or Chicago or New York, burned down the libraries, stole antiques, bombed cities and towns. What would happen?"

"We'd never hear the end of it."

"In two years there would be twenty books and movies about it; that is what would happen."

HE WAS SILENT for a time. On a board near the computer was a picture of Jamal and a young woman in a burka. Farheen, my fiancée, he said, when he saw me looking at the picture. Love marriage. She's older than me by two years. Then he said, one minute, and shouted across the room to a man who was playing a game of bridge on his terminal. The man left the game and came over.

"This is Kumar, Hindu Brahmin. Many of my friends are Brahmins. Kumar has never touched meat in his life."

Kumar said, "Oh, don't talk about meat. I always say animals have more right to exist on the planet than we do."

Jamal asked Kumar to order more tea for us, dismissing him. Now that he'd shown off his girlfriend, his Brahmin, his urbanity, he could return to his subject.

"Anybody can become a suicide bomber if they are pushed far enough. Some of my radical friends say they could easily go in that direction. We, I mean, they," he paused to smile, to let me know he was joking, "they would do it only if they had no other option. You know what they say? There's always something to look forward to if you become a CP." Again he smiled, and said, "Citizen of Paradise."

"What are the attractions of paradise for a man like you? You're not powerless and angry."

HE SAID, I went to a Christian college and my friends are Hindu but I'm Muslim through and through. My father wanted me to get a good education. He chose the best college he could afford, he didn't care which community ran it. I was one of only four Muslim students. The professors were Hindus and Catholics. One day the mathematics professor found me reading a magazine during his lecture. He slapped me in front of the whole class. He said, who do you people think you are? Why are you in India? You should be carrying out jihad in Afghanistan. Then, during the riots, a mob pulled me off my cycle. I wasn't wearing a skullcap. I spoke in Marathi, but still they didn't let me go. I was very young. I broke down. I saw the hijra woman, my father's kaamwali. She was wearing a dress like a Christian. I pointed at her and called her Ma.

I said, Dimple.

He said, how do you think these things made me feel? Powerful? My father made us read the holy book every night. Do you know that about him? Every night: one or two suras. He'd come home stoned out of his head and make me read some verses while his eyes were drooping and drool fell out of his mouth. Jamal stopped, as if he'd run out of words. There was silence for a time. Then he looked at his watch and stood up. He said, my father was an addict. He was addicted to everything. He's become himself now. Go up. He's on the first floor.

NEW BEIGE PAINT coated the walls but the staircase and the banisters were scuffed wood. I went up, past a locked door on the half landing. The door on the first floor was open and a light was burning in the hall but otherwise the house was dim. Rashid sat in an armchair by an open window and the only noises in the room came from the courtyard below, where children were playing. Their voices echoed against the walls, high voices ringing with fury. He stared out the window but there was no sign that he saw or heard anything. There was a crocheted white skullcap on his head and he was counting prayer beads. I was surprised by his thinness, the expression of unreachability on his face, and by the clothes he was wearing, a blue shirt and new black trousers, Rashid, whose color had always been white.

Rashidbhai? I said. He flinched and looked wildly around the room. I introduced myself. I said I had been away for many years and had returned only recently. I said it was a pleasure to see him and introduced myself again and the stiffness left his posture.

"All that was a long time ago."

He had given up drugs and become a thin man. But he'd lost more than weight. There was nothing about him that was recognizable to me. He'd gotten thin and his charisma was gone.

"How are you?"

He nodded. Then, changing his mind, he shook his head to indicate he wasn't well, or that he didn't know how he was, or that he didn't care. A girl came in with tea.

"I often think of those days, when your khana was the best in the city. Some people said in the country."

"Useless. It was my mistake, that stupid business."

"Not such a big mistake. At least you're still here."

"I'm not here."

"Dimple?" I asked.

"Dead."

"Bengali?"

"Dead."

"Rumi?"

"Dead."

"And yourself?" I said. "Alive?"

He was already drained by the conversation. He blinked at me, meeting my eyes for a moment. Then he shook his thin white-bearded cheeks.

"Worse each day. And alive."

The girl came back with a plate of grapes, washed and peeled and set on a white plate. Too much, he said to her. But he reached out his fingers and took some and pushed the plate to me. I took some too. There was silence in the room.

I said, "What happened to Dimple?"

The girl offered more grapes.

"No, no, no," he said.

HE LOCKED UP the office. He picked up his phone and keys and went up. His father was sitting in his room with the fan off and the window open, doing, as far as he could see, absolutely nothing. He sat all day in the same position, staring out the window. Sometimes Jamal heard him talking to himself, very softly, as if he didn't want to be overheard. His father left the room only occasionally, sometimes for a walk, sometimes to the apartment on the half landing where the kaamwali used to live. What he did in the apartment Jamal couldn't imagine. The place was full of junk and mold and things that needed to be thrown away. Jamal went into his own room and washed his face and neck at the sink. He picked up a towel and thought of Farheen, of her tummy fat, which never failed to excite him. She wore burkas that she designed herself, patterned burkas cut like a lab coat, tight around the hips and belly. She reminded him of his father's kaamwali. Once, in a guesthouse in Lonavla, he came so many times that he wanted to keep count. Number seven, he said, what do you think of that? I wish you also thought of pleasuring me a little, Farheen replied. Sometimes I wish you were older, or that you acted older. To this he said nothing, because he was the age he was, younger than her by two years, and there was nothing he could do to change it. When he thought about it, about her calm appraisal of him as they fucked, the way she kissed him, the way nothing he did surprised her, as if she'd been fucked many times by many men, and the fact that she never talked about marriage though she was a spinster of twenty-five, already older than his sisters when they'd been married, and when he brought it up all she would say was that he wasn't ready—it maddened him, it made him want to own her. He ran his fingers through his hair and checked his shave and then he turned off the lights and went out.

RASHID WAS IN his room, thinking about indifference. He and his son rarely spoke because conversation was Jamal's weapon, a way to antagonize his father. He said whatever came into his head, or, more likely, things that had never entered his head before, strange turns of phrase with no relation to reality. The last time they spoke, Rashid had complained about household finances. He'd said that Jamal was not putting enough aside for unforeseen future occurrences. Jamal's reply: Who gives a shit about all that? Tell the future to go fuck itself. At that point, the conversation had come to an end and Rashid had returned to his apartment, where he'd picked up his prayer beads and gone to his armchair and wondered if some types of communication were better achieved without words. Communication between animals, for example, was wordless and highly effective. Perhaps communication between father and son should be the same, mostly silent. He thought of the strange one-word text messages Jamal and his friends sent each other: "gr8" and "rotflmfao" and "ftds." It was as if they didn't care whether they were understood, or they took pleasure in being misunderstood, or they'd decided that the rewards of obscurity outweighed the rewards of clarity. They had distilled communication down to its essence: guttural exclamation, partial understanding, indifference. They did not worry about words and what words meant. They were unmoved by tradition. He thought of the burka-clad teenage girls he saw on the street, openly smoking on their way to or from school. The sight always gave him a small shock. Now it was time to learn something from the young, in this case the usefulness of indifference. Or it was time to relearn it, for it was a lesson he had once known. He went back to his prayers, his thumb and index finger beginning the count. From the courtyard below he heard the sound of children. It was the sound he heard most days, the shouts and cries of small children, a vast army of them, and it seemed to him at those moments that the city was a pen for unchaperoned children, wild boys and girls who were bringing themselves up on their own, begging, stealing, selling, stoning, and that his son was among them, and there was nothing he could do about it because after all this was Bombay and how else could it be?

IT WAS a Saturday night and there was a crowd at the door. The club was couples only, so he'd picked up Farheen and they'd ridden to Juhu, an hour in the traffic and more time waiting at the entrance. After twenty minutes he called a number he'd been given and told the woman who answered that he was there, waiting outside, and he didn't mind leaving if they were full, but he wasn't going to wait any longer. She came down personally, introduced herself as Natasha, and escorted them upstairs. They rode up in a glass elevator fixed to the side of the building. She had an accent he'd never heard before, South American, maybe, and all the way up she was talking on a cell phone, a second phone gripped in her free hand. I'll try, she said. I promise you, I'll try. All the way, for three floors, she repeated the promise. Once they were inside, Natasha vanished. Jamal and Farheen wandered around looking for a table but there was no space anywhere, not in the lounge and not at the bar, and the crowd was thicker than Grant Road Station at rush hour.

"Is it hell?" Farheen whispered, buffeted against him by the crowd.

"No," Jamal said, "it's cocaine."

Which it surely was, a cocaine fantasy directed by a maker of Bollywood extravaganzas, because every surface, wherever he looked, was shiny, the bar tops, the low tables, the armchairs and stools. People brandished new cell phones and laptops, and these devices too were shiny: aluminum or steel or white plastic. The ceiling was hundreds of cylindrical light fixtures that changed color with the beat. Even the toilet tanks had ridges on the side, to keep your drugs safe. He could see it on the faces and smell it in the air, cocaine and MDMA and ecstasy, new drugs for the new Bombay.

The Russian he was supposed to meet was sitting alone in a lounge area near the restrooms, an area designed for men or women who were waiting for their partners. And what were their partners doing? The skinny women and buff men he saw around him looked like they wasted no time on ordinary activities such as pissing and shitting. They took their time in the toilets and returned with sniffles and frozen smiles. The smile on his own face was genuine enough. He knew what he was looking at, a vast opportunity made up of many separate smaller opportunities. He tried not to let his excitement show as he negotiated with the Russian, a big man in a coat who never smiled. They did the deal right there at the table,

Jamal handing the Russian the coke and the Russian giving him cash. Then the man said he was going to try a little taste. Did Jamal want some too? Jamal replied that he didn't do coke because it wired him and if he wanted to be wired he preferred coffee, which was cheaper and more reliable. The Russian looked at him in surprise and said Jamal was probably right but it was a good idea to keep such opinions to himself, since he wouldn't want the word to get out among his customers.

"Are you Russian?" Farheen asked the man.

"Yes, Russian," he replied.

"I never met a Russian before," Farheen told him.

"I'm Boris," said the man, "like Boris Yeltsin, except I don't drink so much."

Farheen said she didn't know who Boris Yeltsin was.

Boris said, "When I was growing up I watched Indian movies, *Awara, Mera Naam Joker*. I like Raj Kapoor."

Farheen didn't know who Raj Kapoor was, and said so.

Jamal smiled and said, "She's never heard of those movies, she's too young."

The Russian didn't smile. He said, "Young or old, you should know Raj Kapoor. He is great Indian artist."

"We have great actors too, have you heard of Dilip Kumar? Great, great, better than Raj Kapoor. You know Dilip Kumar's real name? Guess."

The Russian got up and gathered his cigarettes and cell phone and heavy silver lighter. He hesitated for a minute before he left the table.

"Yusuf," Jamal shouted as the man shouldered his way through the crowd. "Yusuf Khan!"

FARHEEN WAS WEARING JEANS, because he'd asked her to, and her shoes were so high she was almost as tall as he. She said she wanted a drink, because that's what people did when they went to a club, wasn't it? She spoke as if she expected an argument. Get me a nice one, she said, pointing to a black woman in a dress who held a pink cocktail in a long-stemmed glass. When he came back with Farheen's drink, she took a sip and smiled her thanks. She looked at the lights on the ceiling, which turned from gold to blue, and she looked at the crowd of people around them, dancing, or moving where they stood. She asked if he felt bad about giving drugs to people who had never learned how to say no, who were paying for their own destruction. Jamal fixed her with a look. He said, look around, these are my customers. Do you see any Muslims? She said, how do you know there are none here? Look at us, we don't look Muslim but we are. This wasn't strictly true. Jamal had started to grow his beard, though he still shaved his cheeks and upper lip. And though she wasn't wearing a burka, she was covered up, she was decent, which was more than could be said for the women around her, women of many colors and ages, who came alone and danced alone. They danced and watched themselves in the mirrors. Men bought them drinks and told them jokes. They spoke very little Hindi and some English, but they were fluent in unidentifiable other tongues.

"There are no Muslims here," Jamal told her, "which means there's nothing wrong in selling them drugs."

Farheen laughed.

"In fact," she said, "it's your duty."

HE DIDN'T LIKE to dance: it made him feel foolish. Come on, soldier, Farheen said, I'll show you how. If he refused, she would have danced alone. So he let her lead him to the floor. The dance was crazy and beautiful, people of all races and classes, all moving to one beat. Some swayed as if they were too high to stand, others hardly moved, or they moved only their hips. The metallic light fell around him in washes. It was like being on a stage with nobody looking. He felt a woman's breasts against his back, and other bodies against his hips and thighs. Then Farheen kissed him. She put her tongue in his mouth and her lips were cold and wet from the cocktail. They stood absolutely still for a moment, but she pulled away to shout in his ear. Dance, she said, dance or we die.

3.

The Enfolding

I went back the next day and found Rashid in his room, sitting in his chair by the window with the prayer beads in his hands. I asked if he was feeling better.

"I'll never be good or better, I'm past the age for it. Now there's only bad and worse."

I said I had come to pay my respects.

Rashid said, "I'm an old man. I don't want to talk about the old days." But he brought it up himself.

"Garad wrecked everything. If we'd stayed with opium my place would still be open. I'd be making money every day instead of sitting on a chair saying, if, if, if. So many people would be alive, Dimple, even your friend, the crazy one with the hammer. No, maybe not that sisterfucker."

Instead of saying *bhenchodh* like everyone else, Rashid's variation was *bhen ko chodhu*, and the way he said it made the words sound Arabic, a guttural clearing of the throat.

I said, "Rumi."

"Yes, him. Came here with a set of teeth, old dentures in a jam bottle. He said they were Mahatma Gandhi's and tried to sell them to me for ten thousand rupees. I told him, chief, you're a crazy man and this is a chandu khana not a pagal khana. He liked that. He said the dentures were Gandhi's, totally genuine, money back guarantee. He said he got them from a man who got them from a man who stole them from Gandhi's son, the drunk, who was neglected by the father. He said the government would give me a cash reward, saying all this loudly, and people laughing at him. I imagined the newspaper headlines: MUSLIM DRUG TRAFFICKER BUYS GANDHI'S TEETH. I told him to get them out of the khana before there was another riot. So this pagal smokes some garad and goes away. The jam bottle with the teeth, he leaves behind."

The girl came in with a tray of tea and biscuits.

He said, "Years later I went for a talk at Bhavan's College by one of Gandhi's grandsons, a scholar of some kind. Afterwards I asked him if it was true, what Rumi said, that the old man had neglected his family. You know what he told me?"

"I can't even guess."

"He said the children may have suffered slightly from inattention, but the next generation made up for it. Of course he was bragging. He said the sins of the fathers may be visited on the children but the good is visited on the grandchildren. He was a tall corpselike man with glasses that were too big for his face. He seemed annoyed. He told me I didn't understand a thing about Gandhi, nobody did, no one understood that for him the most important thing in the world, more important than ideas and politics, were the simple facts of living. Life lived in quest of itself was the greatest art form. But the way he was saying these things, it was as if he didn't believe his own words."

"How did Rumi die?"

"Someone smashed his head with a piece of concrete pipe. They say it was the Pathar Maar, but I don't think so. I think the Pathar Maar died a long time ago, or moved to some other city. Maybe Rumi met a copycat. Case is still unsolved."

Rashid got up slowly. He took a set of keys from his pocket and gave it to the girl. He told her to take me to the flat on the half landing. He said, Zeenat's old place. There's a trunk under the bed. She'll help you bring it up.

IT WAS AN old Bombay apartment with high ceilings and tiled floors. The front door opened into the living room, which had a marble-topped Irani table and some chairs. The rest of the space was crowded with computer equipment and obsolete or broken keyboards and terminals. The girl went through into the back and nodded at a tin trunk that lay wedged under the single bed. I pulled it out and between us we carried it up to Rashid. He unhooked a clasp and threw back the top and a handful of newspaper cuttings and documents fell on the floor. They were in Chinese and there was a photograph of a young officer in uniform. Rashid pulled out a striped shopping bag, the kind Bombay housewives stuff to the brim with coriander, onions, and tomatoes. Inside was a pipe, the only one that had survived. He handed it to me. I sniffed the bowl for its long-gone scent and I thought I smelled it, like molasses and sleep and sickness.

"You can have it," Rashid said. "I don't want it."

I saw a jar, with the dentures Rumi had tried to sell Rashid, and I asked if I could have them.

"What will you do with it? Sell it to the government for millions of rupees? Take whatever you want. Jamal wants to throw it all away."

I picked my way through the things in the trunk, making two small piles. The opium pipe and dentures I put in one pile. I added a newspaper cutting from the *Indian Express*, a copy of a school textbook, some notebooks, and an issue of *Sex Detective*.

Rashid said, "What will you do with all of this?"

"Who knows? Make a museum exhibit, maybe."

"Yes, why not? Put our shame on display, so people understand the lowest of the low, prostitutes and criminals and drug addicts, people with no faith in god or man, no faith in anything except the truth of their own senses. This is a worthwhile thing to you?"

His voice was very weak, as if it had to travel a great distance to be heard. The light in the room began to fade and there were shapes in the air outside, small whiplike shapes moving between the mango trees. We sat together as the room got dark. The girl put on the lights when she left, but the table lamps only made everything dimmer, bathing each object in a weak yellow gleam. Rashid was immobile, but when I got up to leave he got up too, and in the twilight, with the old ghosts swimming in the air between us, I saw the confusion in his eyes.

I WANT to tell you something, he said. I know what you did. You put her in the center and that was a good thing. But she came back. Did you know that? When she was sick, she came back to her old room to die. I knew she was sick because she spent most of the day sitting in a chair, just sitting, like an old man. And then, the week after Id, she got worse and Dr. Belani came to see her, our old Sindhi family doctor. He whispered to me that she was very ill, but with her he joked, told her she had the constitution of a bullock, and Zeenat, also joking, said it was not a flattering comparison. Later she told me, I know what he said to you, there's nothing wrong with my hearing. She told me not to worry, that she wasn't planning to die just yet. But almost from that day there was a change in her. No, no, not then, it was after she came back from the hospital. We had to take her to hospital for the treatment, the terrible treatment, which made her hair fall out and gave her more pain than the sickness. And when she came back she was changed. She told me there was a window in the back of the ambulance that carried her to the hospital, and as she lay there she looked out and caught a glimpse of the sky and some trees, and she could see the attendant and the driver, and these ordinary sights filled her with joy and gratitude. Why joy, I asked her, why gratitude, of all things? Because, she said, I knew what a lucky life I was given and I understood everything: the exact meaning of the sun in the infinite sky and the trees trembling around us and the people hungry for affection, and I understood how foolish it was to be proud or angry and, most of all, how wrong it was to withhold affection from those who need it most, which is to say, everyone. That's all. I understood how lucky I was to know this at last, maybe a little too late, but at least I knew. I thought it was her sickness that made her say those things, but still, Nasrani, it brought tears to my eyes to see her so radiant, and the way she spoke, as if she was in some kind of ecstasy. I am beloved, she said. And you, dear friend, you're beloved too. This is what she said. After she died, I gave up the business. I learned to pray, not five times, but six, eight times a day. I prayed all the time, but the worm could not be killed by prayer. It was still inside me. You see, I realized I wasn't praying to praise god, I was praying for my own

selfish reasons, but such is god's mercy that he listened to my en-
treaties. This is the meaning of mercy, wouldn't you say, when it
is offered to the undeserving? So I sat in my chair and I prayed
and eventually I was rewarded. One evening I heard a door closing downstairs, in Zeenat's apartment. I heard a toilet flush and a
chair scrape against the floor. This is a quiet building, sound carries
in the night. I didn't do anything at first. I continued to pray, but
I knew where the sounds were coming from. Some nights later, I
heard a door bang and I went down. The room was as she left it,
it still is, you saw. I sat on the bed and waited. The door was open
and I thought it was only a matter of time until she appeared. But
she didn't, she didn't appear. I went back to my routine, I prayed, I
slept, and again one night I heard something downstairs. This time
I decided I would wait all night if I had to, but I fell asleep. When I
woke, I realized she wouldn't come. I went to use the toilet and that's
where I found her, sitting on the seat. Her eyes were full of fear. I
asked, what took you so long? I told her about my life, about how I
had given up nasha and filled my mind with prayer. I talked about
my family, about my loneliness, about her. I told her how much I
missed her. I asked her again, what took you so long to come? I said
I'd been hoping she would return to haunt me. And that was the
only moment when she seemed her old self. She said, haunt? Listen
to me: I'm not a ghost. I'm still here. I've been here all this time but
I kept out of your way. Dead do not always become ghosts. We are
like dreams that travel from one person to the other. We return, but
only if you love us. I told her she didn't have to explain anything to
me. I said I would be happy if she were only to sit with me for a little
while. You see, Nasrani, I've become a foolish old man. I still talk to
her, more and more as the days go by.

WHEN I GOT BACK to the apartment in Bandra, I looked at the papers I'd salvaged from Dimple's house, the magazine advertisements for Duckback rubber sheeting and semiautomatic washing machines and Sri Balaji's instant bumper lottery, first prize Rs. 10 lakhs; the photographs of congressmen and criminals; the opinion pieces on sex and money and the city's crumbling infrastructure, and it struck me that the pieces could, with minor changes, be reprinted in that day's newspaper and no one would be any wiser. In a notebook I found unfinished lists: the names of night watches; a comparison of smells, for instance, the smell of cordite against that of sulfur; several definitions of the word *remorse*; and handwritten pages, a story or dream, titled "The Enfolding," in which a small child falls asleep in a house from which the adults have vanished. The child runs around the house in panic. Then he learns. He waits in the empty rooms and mazelike gardens. He tends the flowers. He grows into young adulthood. He keeps himself fit and alert and he waits. He lives in "a world," wrote Dimple, "in which only pain was real." Most of the story was taken up by the closing paragraph, in which the boy waits by a parapet near the ocean. Behind him, the old house and the sky reeling with birds. He looks out to sea, waiting for the lights of a ship. He imagines he can see tiny yellow or blue pinpoints that grow larger in the night but vanish with first light. Who is he waiting for? How long must he endure the rigors of his vigil? What are the bearable consequences of loneliness? These questions are raised in the course of the story, though they are nowhere answered. I fell asleep reading and late at night I heard footsteps on the ceiling, things dropping, coughs and whispers.

I woke up saying, who is it? I thought I heard voices outside my door. My neighbors on the left were a family of four in a space as small as mine. I never saw the father, a laboring man who came home only to sleep. They kept their doors and windows open all day, there was no other way to live in the tiny space. The younger child, a girl of about six, read her homework aloud. I sat on the couch in my room and listened to her real voice. "When the sun rises we say good morning." When I opened my door at noon, she and her mother looked at me with curiosity, or pity. If I could hear them, they could surely hear me, talking with my invisible guests. I introduced myself. I said: Ullis's my name. These are my friends. This is what we did. These are the things we said and dreamed. Mother and daughter looked at me and then they looked behind me, as if they too could see the shapes that filled the air. Late that night, after my neighbors had gone to bed, I cleared a space in the small room and set up an oil lamp and the pipe. This is the story the pipe told me. All I did was write it down, one word after the other, beginning and ending with the same one, Bombay.